Praise for *The Wreckage*

'A terrific debut exploring the vulnerabilities and co-dependency of damaged individuals. I loved the wonderfully subtle but insistent tone of menace woven into the narrative, winding me into the colliding worlds of Ben and Alice and pushing me on to finish it. Clever and compelling!' – Fiona Barton, *Sunday Times* bestselling author of *The Widow*

'Artfully written – the focus on Adam and Ben's internal conflict was a welcome reversal of stereotypes often found in psychological thrillers.' – LJ Ross, international bestselling author of *The DCI Ryan Mysteries*

'An astounding debut – disturbing and utterly compelling.' – K.L. Slater, author of *Blink*

'*The Wreckage* is an exceedingly good debut novel that tackles serious issues with real compassion and empathy, allows the characters to draw you in and feel their pain, and keeps you guessing.' – Joy Ellis, author of *The Jackman And Evans* series

'This is a terrifying psychological thriller – credible & gut-wrenching. We are cunningly forced into the pit of obsession. Completely successful, an exciting new writer. I loved it.' – Miriam Margolyes

THE
WRECKAGE

After graduating from Cambridge University with a First Class degree in Modern and Medieval Languages, Robin Morgan-Bentley worked for five years at Google. Since 2014, he has worked at Audible, where he runs their podcast, *Audible Sessions*. He has interviewed multiple crime authors including Paula Hawkins, Fiona Barton, Clare Mackintosh, Ian Rankin, Val McDermid, Anthony Horowitz and Jeffery Deaver, and these conversations inspired him to start writing.

THE
WRECKAGE

Robin Morgan-Bentley

TRAPEZE

First published in Great Britain in 2020 by Trapeze Books
an imprint of The Orion Publishing Group Ltd
Carmelite House, 50 Victoria Embankment
London EC4Y ODZ

An Hachette UK company

1 3 5 7 9 10 8 6 4 2

A CIP catalogue record for this book is
available from the British Library.

ISBN (Hardback) 978 1 4091 9417 0
ISBN (eBook) 978 1 4091 9420 0

Typeset by Born Group

Printed and bound in Great Britain by Clays Ltd, Elcograf S.p.A.

MIX
Paper from
responsible sources
FSC® C104740

www.orionbooks.co.uk

For Pauly

Pause you who read this, and think for a moment of the long chain of iron or gold, of thorns or flowers, that would never have bound you, but for the formation of the first link on one memorable day.
– Charles Dickens, *Great Expectations*

BEN

It's the windscreen wipers first. Shards of rubber and plastic, going back and forth, back and forth, frantically scrambling to clear my way. There's no road in front of me, just flashes of grey and wet, grey and wet.

And then the sounds. The low, dull whirr of my engine, punctuated by the zip of other cars, more eager, more urgent, overtaking me on my right. The sharp, sudden whip of thunder cracked onto the roof of my car, causing me to jump each time, my legs shaking in anticipation of the next strike.

And then the morning mist. The dial on the heater is broken, so I lean forwards and rub the windscreen clear with the edge of my sleeve. I notice a milk stain on my left cuff, the remnant of a rushed breakfast.

The wipers, the zip, the thunder, the mist, the dial, the stain. Always in that order.

And then there it is: the flash of white – one glimpse, one frame, then chaos. A cacophony that I remember and describe differently every time: a thump on impact, a smash of the head, a screech as I hit the brakes and swerve to the side. If the sequence of visuals is set, the sounds are on shuffle. What came first, the screech or the smash? After the sounds, other sensations: ears popping, stomach dropping, a warm, sensual urge in my groin. And then the smells: the whiff of burnt rubber and that sweet, warm scent of rain trickling in through the broken windscreen. And just one taste: the metallic tang of blood.

I switch off the engine, unbuckle my seat belt, lean forwards and run my finger across a crack in the windscreen. I shuffle across, open the passenger door and climb out. The roar of the traffic drowns the ringing in my ears. And it's pouring, that uniquely British brand of rain that cuts across diagonally and feels much heavier than it looks.

I walk behind my car to the edge of the hard shoulder. I can see that people are stopping now, so maybe one of them can help me to get back onto the road. It's still dark but the lights of the gathering cars shine around me, from the road to the hard shoulder, and onto the verge to my left. That's where they all seem to be going, that's where there's a commotion. Another clash of thunder, and as I jolt forwards, my stomach drops and I vomit onto the tarmac. I've just seen the white again. A pair of white cotton trousers, stained with mud at the hems, lying on the verge. There's a man on the side of road. He's there because I hit him with my car.

There are a good few seconds that go missing here. When I return, I'm walking down the hard shoulder, facing the rush of traffic. My legs feel numb – like pins and needles but colder, even more detached. I'm stumbling towards a flashing blue-and-red light, where I can see a police officer. As I approach him, my legs return, but I feel a strange pull in my upper body now, as if a force quite separate from my realm of control has taken over. By the time I reach the officer, I'm drenched, shivering through sodden clothes, my hair plastered across my forehead.

'I'm sorry,' I yell, my arms raised high above my head. 'I'm sorry.'

ALICE

Tuesday, 9 January, 7.15 a.m.

It's not the first time I've woken up and turned over to an empty pillow. He's been an insomniac ever since we first started seeing each other and, apparently, all his life. On our second date he told me he was 'a thinker', which at the time struck me as condescending, as if the rest of us spend most of the day staring blankly into the distance.

I look up to check the time: Adam has one of those tacky clocks that projects onto the ceiling in bright blue neon. He always likes to know what the time is, even though I tell him that it doesn't help with his sleeplessness. It's 7.15 a.m. I'm surprised I haven't been woken by Max yet. He sleeps quite well for a seven-year-old, but he's usually in here by now, asking for breakfast and grabbing the duvet off me.

I get out of bed, put on a dressing gown and walk over to the window. It looks like it's been a rough night. It's still raining a bit, and I can see that it must have been heavy because the lawn looks flooded and the clothes line has been floored by the wind. On the news, they've been talking about Storm

Jolene, sweeping over from the southern states of America, and it certainly looks like she's had a little stopover at our house. I'm not sure there are many people called Jolene in Rickmansworth, or in all of Hertfordshire for that matter.

I head across the hallway and into Max's room. He's still asleep, gently snoring. I kiss him on the forehead and he stirs but then settles, so I step out of the room and go downstairs. This house is so much bigger than we need and it feels extravagant, but Adam calls it his 'forever home' and who am I to argue with that? I feel lonely sometimes: when Max is at school and Adam is locked up in his study at the end of the garden, tearing his hair out and being excruciatingly creative in his attempts to write his almost-but-never-quite-finished screenplay. I was an accountant in the City before Max was born, and I thought about going back to work a couple of years ago, when he started primary school, but Adam was against it and, thanks to his father's oil business, it's not like we need the money.

I head into the kitchen and put on a pot of tea. I can see that Adam has already made some for himself because there's a teabag in the sink. He must be in the outhouse, writing. I put on three crumpets, dollop butter on them, stick one in my mouth, wince as I squeeze my feet into the trainers by the patio doors and head outside. The garden really is in a state – branches have leapt off the trees, flowers have collapsed from their beds onto the lawn and the clothes line looks finished. I screw up my face as the drizzle soaks me and the bottom of my dressing gown is soiled as it drags across the ground. The tree house that Adam started building with Max in the summer hasn't fared well. It's a good job they didn't get very far.

The door to the outhouse is wide open. I approach carefully, as I know Adam doesn't like to be disturbed while he's writing and I can't be bothered with a shouting match. But he's not in here. The place is an absolute tip. All of his books, usually so neatly stacked and ordered by theme, are strewn across the floor. I step over shreds of paper, discarded manuscripts, scenes from his latest play that he's no doubt agonised over for hours before discarding in a temper. And the lamp, his mother's porcelain lamp – ghastly but treasured – is shattered into pieces and scattered on the tiled floor. It's as if the storm has made its way inside the outhouse and turned Adam's room upside down. And where the hell is he?

I start picking up the pieces of porcelain first, because I know that when Max wakes up and realises there's no one in the house, he'll come and find me here. As I step out of the shed, I almost trip on Adam's slippers. Has he left the house without shoes? I gather pace as I head back towards the house, running up the stairs to grab my phone. I call his phone: straight to voicemail. I scramble back down the stairs, burst into the garden and back into the outhouse. The panic has set in: I've been here before. I riffle through the mess on the floor, the notebooks, the loose pages, cutting my finger on a piece of lamp. And then I see it, perched on the seat of his chair. A stuffed brown envelope and on the front a few simple marks in Adam's beautiful calligraphy:

Tell Maxy I'm sorry.

I run back through the garden, into the house, leap upstairs and into the bedroom, snatching my car keys from the bedside table and dabbing my bleeding finger on a torn old tissue. I need to get Max out of bed.

'Max, sweetheart. Wake up. Wake up, please. Here, put these on.'

I open his cupboard and grab the first T-shirt and shorts that I see, throwing them on his bed as he rubs his eyes.

'Where are we going, Mummy?'

I need him to get the urgency, but I can't tell him what's going on.

'Max, I'm going to take you over to Mrs Turner. Mummy needs to do something quickly. Come on, get out of bed.'

It's one of the privileges of suburbia, having a de facto babysitter living next door. Mrs Turner has always had a soft spot for Max: he's one of those kids who impresses strangers, particularly older ladies, and as Mrs Turner has lived alone since her own child died of meningitis in the early nineties, I like to think that taking Max round there from time to time is an act of charity. Today, she is visibly perturbed by my sudden appearance at her front door so early in the morning, and she looks me up and down in consternation when she notices that I'm wearing my summer dressing gown in the depths of the winter. I don't have time to stop and explain, and usher Max towards her before she knows what's hit her.

I rush straight from Mrs Turner's to my car, the back of my dressing gown cold and damp as I shut the door and turn on the ignition. As I reverse out of the driveway and through the gate, I see the sun rising in the rear-view mirror and feel a shot of adrenaline run straight down my spine. There's never been a fucking note before.

I race into town, past the railway station and onto the main road, noticing every early-morning stroller and hurried commuter. I know his usual haunt. In the past, when he's disappeared, he has just needed space, heading into the park to sit on the bench and pull himself together. I drive as close as I can get to the entrance, ditch the car and cross the road into the park, dodging stray branches and landing in puddles as I go. Through the turnstile, past the roundabout and swings, towards the bench in the distance. I'm running, screaming his name, but I can already see that there's no one sitting there.

What a sight I must be: a heffalump in dressing gown and trainers, with streaks of last night's make-up trailing down my cheeks, yelling into an empty, sodden park. My body is not made for this, and I'm wheezing and gasping as I cross to the other side and head towards the high street. I should have taken my inhaler. The man who runs the launderette has just arrived, putting the key in the shutters to open up, and he turns round and looks at me as I gasp for air, scuttling away from him, crossing the road in between moving cars, past the betting shop and towards the police station.

As I approach the automatic doors, I stop to catch my breath and notice the patch of sweat from under my left tit that has seeped through my satin dressing gown. Through the doors, to the reception desk, one last deep breath and . . .

'Hello, I'd like to report my husband missing. Yes, missing. He, he . . . there was a note and I think he might be in trouble.'

BEN

'Let's get out of this rain. Would you mind joining us in our vehicle for a quick chat?'

'I did see a flash. I saw a white flash as I was driving along and heard a bang and I thought I must have hit something. I swerved to the left and then got out to see the damage and only then did I see him, I didn't . . .'

'Let's go and have a proper chat. Come on, now. Have you got the keys to your car?'

'Keys? No, I mean they're still in the . . . Is he dead? Is the man dead?'

'Please, sir, try to stay calm. Our car is this one at the back here; it'll be nice and warm in there. Let's go.'

The officer signals to a colleague and I watch as he heads towards my car. I trundle across the road towards the police car in the near distance and I can feel a cold squish of rain that has seeped into my left shoe. It's particularly cold on the heel and this makes my gait heavy, my foot a bit harder to lift. When we reach the car, the officer opens the back door for me and I slide in. My breath's gathering pace: I can feel my upper torso rise and fall with each inhale and exhale, my face dripping with a mix of rain and sweat from the top of my hairline. The officer closes the door and takes the driver's seat.

'OK, great. So, just a few routine questions now. What's your name please, sir?'

'Benjamin Anderson.'

'Age?'

'Thirty-two.'

'Lovely. Now, can I call you Ben?'

I can see the officer in the rear-view mirror and nod. I don't say a word, because I can feel a lump developing in my throat and my eyes glazing over, the first sheet of tears forming.

'Good stuff. I'm DC Ed Parsons. Now, first things first. Where were you off to this morning?'

'Work – I teach at a school near Bricket Wood. But what happened – is he dead? I need to know what happened. Let me out of the car, I need to go and see . . .'

I lean across to open the door and hear the crunch of the lock. I pull anyway, pull and pull and pull.

'Ben, we need you to remain where you are, please. There's a medical team at the scene now doing everything they can.'

The officer reaches into his glove compartment for a packet of tissues and offers me the box. I grab one, blow my nose hard and look into the tissue.

'Everything will be OK,' he continues. 'Our friends from the ambulance know what they're doing and they're already here, doing what they can to help him. Now, can you tell me about your movements this morning? The more you can tell me, the better; it just helps us to get a picture.'

I take another tissue, rubbing it over my hair, down my face and across my neck. I fold up the tissue, dab my eyes, take a deep breath and start talking.

'Well, I woke up, as usual, at 5.45 a.m. I had a shower, got dressed and then left the house at about six fifteen. It usually takes about fifty-five minutes door to door. I like to get in early to do some lesson planning before the kids arrive.'

I've sometimes thought about moving closer to the school, but I love my flat and I don't mind the drive. It gives me time to gather my thoughts for the day. When I was offered the job at this school five years ago, I couldn't quite believe my luck. I was only twenty-seven, the youngest teacher there, and I knew the kids would be stimulating to teach. My last school was in Central London, one that inspectors describe as 'challenging'. When I started, I saw it as some sort of moral calling, but in the end it was an achievement just making sure that all the kids had been given some-thing to eat for breakfast. My new school is in an affluent suburb, and my students are the kids of bankers, solicitors and actuaries. I suppose I feel honoured to be trusted with 'the leaders of tomorrow', as the prospectus puts it.

'And what about your mobile phone? Where was that while you were driving?'

'I wasn't texting or anything, if that's what you mean. No, look, my phone's here in my pocket. I always keep it there and don't even touch it if it rings while I'm driving. It's pretty battered now.'

Not strictly true. I've been making an effort to keep my phone in my jacket pocket, but if I'm honest with myself, sometimes I do get it out and check for texts when I'm sitting in a traffic jam. That's normal, isn't it?

'OK, Ben. We're just going to ask you now to do a quick breathalyser test. Have you done one of these before?'

Breathalyser test? How can he possibly believe that I've been drinking at 7 a.m. on a Tuesday? He's obviously never had to stand in front of a room of eagle-eyed eight-year-olds, with their acute sixth sense for vulnerability. I suppose it's just a box-ticking exercise and so when he hands me the contraption, I accept it with grace and place it in my mouth.

'That's it, well done. And if you can just take a deep breath and blow into the tube, please. That's it.'

I hand it back to him, my mind spinning as I try to remember when I last drank. I had a glass of wine a couple of nights ago with dinner. Is there any chance that might still be in my system? I run my tongue across my front teeth and can still feel the sting of mouthwash that I used this morning. What if I swallowed some?

'All clear, son. OK, we're just going to run you down to the station now, to take an official statement.'

If I need to make an official statement, shouldn't I have some support? I don't know what I'm doing. Maybe I need a lawyer in case I say something that I don't mean. And Dad. I want to call my dad. He's always good in situations like this. He'll know what to do.

'I'd really like a lawyer to be present, please. And am I allowed to call my dad?'

'Sure, go ahead, son. Take this. And yeah, there'll be a duty solicitor down at the station, so when you're ready we can head down there.'

The officer passes me a phone and my hand is shaking so much that I can barely dial. I have to hold the phone down with my left hand and press the screen with my right. As the phone rings, I feel tears streaming down my face, proper tears this time, and an itch on my cheeks that is relieved when I wipe them away. It rings once, twice, three times, and I scramble to figure out what to say. How to phrase it? How do I break the news?

'Dad – I need you. I need you to come – I'm with the police, we're going to the station. I ran someone over, Dad. He was on the side of the motorway and stepped out in front of my car. Dad, I think I might have killed someone.'

And there it is. The first time I've said it out loud.

ALICE

Here I am, in someone else's coat, slumped on a chair in a waiting room in Rickmansworth Police Station. Someone's given me a coffee, but one sip's enough because it tastes like crushed paracetamol. I bite down into the top of the polystyrene cup, leaving teeth marks. I look around for a mirror but am relieved not to find one – my forehead feels like someone's plastered it with glue and I can taste last night's mascara that's trickled into my mouth.

'Mrs Selby?'

A stumpy man is coming towards me. He can't be more than about five feet four and he's got a bulbous belly. He's also got a mole to the right of his top lip, which he should really get checked. I'm transfixed for a good few seconds: an intermission to worry about a stranger's future before having to face the reality of my own.

'Yes, hello. Hi. Alice, I'm Alice Selby.'

The stocky man pulls a handkerchief out of his right trouser pocket and wipes his brow, mouth and chin before reaching out a hand.

14

'Won't you please come with me? Have you been offered a drink?'

'No, I mean . . . yes, I'm fine, thanks.'

I follow him down a damp, dingy corridor, my shoes squeaking on the cold concrete floor. He leads me into Interrogation Room 2 – a desk, three flimsy blue chairs and four pale, blank walls – and he pulls a chair out for me before taking another opposite. I wince as he lowers himself, unsure that the plastic can take his weight.

'Mrs Selby, I am DI John Cousins, in charge of the Rickmansworth service here today. We've been informed of an incident out on the M1 this morning and we have reason to believe your husband has been involved.'

'What? It can't be him. He never drives on the motorway. Must be someone else. Adam will be somewhere around the park; he's done this before. My car's just outside. I can show you where I found him last time, just behind the . . .'

'Mrs Selby, Mrs Selby, please listen to me. We believe your husband has been involved as a pedestrian.'

Gut drops. Throat closes. I can see where this is going but feign ignorance for now.

'A pedestrian on the motorway?'

'Yes, that's right. Now, sorry to ask, but do you have any reason to believe that he might have attempted to take his own life, Mrs Selby?'

Fuck.

'How do you even know it's him? Surely this kind of stuff happens all the time. What evidence do you have that it's Adam? He promised me he wouldn't try to do this again!'

The fat man reaches for something on the chair next to him and slides it across the table. In a flimsy freezer bag, I recognise it immediately. Real Italian leather, from a market in Turin and frayed at the edges: a wallet with his initials.

In a whisper, I say, 'Where's his body?'

'Watford General. He's still alive, Mrs Selby, but I'm afraid he's in a very critical condition.'

Critical condition. I need to get out of this room, right now.

I stand, shed the charity coat and run down the corridor, past the coffee machine, through the double doors and into the world. It's raining and as I look up to the sky, grey clouds are closing in. I take a seat on a bench outside the police station and start rocking. Rocking and sobbing in my newly see-through dressing gown. A crazy woman in the elements.

BEN

Tuesday, 9 January, 7.12 a.m.

I have no concept of time or place. As we drive towards the
police station, all I feel is a sequence of dread, guilt, fear and
regret. My senses are raging and there are sounds coming out
of my mouth that I don't recognise as my own. I'm howling
and gasping for breath, moaning in pain like an injured
animal. I catch a glimpse of myself in the wing mirror and see
a child: my eyes red raw, with snot hanging from my nose
to my chin. I look down at my seat belt and the red of the
button grows bigger and bigger. Why have I got a seat belt
on? This is not something I deserve. I bang my head with my
palm and this provides some relief. I bang and I bang and I
bang. Maybe if I keep on banging, this will all be over.

And then everything goes quiet. I stop crying and I sit on
both of my hands, tying myself down and rocking myself
to a gentle calm. My forehead is sore and I crack open the
window for some fresh air. My breathing starts to regulate
and I grab another tissue from the box that's now at my
feet, wiping my face and rubbing my eyes.

'I'm sorry, I don't know what came over me, I just don't know how . . .'

DC Parsons looks into the rear-view mirror, straight at me.

'It's the shock, Ben. I'm sure the trauma of the whole thing would set me off, too. Not much I haven't seen before, I can tell you that for nothing.'

As we drive, more slowly now, through the streets of Rickmansworth, I think of my mother and what she will make of all this. She's always warned me about cars. She never learned to drive as she didn't trust herself and while that approach has always seemed uptight and ridiculous – as are so many of her takes on the world – now I see this perspective in a new light. How ridiculous is it that we are allowed to take the wheel after a cursory test and drive around the streets with such power! Are cars any less lethal than handguns? We all drive around with this collective trust, an unspoken agreement that we rate each other's skills with this deadly, complicated weapon.

I hear a crackle on the car radio and a woman's hoarse Cockney voice. 'Hi, lads. We've got an ID on the victim. Adam Selby. He's en route now to Watford General. Still breathing, apparently.'

Adam Selby. The victim. Why is she calling him a victim? If he's the victim, am I the perpetrator? But breathing, he's still breathing. I bite the middle finger on my right hand and the sting of the cut keeps me distracted. I suck until the blood stops and then the car comes to a halt. I hear the crunch of the handbrake and the zip of the keys being removed from the ignition.

'Come on, son. We're here.'

As we step out of the car, it's still pouring with rain, so the officer hovers an umbrella over my head. I've never felt so dependent in my life: like an invalid being escorted between institutions, drenched to the skin, eyes heavy from all the crying. I step up onto the pavement, taking a few more confident steps and striding ahead of the officer, determined to make my own way inside.

Suddenly, everything comes into focus and I take it all in. I look at this officer properly for the first time: a distinctive face, with a scar just above his right eyebrow. A row of parked police cars, one of them with a smashed windscreen. Automatic doors and a computerised, transatlantic voice that says 'Doors opening'. Mud stains that I'm leaving on the ground as I trundle into the police station. And Dad, who stands and rushes towards me, hugging me harder than I've ever been hugged before.

BEN

'OK, Ben, we've got your statement now, all the tests are clear, so you're good to go. Chances are there will be some future investigation, particularly if the gentleman does pass away. In the meantime, try to take it easy, yeah? Don't be too hard on yourself. As I said before, mate, we won't be pursuing dangerous driving charges – you couldn't have done anything differently. It's all just very unfortunate.'

DC Parsons thinks I'm a nervous wreck, but who wouldn't be in this scenario? For him, it's just another day at the office. People must get run over all the time on their way to work. For me, it's a major life event that I can't just shake off with a few words on a piece of paper.

'Can I go to the hospital? Or at least call to see what's going on? I need to know what's happening.'

DC Parsons sighs, looks over his shoulder and lowers his voice.

'Look, I know it's hard, but you need to leave it in the hands of the professionals now. Come on, now.'

He leads me out of the interrogation room and I meet my dad at reception. He looks concerned, tired, and puts his arm round me as we head to the exit together.

'Come and stay with your mum and me for a couple of days, yeah? Shake it off.'

And so he drives me back to their house in Edgware – about half an hour's drive – and we listen to talkRADIO. There isn't a single mention of the accident on the news, or even on the traffic updates. Dad wants to chat, but my head is spinning and I just don't know which words I'd spit out first. I'm sorry? Help?

When we reach the house, I head straight up to my old bedroom and shut the door. I don't even take my clothes off or bother going under the covers – I fall flat on the bed. When I wake in the middle of the night, the lights are off and I'm tucked under the covers in my boxer shorts, my clothes folded neatly on the chair by my table.

I get out of bed and find my phone, which is charging on the desk. I take it back into bed with me, frantically checking the BBC website. And then google:

Road accidents 9 Jan
Collisions 9 Jan motorway
9 Jan motorway deaths
9 Jan Adam Selby

But nothing's coming up and I think that must be a good sign. If Adam were dead, surely they would be reporting on it by now?

And then I get sucked into a vortex of searches about the man himself. This man, Adam Selby, whose life I have suddenly altered, whose whole existence has been threatened by the fact that I drove my car into him. The trouble is, it's quite a common name. I find Adam Selby, Finance Director of Beat Communications; Adam Selby, freelance photographer specialising in wildlife portraits; Adam Selby, playwright, winner of the Laurence Olivier Award for Best New Play for *The Girlfriend* (2009); Adam Selby, champion gymnast, currently training to represent Team GB at the next Olympics. Which of these Adam Selbys is my victim?

The next morning when I come down the stairs, just in my boxers, it's like I'm the prodigal son, returning from a gap year in Peru. Mum has made one of her famous 'family breakfasts' – reserved in the past for birthdays and exam days – and she pulls out a chair for me as I approach the table.

'You must be starving, love. Didn't eat a thing yesterday, did you?'

Mum doesn't hold back with the food: she's always been a keen eater, yo-yoing from one fad diet to the next. At the moment she's on some kind of protein-only regime, and piles her plate full of smoked salmon and kidney beans. And I am hungry: food hasn't really crossed my mind since the crash, and although I vaguely remember being offered a chocolate bar in the police station, I wasn't in the mood. I help myself to a bit of everything.

'We called the school and spoke to the headmistress. She's a lovely lady, isn't she? Said to take as much time off as you need.'

'Mum, why did you do that? Did you tell them what happened? I don't want them to know.'

'Don't be silly, Benjy. Just eat up your breakfast and we can all chat together afterwards.'

Oh, shut up, Mother, I'm not a child. I have no intention to chat. Chat about what? I don't know why I expected Dad to keep all this a secret from Mum, but I feel really put out that it's been the topic of conversation in my absence. Mum has a knack of foreseeing the worst possible potential outcome in the most harmless of scenarios and it had never occurred to me how she might react when the shit really did hit the fan. What do they want to chat about, anyway? Chat about the fact that I ran over a perfect stranger? Chat about the state of that poor man, either dead or comatose in hospital, struggling for his life because of my driving? No, no chat for now.

I finish my breakfast, brush past my mum and head back up to the bedroom. It's chilly and I'm still in my under-wear, so I find an old dressing gown in the cupboard; it has that distinctive smell of home. I wander over to the CD rack, running my finger down the dusty collection. I pick up Alanis Morissette's *Jagged Little Pill*, place it in the ghetto blaster and leap onto my bed.

And, in this moment, I feel quite content: in the four walls of my parents' maisonette, I needn't have a worry in the world. No one can touch me, or accuse me of anything. No one can ask me whether or not I was sober or speeding or using my phone or not paying attention. And, obviously, in this room everyone else is safe from me, too. There's no viable way for me to harm anyone else. But then I close my eyes and fall asleep, and I have the first flashback. The wipers, the zip, the thunder, the mist, the dial, the stain. The flash of white.

ALICE

Tuesday, 16 January

We've been here for seven days now and it's hardly the Ritz. There's a TV in the far right corner, about 22-inch, Panasonic, on a bracket attached to the wall. A large bay window looks out onto the car park, where I watch vehicles come and go throughout the day. A door that leads to a bathroom, with a cracked toilet and a crusty bath that looks like it would do more harm than good. And then, if I turn and look to my left, I see the labyrinth of wires and tubes, the monitors, the catheters, the liquids and gases all working together to keep my husband alive.

On that first morning in the police station, I jumped to the wrong conclusion. When I heard that Adam had been hit on the motorway, I didn't expect to be spending the next few weeks in a hospital ward. I suppose you instinctively go to the darkest place.

The police gave me a lift from the station to the hospital. It was the first time I'd been in a police car and it almost felt exhilarating: I was on a mission, weaving in and out

24

of the traffic, at the centre of something vital, something urgent. For the first time in as long as I could remember, I felt special, even glamorous, until I caught a glimpse of my face in the reflection of the tinted windows: sweaty and blotchy, eyes puffy and hair strewn across my face.

When we arrived at Watford General, I knew that I had to put my vanities and anxieties aside. It was time for me to step up and be the strong, concerned, assertive next of kin. They seemed to be expecting me as soon as I walked in, and I was led immediately to a room where I was offered another coffee – this one more palatable than the one in the police station – and greeted by a lanky man with a stethoscope round his neck.

'Mrs Selby, my name is Dr Isaacs. I'm one of the doctors on duty this evening at Watford General.'

'You're not a fucking doctor, you're only about twelve!'

I'd read about junior doctors but didn't expect someone *that* junior. This guy was barely out of school. He had acne all over his face and neck and looked like he'd just had a growth spurt and was in need of some new trousers.

'I'm sorry, I didn't mean to . . . sorry.' Bit harsh of me, to be fair.

The junior doctor gave a tight-lipped smile. 'No offence taken. Would you like to follow me, please? I'd like to give you the latest on your husband.'

Was this the moment they'd tell me, ever so gingerly, that my husband had passed away? But then this chap seemed a bit too chirpy for that and his choice of words – 'the latest on your husband' – suggested a transitory state that hadn't reached its end.

I followed him into a busy corridor, dodging nurses and trollies, and was led into a dingy room at the end of the hallway.

'Take a seat here, Mrs Selby.'

The junior doctor pointed towards a black chair, one of those that swivels even when you want to sit still, and I plonked myself down on the seat. It was barely sturdy enough to take my weight and I jolted back as I lowered myself. My heart was pounding fast and I felt queasy.

'Mrs Selby, I'm glad you could make it here so quickly. Your husband is in a critical condition and is currently in emergency surgery. He's sustained quite a few fractures and, most significantly, some serious injuries to the head.'

'Well, can I see him?'

'Mrs Selby, as I mentioned, he's currently undergoing some important surgery and we need to wait while we let the doctors do what they can to help him in this critical period. He's in good hands, Mrs Selby.'

There was something in the way this child was repeatedly using my name that riled me.

'What do you mean head injuries? Is he going to be brain-damaged?'

'I'm afraid it's hard to ascertain the extent of his complications, Mrs Selby. What I can confirm at this juncture is that he is in a critical condition and it's likely that we'll keep him in an induced coma for the time being.'

Who fucking uses words like 'ascertain' and 'juncture'? There was something so calm and officious about the way he was speaking, like he'd just got out of a seminar called 'How to Deliver Bad News to Loved Ones'.

'Induced coma? So essentially he's going to be a vegetable?'

'We don't like to use that terminology, Mrs Selby. He's been placed in a medically induced coma.'

'So what now, then? I just sit and wait for him to come round?'

'Er, yes, Mrs Selby. There are magazines in the relatives' room.'

As he walked away, I saw a faint shake of the head. Dickhead.

A few hours passed. When I looked out of the window and saw that it was getting dark, I knew I should check in on Max. What would I say to Mrs Turner? My phone had long run out of battery, so one of the nurses gave me some change to make the call from a payphone. I dialled her number and, as I waited for her to pick up, I tried to decide how much detail to share at this stage.

'Mrs Turner, it's Alice. Yes, I'm so sorry, my phone ran out of juice a few hours ago. It's Adam – he's . . . there's been an accident.'

Accident. It felt like a suitable placeholder. It's not like I could have opened with 'Adam stepped in front of a car and is now in a coma,' could I?

Mrs Turner agreed to keep Max with her for as long as needed, and when I spoke to him on the phone, I explained that 'Daddy's not feeling great,' and he seemed happy to stay put. I was relieved that he didn't ask any questions and didn't seem that bothered about where I was, where his dad was or what had happened, so I was happy to keep him in ignorant bliss for now. So for the first week I stayed at the hospital, and Max slept at Mrs Turner's. I popped in a couple of times during the week to see him – I had to go home to get some clean clothes anyway – and he was doing just fine.

And so here I am, waiting. I think I'm playing the role of attentive wife quite well, sitting patiently with very little to do but stroke the sections of his right hand not covered in tubes and plasters. Every few hours a nurse comes in and does something: notes down a measurement, replaces a catheter. I wonder how necessary all this is, or if it's all just a charade that they play to give my husband a semblance of humanity.

The nurses try so hard to make small talk, to perk me up, and for the first couple of days I indulged them. But now, I bat away their pleasantries as quickly as they come. It's all very well them smiling, being chirpy and commenting on the weather. Secretly, I bet they're talking among themselves about the man in room 454 who tried to kill himself on the motorway and his stuck-up bitch of a wife who probably drove him to it. And yeah, I'm sure I am coming across as a bitch, but I don't care. I'm not here to make friends and even if I were, they wouldn't make the cut.

'Significant and irreparable damage to the frontal lobe' is the latest diagnosis, and this aside from the two broken legs, two broken arms, cracked ribs, punctured left lung and damaged spinal cord. A consultant came in yesterday, apparently Britain's leading expert in brain trauma: a mild-mannered doctor called Mr Al-Shawawi. He tried to explain to me that Adam may never come to and that if he did, we could expect significant disability: owing to the spinal injury, partial, if not total, paralysis, and because of the brain damage, a marked decline in his cognitive abilities.

He was also kind enough to remind me that he was lucky to be alive – that the speed of the car that ran into him was significant and should have killed him in an instant. I'm not sure if Adam would agree with the 'luck' diagnosis; Mr Al-Shawawi clearly isn't up to speed on the circumstances of the 'accident'.

And as for me, I don't know how to feel: on the one hand, a duty to be traumatised, to mourn the loss of my husband even though he's still sort of breathing in front of me. And it's horrific to watch him, lying there totally dependent on machines to keep him alive, helpless and unaware of his predicament. But then there's another side of me that feels guilty: that he's here at all, that he didn't achieve what he set out to do, that I'm letting the doctors keep him going against his will. And guilty, too, that I couldn't help him more than I did. To what extent am I to blame for these circumstances? Had there not been enough warning signs? Could I have insisted on him getting more help? Shouldn't I, as his wife, the only person who truly loved him, have been able to stop this from happening?

I spend most afternoons going backwards and forwards to the vending machines on the second floor, stuffing my face with coffees and KitKats, bowing my head ever so slightly to avoid eye contact with other patients and their families. No, I'm not very good at making friends.

BEN

Tuesday, 23 January

It's been exactly two weeks since the crash. I woke at five thirty this morning and I watched the clock as the minutes ticked by, doing my best to mark the exact time that the impact happened. I know that it must have been at some point between six thirty and six fifty, because I'd left the house at the usual time and that's when I'm on the motorway. When the LED displayed 06:42 this morning, I felt a funny lump in my throat, so I think that's the moment. I spent that minute thinking about Adam, trying to picture him and what he must be like. I pictured a handsome man, about the same age as me. Blond hair and green eyes; I don't know why. Tall, broad frame, wide smile. A man you'd want to get to know.

For two whole weeks, I haven't fancied going anywhere, or seeing anyone, because stepping out into the world would mean that I would have to start confronting the consequences of my actions. The school have been really good and told me not to come back until I feel ready. I've called Watford General a couple of times, in the hope that they'd give me an update on Adam's prognosis, but as I'm not next of kin they won't tell me anything. I've tried to explain the unusual circumstances, but they just won't budge. And so today I've decided to bite the bullet and take myself down there. See for myself. I need to know what's going on.

As I shut the front door and step out onto my parents' driveway, a sharp wind stabs me between the eyes. I reach the edge of the driveway and then turn back, reconsidering, before doing up my coat and striding with confidence down the cul-de-sac and towards the high street. I stop to buy flowers from the shop that's run by the little old lady who lives next door to my parents. 'Why don't you go for some nice red roses?' she suggests. 'Timeless, aren't they?' She wraps them and I pay with the twenty-pound note in my wallet. I smile, then frown, then smile again and scurry out of the shop. I don't even know what to do with my face at the moment. What is wrong with me?

The first challenge of the day is actually getting to the hospital: the idea of driving plagues me with such a sweep of nausea that I know the bus is the only option. As I look out of the window from the seat towards the back of the bus, everything is a potential hazard: it feels like we're constantly coasting too close to adjacent cars; every time we pull into a bus stop the brakes seem to jolt and I close my eyes at every zebra crossing, convinced that the driver won't notice the pedestrians. After forty-five minutes of torture on the 142, I step out into the brisk cold of day, deeply inhaling the fumes of the bus, unsteady on my feet but happy to be alive.

The ten-minute walk to the hospital allows me to clear my head and as I approach Inpatients, I feel resolute, ready to get some answers and put my mind at rest.

'Hello, I'm here to visit Adam Selby, please.'

'Ah yes. I'm sure he'll be glad of the visitors, sir. He's in room 454 on the fourth floor.'

Glad of the visitors? Is he awake?

I go up in the lift to the fourth floor, a bead of sweat trickling down my forehead as I rehearse, out loud but in a whisper, how to introduce myself. I wipe the sweat from my brow into my hair, adjusting my quiff in the mirror of the lift. I find myself storming down the corridor of the hospital, walking with the assurance of a concerned relative, grasping the bunch of roses carefully between the thorns so I don't hurt myself.

As I approach room 454, I find the door ajar, stop, start, stop again and then stride inside. And there, perched on a chair by the window, reading a newspaper and eating an apple, I see her for the very first time.

ALICE

Tuesday, 23 January

'I'm sorry. I hope I'm not disturbing. I really hope you don't mind my coming to visit.'

A man's just walked into our room with a bunch of roses. I don't recognise him at all.

'I'm sorry, do I . . . Are you . . .?'

There are other people on the same wing of the hospital with a different visitor every day: a never-ending ebb and flow of friends, relatives and colleagues with hand-tied carnations and lilies, magazines and crossword books. They come partly through duty, of course, but also, I think, to satisfy a need to signal their virtue: 'I have such a busy schedule, but of course I can spare an hour to visit my poor friend, who I hadn't called for six months before he ended up here.' I can probably count on one hand the number of people who would even care that Adam was in this state. Adam's dad, Roger, lives in Marbella with his new family and I can't get hold of him. There are no relatives calling to ask for an update, no old school friends coming round to see how he's doing. So, a visitor? This is new. I wait for him to introduce himself, but instead he just stands there, pale and stiff, staring at Adam's face.

'I'm sorry,' I say, 'I don't quite remember meeting you before. Are you . . . How do you know Adam?'

'I don't. I . . . I never met your husband. But I . . . I . . . Mrs Selby, I'm so sorry. I'm the one who ran him over.'

It takes me a second to process this. Sorry, what? What the hell is he doing here? What a funny thing to do, to take responsibility for someone else's attempt at suicide. He must be even more fucked up than Adam. How did he even know where we were? And his name? Where did he get Adam's name?

I hit the roof.

BEN

It couldn't have really gone any worse. I don't really know what I expected, but I thought it was a pretty magnanimous gesture on my part, going to the hospital to see how he was doing. At first she seemed glad to see me, pleased to have relief from the loneliness of being with a man who can't respond. I keep replaying that first conversation over and over in my head. When something important happens, I'm really good at remembering every detail of what's been said. I wonder if she'll remember our interaction so clearly.

'You seem familiar. How do you know Adam?'

And then straight to it, no beating around the bush. All my cards on the table.

'I'm Ben. I was driving the car on the motorway.'

And then silence. Alice – the nurse told me her name on the way out – put a hand to her mouth and stared straight through me. We just stood there, looking at each other, for what felt like five minutes, while she processed my confession and I became accustomed to her face. Beautiful – not in

35

a conventional sense, but with an air of childish wonder in her eyes as if she didn't have a care in the world. I wonder how old she is – can't be more than mid-thirties. I didn't want to be the one to break the silence. I'd said my piece and now awaited the verdict.

'What . . . how . . . What are you doing here?'

Her voice was familiar, like so many girls I was at university with: posh but in check, with a tint of rough, as if to say, 'My family's rich, but I still make my own living.'

'I just . . . I've been feeling terribly guilty, you see, and I wanted to check that everything was all right.'

'Check that everything's all right? Well, where do I start? He's in a minimally conscious state – a coma, essentially – there's barely a bone in his body that isn't shattered and they can't find either of his bloody optic nerves. So yeah, not in a great state.'

'No optic nerve? Does that mean he's gone blind?'

'Sorry, I really don't understand why you're here. You're saying you were driving the car that he jumped in front of?'

Ah! So he did jump. Since that day, I've imagined every possible scenario. Suicide, clearly, was the simplest and most likely explanation. But from time to time I've allowed myself to imagine other scenarios. Perhaps he was merely crossing the road, resting on the side of the motorway during a long journey. Was it my carelessness that landed this man in a coma?

During one sleepless night, I managed to convince myself that he had not been a pedestrian at all but that I had smashed into a moving car, the force of impact jettisoning him onto my windscreen and then onto the tarmac. That night I spent hours on YouTube, watching videos of horrific car accidents, re-enactments of awful collisions, trying to rule out each circumstance, trying to convince myself that suicide was the only viable scenario. Alice's confirmation that he jumped provided the reassurance that I craved.

'How is he? His name is Adam, isn't it?'

'How the hell do you know this?'

Alice was getting angry now and that was the last thing I wanted.

'How do you even know that his name is Adam? What do you want from us?'

'Nothing, nothing, I don't want anything. I just . . . It's just it's on my mind and I wanted to see if . . . I feel so terribly guilty, you see.'

Alice shut her eyes, turned away, walked to the window and then turned back.

'Please, just go. It's not your fault – Adam wanted this to happen. He left a note. I need you to leave, please. I need to be alone.'

And so I left the room, striding down the corridor with tears streaming down my face and a stitch in my chest. I only meant well, but it's not my tragedy. I wasn't welcome and I should never have presumed otherwise. I left the roses with Adam and Alice, for them to take or to leave.

And now here I am, back in my childhood bedroom in Edgware. It's the middle of the night but the light is on, because there's no point in pretending that I'm going to sleep. There's only a certain number of times an hour that I can roll over and look at the green LED reminding me of my insomnia – 02:12, 02:14, 02:18, 03:23, 03:37 – before it's time to surrender.

The visit to the hospital has not given me the peace of mind I had anticipated. I was hoping I would make the trip today and find Adam in a ward with a group of other patients, both arms in plaster and legs akimbo. I was expecting to find a man heavily sedated on morphine, pushing some jelly round a bowl and flicking through the TV channels, desperately looking for something engaging to watch. Instead, I met a man who was in another world: present in body but not in mind, a lump of meat on a slab of bedding. The beeping of his life support machines lingers like tinnitus.

The tears start when I allow my mind to wander even further. It was such a dreary day and I know you're supposed to be more careful when the weather is bad. Was I driving too fast? They say that if you drive under 30 mph and you hit a pedestrian the injury is far less severe. How fast was I going? The windscreen wipers were going crazy. They must have been blurring my vision. I should have pulled onto the hard shoulder and waited for the rain to subside.

I'm really crying now, rocking back and forth like a baby, banging my head with my fist. What will happen in the next few days? Will Adam ever recover? And if he doesn't, what does that mean for me?

My last glance at the clock is at 4.46 a.m. before the instinct to sleep has one more lunge at me and I succumb.

BEN

Friday, 2 February

School called last night to tell me that unless I was ready to come back on Monday, I'd need a note from the doctor. And it's probably good that I speak to my GP anyway, to be honest – I've been sleeping so badly and my mind is all over the place. While I'm asleep, my dreams torment me with flashbacks to that morning on the motorway, and while I'm awake, I spend the whole time reliving my brief exchange with Alice and imagining myself having conversations with Adam. Over the last couple of days, I've caught myself in front of the mirror in my parents' bathroom, rehearsing hypothetical conversations with people who I barely know yet.

'It's good to see you making such a healthy recovery, Adam. I have to say that I didn't think you'd pull through.'

'Alice, do you remember that first time I came into the hospital ward and you told me to go away?'

Is all this wishful thinking? Am I hoping that Adam will wake from his coma? Of course I am, because if Adam survives then I'm free. If Adam wakes and carries on as normal, I, too, can carry on as normal, my record clear. If I'm honest, I know that the chances of this outcome are very low. I never took to biology at school, but I'm now becoming a bit of an expert on the brain and what happens when it goes wrong. It started with a bit of harmless googling:

> *Brain trauma*
> *Brain trauma after car accident*
> *Coma after car accident*
> *Chance of coming out of a coma after car accident*

But ever since that fleeting visit to the hospital, I've been fixated on the small medical details that Alice gave me:

> *Optic nerve damage*
> *Minimally conscious state*
> *Prognosis from minimally conscious state*

And then, before I know it, it's 4 a.m. and I'm watching a video about Greg, a man in his thirties who miraculously woke from a coma three months after a skiing accident, or reading a blog post written by parents celebrating the survival of their child following oxygen deprivation at birth. These stories of survival against the odds give me the hope that I need, at that unearthly hour, to quieten the chatter in my mind and to get some sleep.

I took a taxi with Mum to the doctors' surgery this morning because I still don't feel up to driving. My car is in my parents' driveway, where it's been since the day it happened. As we walked out of the house, I was careful to look straight ahead, seeing the red of my Volkswagen out of the corner of my eye but making a point not to look at it directly.

'Are you never going to drive again, then?'

My darling mother, helpful as always.

I made sure to arrive at the surgery first thing, but when I walk in, there's a queue of people waiting in the foyer already. A motley crew: at the front, an elderly lady with a shopping trolley, glancing repeatedly at her wristwatch and looking me up and down as I come through the door. Behind her is a pregnant woman pushing a buggy, a dishevelled man coughing up phlegm into a tissue and then swallowing hard, then a man in running gear with a huge gash on his forehead. Some are clearly more urgent than others.

I saunter up to the reception desk. Come on, Ben.

'Good morning. My name is Ben Anderson. I'm here to see Dr Edwards, please.'

'That's fine, please take a seat and I'll call you when she's ready.'

I take a seat, the one nearest the entrance, and glance over at the selection of magazines. I pick up an edition of *Take A Break* from October 2013 and then put it down when I find an unidentifiable crust of bodily fluid stuck on the edge of the second page. I reach into my trouser pocket and get out my phone. The screen lights up when I hit the side button, but then immediately starts powering itself off because I was on it all night draining the battery. And so I'm waiting in the surgery, with nothing to occupy me but my thoughts.

As I wait, sitting on a fold-up plastic chair with my mother next to me, I find myself rehearsing dialogue, and when the receptionist calls my name, I'm so deep in my own world that Mum has to nudge me into action.

'Ben Anderson? Dr Edwards – third door on the right.'

Mum and I both stand.

'No, Mum, no. Stay here.'

I can't believe she actually wants to come in with me. She needs to stop treating me like a child. If it were something physical, a cancer scare or something like that, I wouldn't mind. But this is really private. It's hard enough for me to admit it to myself, let alone have her chipping in.

My hands are shaking as I approach Dr Edwards' room and I give the door a pathetic knock.

'Ben, do come in! No need to knock. Nice to see you.'

'Hi, Dr Edwards. Nice to see you, too.'

Dr Edwards has one of those faces that invites you in. Almost perfectly round, a bit chubby and sprinkled with freckles. Immediately, I feel more at ease.

'Take a seat; you know the drill. How's your mum?'

Oh, you know: irritable, overbearing and rude.

'Yeah, she's great, thanks. She's just outside waiting for me.'

'And what about you? What can I do for you, Ben?'

Pause.

'I've been having these headaches.'

Headaches? Where on earth did that come from?

'OK, what kind of headache? All over your head or in one particular region?'

'Umm . . . yeah, kind of all over, a bit like migraines.'

Ugh, what I am doing? I'm dodging the issue. It just seems infinitely easier to report physical symptoms than anything else. It feels like a more valid reason to be calling in sick, a more tangible ailment. What would I say? I'm anxious? Depressed?

'OK and any other symptoms at all?'

'Yeah, well I guess I've been feeling a bit out of sorts.'

'Mood-wise, you mean?'

'Yeah, I had this car accident a couple of weeks back and I can't seem to shake it off.'

Car accident will do – I don't need to tell her any more than that.

'OK. So how do you think I can help?'

'Something to calm me down a bit would be great. And maybe something to help me sleep.'

Dr Edwards looks at me with the slight smirk of a reluctant, disapproving parent and starts tapping on her computer. Touch-typing is clearly not part of medical training – she's only using two fingers. She swivels her chair to the printer, tears off the prescription and scribbles on it.

'There you go, Ben. A low dose, just to get you through the next couple of weeks. You're not a big drinker, are you?'

'Drinker? Not really, no. You know, sometimes when I meet up with friends or whatever, the odd pint.'

'That's fine, just nothing too extreme while you're on these, OK? Can I persuade you to do some talking therapy too, this time?'

I've tried that twice before and it's just not for me. The last time I was here, Dr Edwards gave me a speech about how finding a therapist is like going on multiple first dates: you have a few false starts before you find the person you connect with. But the prospect of talking to a stranger about things that are so personal, so hard to put into words, is terrifying; just the thought of it compounds my anxiety.

43

'These tablets don't have any side effects, do they, Dr Edwards? Like, there's no risk they'll make things worse? Because you hear all kinds of stories, don't you? I've got quite a fragile stomach . . .'

Dr Edwards looks up from her notes and smiles.

'It's a low dosage, Ben. You'll be fine. Do you need a note for work?'

'Yes, please, Dr Edwards. And . . . well . . . maybe if you keep it quite general? Like I don't necessarily want them to . . .'

She blinks twice, nods and turns to her computer. She's hitting the keys really hard and typing so slowly that I can easily read what she's writing over her shoulder:

Re: Benjamin Anderson, date of birth 17/03/1986. I have seen the patient in question and recommend sick leave for a period of two weeks from today while he recovers from a minor car accident.

I wouldn't exactly call it 'minor', but I let it pass.

ALICE

We're in the third week and things seem to be stable, so I've decided that it's time to bring Max in to see his father. A consultant told me yesterday that it's good to talk to Adam as much as possible, to keep him stimulated, but I'm not sure how much longer I can talk *at* him without a response. I find it hard to believe that Adam, in his 'minimally conscious state', is going to notice who is here and when, but I'm going to pass the conch to Max for a while, to relieve the burden on me. And besides, there's only a certain amount of time that I can brush the trauma under the carpet for him. So far, I've wanted to protect Max, to shield him from the tubes, the wires, the ominous bleat of the life support machines. But as each day goes on, Adam's reality seems less and less transitory, and so every moment of procrastination is more and more futile. Max needs to see it with his own eyes, to start the process of adjustment to a new reality.

When I arrive at Mrs Turner's to pick him up, he's already waiting on the front doorstep. His little face lights up as I

45

edge into the driveway and he runs towards the car. I stop just short of him and wind down the window.

'Careful, Max! Are you ready to go? You can sit in the front with me as a special treat.'

As we drive through the side streets of Rickmansworth, I try to think of a way to start the conversation. He feels distant, detached: so much has happened and I haven't really kept him in the loop.

'How are you, Max? Sorry that Mummy's been so busy this week.'

'That's OK, Mummy. I know that Daddy's in hospital.'

'Yes, darling, I'm afraid he's not well. He's not very well at all.'

'Has he got the plague?'

Max has been learning about the Great Fire of London at school and it seems now they've progressed to other great British tragedies.

'No, darling. He's hurt his head and he's having a long sleep.'

'Daddy is so silly and lazy sometimes!'

When we arrive at the ward, Max runs up to his father and gives him a big kiss. He immediately places his treasured bear – named Bear – next to his head on the pillow and sits on the end of the bed by his feet.

'Why has Daddy got tubes, Mummy?'

'That's to help him breathe, Max.'

'But doesn't he already know how to breathe?'

'Yes, of course he does, darling. He just needs a bit of help with a few things at the moment.'

'Did he hit his head very hard, then?'

'Yes, he did, I'm afraid.'

46

Max jumps off the bed and bounces over to Adam, stroking his head and giving him a kiss on the temple.

'When I hurt myself, it makes it feel better when you do kissing on the hurt bit.'

The door opens and in walks Mr Al-Shawawi, the consultant neurologist. It's the fourth time he's seen Adam and I'm sure he's very clued up on science, but I don't like his manner. He's got this fixed, slightly manic smile on his face, as if he's read *Bedside Manner for Dummies* but only got as far as Chapter 1, presumably entitled 'Staying Positive'. This morning, he takes a shine to Max.

'Hello, young man. You must be Max. Have you been cheering your dad up?'

'I don't think so, really. He's in a minimally conscious state.'

I rub Max's shoulder and stifle a smirk. Mr Al-Shawawi's grin remains stuck to his face, but he turns immediately to me.

'How are we doing today, Alice?'

Oh, shut up with your 'we', Mr Al-Shawawi. That must be Chapter 2 – 'We're all in this together'.

I don't respond.

'Well, today, Alice, I wanted to introduce Laura-Jane Mandalay. She's one of our resident psychotherapists.'

Laura-Jane pops up from behind him, her head cocked and her hand outstretched.

'Hello, Alice, it's so nice to meet you. I'd love to spend some time getting to know you, if that's all right with you?'

Oh, fuck off, Laura-Jane. I don't need therapy and you don't need a double-barrelled name.

'Do you know, I think I'd rather . . . I mean, I don't want to leave Max and . . .'

47

'Please, Alice. It's not about therapy; I know you're doing really well. It's important that we speak so that you understand the situation and the options.'

'What are the options, Mummy?'

Well, thanks for that, Laura-Jane. Really helpful.

BEN

I decided not to take the full course of tablets that Dr Edwards prescribed. I took the first dose as soon as we got back from the surgery and immediately started to feel calmer, even sleepy. But then I started to feel funny about the ethics of it all: was it right that I should be filling my body with chemicals to lift my mood?

And then I started googling and read some horror stories about people who had got hooked on the very tablets that I had been prescribed. It's a real problem in the States: doctors overprescribe, patients get dependent – quicker than you'd think – and then the patients end up worse off than when they started. The last thing I needed at this point was to become some kind of junkie, hooked on prescription medication like Michael Jackson.

Then there's another part of me that's so ashamed about the idea that I can't get through something like this on my own. How pathetic to think that I need to pump my body full of chemicals in order to see me through the day.

What kind of a man am I? I can handle this on my own. I've had bad patches before and I've got through them. I can do it again.

I'm on the bus to the hospital again and already I feel better than last time. I've spent the last couple of days weighing up whether or not to make another visit. On the one hand, it's mildly crazy behaviour. I'm not surprised that Alice reacted in the way she did when I went last time: if I think about it logically, this has really got nothing to do with me. But then I feel this impulse, a compulsion to check in on Adam, to see how he's doing. And obviously that's not me being totally selfless – I have a stake in the outcome. Whether he lives or dies makes a big difference to me and it's the uncertainty that's fuelling these horrible nightmares. So, I think it's a good decision to visit again and I hope Alice doesn't get too angry.

I look out of the window and see parents rushing to the school bus with their children, professionals in suits honking their horns when the car in front of them doesn't edge forwards in the traffic at the first possible moment. Everyone getting on with their day. They don't know about Adam. It's just another early morning for them, uneventful and mundane.

I step off the bus and head towards the hospital. I don't need Google Maps this time: I've planned my walk, dodging the main road and going for the more scenic route.

It's a beautiful February day. Cold, but I walk on the sunny side of the road and feel some warmth beating down on my neck. On I go, past A & E, past the row of ambulances and the parked cars, heading towards Inpatients. I don't have flowers this time – I don't want to come on too strong – but it will be interesting to see where Alice has put the roses.

The door to room 454 is shut, so I give it three clear knocks. Nothing. I knock again and then hear a child's voice.

'Who is it?'

I feel a sudden hardness in the front of my throat. Who is that? My mind races, flicking through the possible scenarios, starting with the most catastrophic. Adam is no longer in the hospital because he has died and been replaced by someone else. Adam has moved hospitals and I'll never see him, or Alice, again. Alice has requested a move because she is so traumatised by my last visit. Adam has been discharged because he's made a speedy recovery. It has been a few days since I last came, and there was that case of the lady called Fiona in Massachusetts who woke from a coma one day and was completely back to normal within a week.

'Hello? Is there anyone there?'

Definitely a child's voice. What if it's one of my kids from school? I always find it disconcerting to see them out of context, but this would be unbearable. I haven't had a shave in days, and I am wearing a Radiohead T-shirt and my oldest jeans – not exactly how I want the kids to see me. Surely it can't be one of the students – what are the odds of that? Either way, it isn't Adam and it isn't Alice, so I turn back and speed down the corridor. Maybe the lady at reception can tell me the latest. If he's been discharged, they should be able to tell me that. That's good news and they don't have to tell me where he's been discharged to, so surely that's fine.

I'm about halfway down the hallway when I hear the creak of a door and that same soft voice call after me.

'Are you here to see my daddy?'

I turn round and standing with one foot in the room, one foot in the corridor, is a little boy. He's chubby, wearing a bright orange T-shirt and pink shorts. His nose – that distinctive button mushroom – makes me realise in an instant that this must be Alice's son.

'Hey there, buddy.' I scoot back down the hall, crouching to reach his level. 'How are you today?'

'I'm fine thanks, but Mummy says I'm not allowed to talk to strangers. Are you a friend of Mummy and Daddy?'

Good question.

'Um, not exactly. But I wanted to come and say hello to them.'

'Mummy's just gone to get a cappuccino. She says that I can have a spoon for the chocolate on top.'

'So jealous, that's the best bit.'

'Here she comes! Mummy, your friend is here.'

Alice is striding down the hallway, a cup in one hand and a pain au raisin in the other. She looks a right state and I think is in the same outfit as I saw the other day. I suppose looking good is the last thing on her mind. I feel nervous, expecting her to shout at me again, but there's a small smile. I hold my breath.

'I see you've met Max, then.'

'What a handsome little man! I didn't bring flowers this time. I wasn't sure if . . .'

'Oh, we don't need any more bloody flowers, that's for sure. Here you go, Maxy. Just wait a little because it's still hot. And have this pastry, but eat it slowly, will you?'

Maxy, that's a nice nickname.

'Well, do you want to come in, then?'

I follow her into the room and I can feel a wave of adrenaline surge right from my throat down to the base of my stomach.

'I'm afraid there's nowhere much to sit, but you can take the stool by the window if you like.'

I take the stool and then we stare right at each other for what seems like a good fifteen seconds, taking one another in. I want to say something but I don't know how to pitch it. In the end, she comes in first.

'Um, sorry if . . . Sorry if I was a bit short with you the other day.'

'Don't be silly. I totally get it. It was a bit weird for me to turn up like that. To be honest, I thought you might be angry again and I understand, but . . . how is he getting . . .'

'No change. They've started talking to me about turning the machines off. Not sure if I'm ready for that yet.'

I feel sick and it comes out a bit too suddenly.

'Oh, you mustn't do that. You mustn't. You have to keep hope and you never know when he might come round.'

'And what is it to you?'

'Sorry, I didn't mean to . . .'

'So let me get this straight. You were driving the car, the red Volkswagen, that hit Adam on the motorway. You do know he jumped, right?'

She mouths this so that Max doesn't hear, but he's got headphones on now anyway. Her teeth are remarkably white: must take some upkeep, that.

'Do we know that for sure? I mean, why . . . How can you be so certain? Has he tried it before?'

'You mustn't feel guilty about this, you know. It could have been anyone. You just happened to be in the wrong place at the right time. Or the right place at the wrong time. Or whatever.'

It's like I've got crippling guilt written all over my face. How does she know that this is why I'm here? How does she know that every day that he lies in that state is another day of unbearable angst for me?

'What's your name, anyway?'

'Ben. I'm Ben. And you are?'

There's no point in letting on that I already know her name. And her surname.

'I'm Alice.'

'Nice to meet you.'

And there, on that brisk Monday morning, the start of something wonderful.

ALICE

Isn't it ridiculous that no one ever teaches you how to be a parent? There are so many other things in life that we are prepared for: sex, work, even heartbreak. But no one ever sits you down and prepares you for parenthood. An antenatal class might tell you how to breathe, or even how to change a shit-filled nappy, but when it comes to the important stuff – the stuff that really matters – you're on your own. No one ever taught me how to speak to my son.

Almost a month has passed since that first cold January morning and it's looking like things are about to reach a head. I'm not going to pretend that I expected the outcome to be any different, but I didn't think I'd have to make the decision quite so soon. When we were standing in front of each other, eight years ago, swearing to be with each other in sickness or in health, I didn't know how near sickness would be, nor how instrumental I would have to be in its fateful resolution.

And so the early death of my husband is one more tragedy I'll add to the list. Before Max came along, Adam was really the only family I had. My parents died in a plane crash when I was eight. They were on a tour of America, having left me, their only child, with my mother's sister, Lydia, a bitter old spinster who made me drink cod liver oil on a spoon. They'd taken a small aircraft from Las Vegas to the Grand Canyon and, on the way back, the plane seemingly lost control and launched itself straight into a hillside. There were ten people on board and everyone died instantly.

I was flown out to Vegas with Aunt Lydia and the press had a field day: I was on the front page of some trashy tabloid, a chubby blonde girl in pigtails, standing alone clutching a doll, with the headline: They'll Never See Me Grow Up. Aunt Lydia, Dickensian in every way, then proclaimed that her nervous disposition was too acute to take on a little girl full-time and so she sent me straight to a boarding school, miles away from where she lived. I had to learn to fend for myself and soon nurtured resilience.

That resilience is coming in pretty handy now. When they first started talking about 'options' in relation to my coma-tose husband, it didn't take me long to realise that this was a euphemism. When your husband is in a coma, dependent on a machine to make his heart beat, the 'options' are ON or OFF – binary, yin or yang, yes or no – and there's no talking that can make that easier.

'So, Mrs Selby, you see, given the brain stem is completely unattached, there is, I'm afraid, no hope of future conscious-ness. Miracles do happen, but in the case of your husband the cards have been dealt.'

I'm definitely showing more patience with the hospital staff than I was, but this is not the time for metaphor or idiom and Mr Al-Shawawi's turns of phrase are getting on my fucking nerves.

'Talk to me straight, Mr Al-Shawawi. He's brain-dead?'

'Yes. Technically, he's still alive, but from a medical perspective we have to consider him fully dependent and, should one of these machines be withdrawn, he will expire. As Adam's next of kin, it's your prerogative to decide what we do next with those machines, Mrs Selby.'

Expire. Go off like a slab of chicken.

I imagine others in this scenario have people to talk to – someone to call in hysterics, to talk to at length, to consider this with. I get to skip that part because there is no one I can face sharing this with. I go straight to the decision, which seems pretty clear to me.

'Let's turn it all off.'

'Mrs Selby, I know you don't want to speak to any of our resident psychotherapists, but in our experience it really does help to take some time to think this through and . . .'

'Do you really think it takes much deliberation, Doctor? Do you really expect me to sit here wondering whether I'm doing the right thing for my husband? The man stepped in front of a car. He made his wishes clear.'

And so it is to be: all the machines will be turned off. And where does that leave me? A widow at thirty-one. There's another role I'll have to play: mourning widow in a black dress, head bowed, tears rolling down my face, clutching a child to my breast. It's not a role that I've rehearsed for, never what I expected for my life, but somehow I'll muddle through.

And will I ever love again? To be honest, I'm not sure I can be bothered. It seems too hard, too time-intensive, to meet someone new and fall in love all over again. And for all his faults, I truly believe that Adam and I were made for each other. Not in a mystical, soulmate sort of way – I don't believe in that bullshit – but in a much more practical sense. We have the same sense of humour, the same way of looking at the world. For all these years it had been Adam and me, united in our acerbic disdain for just about everyone else. And Adam loved me, in the purest sense of the word. He would go to the end of the earth for me and do anything to keep me safe, to keep me close.

I knew that I didn't have very long to explain to Max what was about to happen. There wasn't enough time to rehearse what I'd say, how or where I'd say it. So today, we left the hospital a little earlier than usual. I was planning to talk to him at home, when he was tucked up in bed, but it was as if he knew it was coming, on that drive home, and his line of questioning took us right there. We were barely out of the car park when the interrogation began.

'Mummy, how come that man came to visit?'

Ben came again today. The man who says he was the one who ran Adam over. I managed to keep my cool this time and engage in some kind of civil conversation with him. The bloke is a mess. He looks horrific – like someone who hasn't slept in days, big grey bags under his eyes and a vile red crust under his nose.

'Well, Max, it's quite hard to explain, really, but that man was there when Daddy had his accident. He's a nice man, I think, and he just wants to know if Daddy is OK.'

'And is he going to be OK, Mummy? I'm worried and I miss talking to him.'

'Oh, sweetheart. I miss talking to him, too.'

'When is he going to get better?'

Is there any way to break this to him that isn't going to damage him for ever?

'Sweetheart, in about a week we're going to have to say goodbye to Daddy. He's going up to Heaven.'

'Trudy says Heaven is made up.'

Trudy is in Max's class and seems to be wise beyond her years. That girl needs to pipe the fuck down.

'The important thing to remember, Max, is that he will always love you. Very, very much. And that Mummy is always going to be here.'

I looked in the rear-view mirror and Max caught my eye, stared, sat back and stuck his thumb in his mouth.

And now it's 9.30 p.m. Max is in bed and I'm looking out into the garden, a glass of Merlot helping me to wash down the remains of Max's fish fingers and potato wedges. I should be thinking about Adam. The mourning process should have begun; I should be rocking back and forth in my chair, hysterical. But as I look out into the black of the night, all I can think about is Max. My poor, undeserving child who is about to lose his father, a few months before his eighth birthday. What does the future hold for him?

ALICE

Tuesday, 13 February

Ben turned up again today – this is the third time now – but later in the day, just as they were closing the wards for the evening. I passed him on my way out, pleading with the nurse at reception. The desperation on his face was palpable and pathetic.

'Please, I just want to say hello. Give me ten minutes. Please.'

'I'm very sorry, sir, visiting times are over now and as you're not next of kin—'

I interrupted her.

'Ben, hi. Do you want to . . . Let's go to the café, shall we?'

His face lit up and so we headed down to the hospital café. It felt funny to suggest it, because having coffee with another man is not something that would ever have crossed my mind while Adam was alive. I had a double espresso – not that the caffeine was having any impact on me anymore – and Ben panicked into ordering the same thing and then proceeded not to touch his cup. As we approached the table, he pulled out a chair for me.

'Thanks, Alice. Thanks for this.'

And then there was an awkward pause. We stared at each other – waiting, I think, for the other to start the conversation. He has big blue eyes, not dissimilar to Adam's, and I allowed myself to get lost in them for just a moment.

'So, Ben, what I want to know is how you find so much time to come and visit us in hospital. Don't you work?'

However hard I try to be sensitive, it's not in my nature: that was me trying to be nice.

'I . . . I . . . I've been off work for the past month.'

'Why?'

'Well, since the accident I've been kind of out of sorts. You know, depressed.'

Blimey.

'What do you do, then? For a living, I mean.'

'I'm a teacher. At a primary school in Bricket Wood.'

'Ah, well that's understandable. Can't have the teacher standing at the front of the classroom in pieces. Mind you, at least you're qualified. The teachers at Max's school are barely out of primary school themselves.'

'I'm hoping to go back to work next week, actually. I'm feeling a lot better and I want to get back there before the supply teacher sends them all off the rails.'

'That's good. You know, you mustn't feel guilty, Ben. You mustn't. He's tried this before. Suicide, I mean.'

'But I guess there's always hope, isn't there? That he'll wake. I mean, suicide is only suicide if it actually, you know, ends in death.'

I had a few different options. Tell him the truth – that all it was going to take was my signature on a document and the machines would be off, putting Adam out of his misery. Or lie and let him keep the illusion that the future was uncertain but hopeful. I could have asked him not to come again. Told him that recovery was likely but that I'd rather he didn't visit. Spare the man from his own misery. But I'm not Mother fucking Teresa. If I could deal with this, so could he.

'I've agreed to let them turn the machines off now.'

'But it's your decision, isn't it?'

'The doctors say there's no chance of him ever being able to function independently. I think it's the right thing to do.'

There we go, I thought. Cue the crazy reaction.

'Oh, but you mustn't! You mustn't, Alice! Isn't that . . . How is that even . . . But what if he wakes?'

'Look, Ben, this isn't a decision I've come to easily. Trust me, I'd rather keep all avenues open. Let there be a chance that a miracle will happen and everything will return to normal. But anyway, I'm not sure it's something that I need to justify to you. And, quite frankly, I'm not even sure why you're here.'

This is a meek man, I thought. A man not used to women like me. He looked horrified that I'd confronted the situation so directly. But why was this man taking such an interest in our lives? I know a sensitive soul when I see one – I've been married to one for years – but this guy really could take a prize for sentimentality. Imagine this in reverse: I'd knocked over his wife or girlfriend when she'd darted in front of my car. Don't get me wrong – I'd be shaken up.

I'd feel sick. But I'd give my statement, take my breathalyser and drive off, getting on with my own little life. Life's too short to dwell on other people's tragedies, and even if this man had a small part to play in Adam's, it was only in the logistics of it, the practicalities, the execution. He was not a vital player. He obviously saw things differently. He was sobbing, sobbing and moaning.

'I'm so sorry. I don't know what to say. I can't . . . I mean, this shouldn't have . . . maybe if I had been driving a bit slower, I'd have seen him coming and . . .'

I reached into my pocket and took out a packet of tissues: sealed, not yet started. I slid the packet across the table and he grabbed them without even looking.

'I don't know why I'm the one crying. I'm so sorry, Alice, I'm all over the place. I just never thought I'd be responsible for ending someone's life. When is it going to happen? I mean, when are the machines, you know . . .'

'Thursday. Day after tomorrow.'

'And then what? A funeral?'

His eyes are red raw and searching. He's reaching out, asking for something.

'A funeral. If you give me your phone number, I'll text you the details. You should come.'

Ben takes another tissue out of the packet, wipes his nose, reaches into his pocket and slides his phone across the table.

'Here, I can't remember my number. But you enter yours in mine and I'll give you a missed call. Then you'll have my number, too.'

BEN

Wednesday, 21 February

She looks different, but I can't put my finger on it. Is it the hair? Maybe a little shorter. It's probably just the outfit; I've never seen her dressed like that, or wearing make-up. She shuffles to the front of the church, tissue in one hand, crumpled paper in the other. I'm on the fourth row: near but keeping a respectful distance. As she stands behind the lectern, she looks vaguely in my direction. I think she's seen me, but I don't get an acknowledgement.

'Adam and I first met in our university halls. It was the second day of the first term of the first year and I guess you could say we hit it off right away . . .'

I admire her bravery. What a time she's had, the last few weeks; plunged into the kind of scenario that we know happens but think only ever happens to other people. She is standing there with grace and I can't help but imagine myself in that scenario. I couldn't stand there like that, talking to the whole congregation. I didn't know the man, never met him while he was alive, and yet I'm a wreck.

'Sometimes life deals you a card that you don't expect. And then, when it does, you make the best of it. So I'll remember Adam as a passionate man, a friend, a deep thinker, a learner, a writer and, above all, a great father to Max. I know that he and I will miss him more than words can say. Thank you.'

It's funny, because while I've always been sensitive, I've never been a big crier. Now, though, all it takes is the slightest sense of emotion from someone else, the smallest inkling of tragedy, and the tears flood out. I'm sitting here, sobbing uncontrollably. I can't help but imagine all the scenarios that Adam will miss. I guess it's thinking about Max that gets to me most: he's not here today – good decision, Alice – but smart as he is, how much can he understand of what is going on? And even more worrying: how much of his father will he even remember? What can I remember from when I was seven? I couldn't name a single thing. But then I suppose nothing quite as traumatic happened to me at such a young age and maybe a critical event like this puts a marker down as if to say, 'Keep hold of this, you'll need this later on.'

I'm crying so much that I stand and head to the toilets to escape further embarrassment. If I do get the chance to speak to Alice, I don't want her to see me like this.

As I'm walking, I look around and am relieved to see that I'm not the only one in this state: there's a group of old ladies in a row towards the back sobbing into their handkerchiefs, and there's a general soundtrack of whimpering, sniffing, nose-blowing and even the occasional moan. I wonder who all these people are: I imagine a lot of them came for the morbid curiosity. It's disgusting, if you think about it, but there's nothing better than the tragic death of a young man to bring a community together. What is it that drives this behaviour? Is it smugness? An expression of the relief that you and your loved ones are fine, unscathed? Or is it rehearsal, for the day when that terrible something happens to you?

I stand at the urinal and push out a wee – something I always have to do if I go into a public toilet whether I need it or not, because I think it looks weird to come in just to stare in the mirror or wash my hands. When I've finished, I head to the sinks and stare at myself in the mirror. I look exhausted: huge bags under my eyes and redness in my pupils from all the crying. I dip my hand under the tap and use a bit of water to flatten down my hair. I let out a deep sigh, doing up my flies as I step out of the safety of the toilet into the wide expanse of the mourning throng. The door creaks, and people turn and look at me. I even get a sympathetic smile from one of the old ladies at the back.

When the service is over, everyone shuffles out in silence. There's an orderliness that seems to work itself out: first, the back row on the left, then the back row on the right, then the next row on the left and so on. Everyone is doing something physical to acknowledge the scenario: a bow of the head, a deep stare into the distance; one lady is even shaking her head as if to say, 'How could something like this happen to someone so young?' I am waiting for someone to look at me directly. I wonder how many people know about my involvement in this. Has Alice told her closest girlfriends about my visits? I see a young woman whisper something in her husband's ear as I take my turn to file out and I assume the whisper is about me:

'Him, that's him. The one who ran him over.'

As I walk towards the exit and the parade of people heading towards the grave, I turn back twice, looking to see if they still have their gaze on me.

Stepping out, I inhale deeply and appreciate the fresh air. It's chilly, but the sun is shining. I like to think that Adam would have had his spirits lifted on such a day.

The crowds are dispersing now, some making for cars scattered around the circumference of the church, others hanging back to wish Alice and family all the best. I think I'll head off now: I've paid my respects, done my duty.

'Ben, thanks for coming. I really appreciate it.'

Alice is running after me, lifting up her long black dress as she struggles in her heels.

'It can't have been easy for you, Ben. Really, thank you.'

I freeze in that moment and don't know what to say. I want to run over to her and give her a massive cuddle, cry into her shoulder and apologise for what I've done. I want to beg for her forgiveness. Instead, I force a smile, wave and run out of the churchyard.

ALICE

Adam always said that he wouldn't want there to be 'too much of a hiatus' between death and burial.

'I don't want to be rotting in a mortuary for weeks on end,' he once said while we were shopping for Max's Christmas presents in Bicester Village shopping centre. 'Seriously, Al, I was reading about this veteran in a bedsit in South London. Only dead for a few days, but the neighbours from the flat below called the police when maggots started dripping through the ceiling. Totally vile.'

So it's not even a full week since he died and we buried Adam today. I was surprised at how many people turned up, because I could count on one hand the number of people Adam actually considered significant in his life. When we first met at university, one of the things that he and I bonded over was our unfortunate family histories. We lay awake, the night after we first slept together, squashed in the single bed of his room in halls, our limbs entangled and our foreheads glistening with sweat, comparing notes about our tragic lives. I told him that my parents were both dead and he instantly softened, curling his body into mine.

'I don't really have any happy memories with Mum,' he said, looking just past me, a sheet of tears forming in his eyes. 'She was in and out of hospitals – institutions, really – for as long as I can remember. Bipolar, I think. One of my first memories is of her being sectioned at my ninth birthday party. The police came round – all the kids were sent home. She ended up killing herself when I was fourteen and they didn't even let me go to the funeral because they thought it would be too traumatic.'

I wonder how common it is for suicide to run in the family. It provides some comfort to me, as I bury my husband, to know that his troubles may have been inherited, that there is a physiological, genetic, hereditary explanation for this. It stops me from blaming myself.

Adam's dad, Roger, gave me a nod as he walked in and then sat in one of the back rows, avoiding eye contact. I did my very best not to say a word to him all day. It might seem ungrateful of me to be so disparaging of this man, whose family legacy in the oil trade continues to provide financial security for Max and me beyond anything I could possibly ever earn myself. But money can't account for everything.

He left Adam and his mother when Adam was just five, fulfilling every cliché by running off with his secretary, Leanne, fifteen years his junior. While Adam's mum was battling depression, hooking herself on lithium, and Adam was left virtually fending for himself, Roger and Leanne got married and started a new family. Before the divorce had even gone through, Leanne was pregnant and then went on to have four children, each of them more precocious than the previous one.

The kids stayed away from the funeral, thankfully, but Leanne was at the back of the church with Roger, lurking in a corner like a reluctant infant. She looked fucking ridiculous: bursting out of a little black dress, her collagen-filled lips so far removed from the rest of her face that it's as if they had a life of their own.

Adam had barely spoken to his dad since his first suicide attempt at university. A member of staff called Roger to say Adam had taken an overdose of antidepressants, but he did not visit Adam in hospital. Instead, he turned up at his rented house a week later to tell him he was weak like his mum and needed to 'man up'. He said Adam had betrayed him by going to the doctor and getting the same pills that had 'ruined' his mother.

What did Roger feel while he was sat expressionless in the church today? Validated because he was proven right? Relief? Guilt? Did he go home and cry?

Plenty of other people came out of the woodwork: girls from university who wouldn't give him the time of day when we were there together but were now seeking some kind of redemption at the eleventh hour, as if their reluctance to socialise with him then was somewhat instrumental in his suicide. His aunt, June, who dramatically left her husband of forty years on Christmas Day last year and ran off with an ex-Quaker lesbian called Dawn. June's son, Jack, also made an appearance, creating some kind of origami duck out of the order of service.

The priest asked me if I was planning a spread after the funeral and I did think about it but couldn't be bothered in the end. I kept thinking about what Adam would want and I knew him well enough to know he wouldn't want a bunch of virtual strangers at the house, scoffing Scotch eggs and dropping crumbs all over the floor. When I told the priest that I thought it would be best if we just did the ceremony and be done with it, he looked a bit taken aback, but I'm not about to be judged by a priest, whose own life decisions are, by dint of him being a priest, questionable.

I didn't cry during the ceremony. Not because I'm not sad. Of course I am. But I've done the grief bit, I think. I did the hysteria that first morning. I've spent days and days waiting and thinking by Adam's hospital bed. The only tears to be heard in that hall today belonged to other people who were thinking about this for the first time. Apart from Ben, who was more distraught than anyone.

The guy really needs to go and see someone – he was all over the place. I think he tried to be discreet about it, but everyone noticed when he had to excuse himself and head to the toilets. And then he was always just *there*: it felt like every time I looked round, he was lurking somewhere nearby. Every time a new person approached me with an attempt at pity or an expression of grief, he was on the periphery, listening, wanting to be part of it.

The man needs to move on. It's not his tragedy.

ALICE

Tuesday, 13 March

I've always thought that mindfulness was a load of rubbish:
it seemed too trendy, something for Buddhists, or for people
who call themselves Buddhists, or for hippies in east London
who wear trousers just that bit too short and shoes without
socks. When the old lady at Adam's funeral gave me the
leaflet, I intended to throw it away as soon as I got home.
None of her fucking business. As it happens, I left it in one
of the kitchen drawers and came across it last week when
I was clearing away. I went on the website and watched
a testimonial from another woman who had recently been
bereaved, convincing me when she said that it had helped
her to get out of a rut. So I decided to give it a go.

I arrive fifteen minutes early and nearly turn back as
soon as I get out of the car when I see the other people
entering the building: one woman in some kind of robe
with a shaved head, a man with track marks on his arms
who looks like he has bigger fish to fry and a goth who
can't be more than about nineteen, with headphones in and

a face that would make Wednesday Addams seem upbeat. This isn't my crowd.

When I enter the room, there are ten chairs laid out, in a horseshoe. The course leader is already sat there, an obese woman in her sixties, and most of the other chairs are also taken. I take the one nearest the door.

'Welcome. If you can take your shoes off, please, and just leave them outside.'

Shit. Wearing odd socks.

'We'll get started in a moment. Just a couple of people who we're waiting for and then we'll begin.'

An uncomfortable silence. In any other setting, at this point everyone would suddenly be very busy with their phones, sending emails or furiously scrolling through Facebook. With no phones allowed during the mindfulness sessions and very little else for distraction, the only thing we can do is look each other up and down. Some people are avoiding eye contact; others are looking at me straight on with an awkward, sympathetic smile as if to say, 'You must be going through some kind of trauma, too.' And then, just as I'm about to close my eyes to avoid these uncomfortable exchanges, the door creaks open and a man runs in, breathless and apologising.

'Sorry, sorry I'm late. The Tube was delayed and . . .'

Flustered, the man takes a seat opposite me, removes his shoes and wipes the sweat off his forehead. Fuck. It's Ben. What on earth is he doing here? I cast my mind back to the funeral, when the old lady handed me the leaflet. Ben was lingering; I *knew* he was listening. Is this man following me? I feel indignant and start playing out confrontations in my head, a showdown at the end of the session. But it also feels thrilling and in some ways I guess I'm flattered.

As the evening progresses, I find myself catching little glances of him from the corner of my eye, looking at his face in more detail. He is a handsome guy and I'm pretty sure I'm not the only person in the group making that observation. Another lady clearly has her eye on him: one of those bigger girls in her early thirties who may as well have 'I'll Take What I Can Get' written across her forehead, spending every waking hour scoping out options for a husband before her ovaries dry up. Not that I'm checking Ben out. Fuck knows, if I wanted him I could have him.

Shirley, the instructor, is so overweight that she must make me seem like Kate Moss. What she's wearing isn't doing her any favours – she's squeezed herself into a horrific floral dress and it looks like she's done her make-up in the pitch-black, her teeth covered in red lipstick and her eyeshadow so thick it looks like a badger's paw. And then a bell sounds to signal the start of the meditation and my mind goes immediately to Adam.

I try to go and see him once a week. It's a weird practice, laying flowers for a dead person. It's not as if he's around to enjoy them, or to comment if last week's flowers are wilting. He's buried in a relatively sparse area of the cemetery, at the back on the right when you go in. It looks like a new patch and I can see that spaces have been left around many of the graves near him, presumably for loved ones who have yet to call it a day.

The church administrator sent me an email a few days after the funeral, asking if I wanted a space left next to him for myself. I didn't answer, not necessarily because I don't want to be buried next to him, but because I felt like I'd be tempting fate to make a decision either way at this stage. Soon, I'll have missed the chance. Give it another few months and some old dear will be laid to rest in the place that could have been reserved for me.

I don't spend very long at his grave. I'm not one of those weirdos who talks to him and tells him about how my week is going, asking for his advice on whatever's going on in my life. There's that scene in *Forrest Gump* at the end where he does that – that always struck me as a bit pathetic.

I took Max to the cemetery for the first time last week. I left him at Mrs Turner's on the morning of the funeral, after much deliberation, because I decided that the whole thing would just be too horrific for him to endure. There's something so stark about a funeral, so lacking in nuance or subtlety, that it didn't feel like the right atmosphere for a seven-year-old. Besides, he's never stepped into a church before and I'm not about to start making a habit of it. I'm quite happy to keep Max protected from the pomp and mystery of religion.

It was a crisp, sunny afternoon and so instead of going in the car, we walked, hand in hand, the mile and a half between home and the cemetery. At first, the conversation was mundane and chirpy. Max had spent the morning watching a *Harry Potter* film, the first one, and so I asked him to tell me the story, even though I couldn't care less about that pretentious wizard and the scar on his forehead. I was distracted, exhaling deeply and feeling a sting in my chest, waiting for a gap in the conversation and the right moment to steer things to the matter at hand. It's not an easy subject and up until now I hadn't done a very good job of talking everything through with Max. It had been easy to prioritise other things, to put off the difficult conversations. But my child had just lost his father. I needed to be there for him. We needed to get things out in the open.

'Max, sweetheart, you know it's OK to feel sad about Dad, don't you?'

This took him aback, because he stopped walking and looked up at me, and I saw for the first time sadness in his eyes, as if he'd been waiting for permission to grieve.

'I do feel sad, Mummy. I miss him so much.'

I felt relieved to hear him being open about it and lifted him up, burying my face in the hair on the back of his head and kissing him repeatedly. I could feel my eyes welling, a chill on the back of my neck, and I swallowed hard to keep myself together.

'Well, Max, he might not be with us here in person, but he'll always be in our thoughts and I think he'll be thinking of us, too. Wherever he is.'

'I know, Mummy,' he said, 'but I can't play with his *thoughts*. Who's going to help me build the tree house in the garden?'

'I can help, darling. You'll have to take charge, though! You're so much better at it than me.'

'Yeah, I'm good at building. Don't worry, Mummy, I can teach you.'

At this, I put Max down, took his hand again and rubbed his little palm with my thumb.

★

Bell tolls, eyes open, back in the room. Is that it? That was hardly relaxing. This has not made me feel any better and I'm in a foul mood. As all the misfits pack up their belongings, smiling bowing their heads apologetically, Ben approaches me.

'Alice, so good to see you. Do you want to grab a drink? I'm not actually drinking at the moment – no alcohol, no caffeine even – but there's a great juice place one minute away?'

I really can't think of anything worse right now.

'Ben, sorry. I really need to head back to Max.'

'How is the little guy? How is he coping? Is he back at school yet?'

The little guy? Really?

'He's doing well, thanks.'

'Well, tell him I said hi, will you?'

I smile, place my bag on my shoulder and run down the stairs towards the exit.

BEN

'OK, so if you want to find a comfortable position, close your eyes if you find that helpful, and when you hear the bell, we'll begin.'

BONG.

The first few minutes of the session are hard. It takes a while to settle down, to quieten the chattering monkey in my head. I'm too hot and I'm conscious of a bead of sweat making its way down my forehead. And everything's a bit itchy: the bridge of my nose, my left temple, my right earlobe. But after a while I settle, and soon enough I'm focusing on her voice: soft, soothing but with an authority that commands attention.

'Focus now on your breathing. Every breath in and out. How does it feel when you inhale, and then exhale? Which sensations do you feel? Maybe you sense a loosening in the chest, or a flutter in your stomach. Whatever you feel, accept that feeling. Let it be and then allow it to pass. And if you do find your mind wandering, accept that and bring your thoughts back to your breath.'

I'd been thinking for a while about trying mindfulness, and when I heard someone mention it to Alice at the funeral, I made a note of the recommendation and googled it when I got home. It really feels like coming to this course is a vital part of me getting back to my old self. The year didn't get off to the best start and by the time it came to Adam's funeral, things were somewhat out of hand.

After the funeral, I went to the cinema. It's an unusual thing to do, but for years a trip to the cinema has been a relaxation technique for me, a way of taking my mind off problems. I first did it when I was in the lower sixth; I had no plans for the whole weekend and instead of moping about feeling sorry for myself, I took myself to the multiplex cinema down the road from my parents' house. I arrived at the screen at the last possible moment, minimising the risk of seeing anyone I knew at the popcorn stand. It's stupid, really, as going to sit in front of a screen for two hours in silence is the least sociable of activities, but somehow convention dictates that it's something that should be shared.

The trouble is that often I've got so many things on my mind that it's hard for me to find a film that doesn't trigger one anxiety or another. A particular low point was crying during *Finding Nemo*, not because I was sad for the poor fish who had lost his family, but because it reminded me that I was still single, that I may never even find a family to love or to lose.

I'm letting my mind wander again. I go back to focusing on my breath but keep one eye open to see how all the others in the group are getting on. Everyone else seems to be in the flow of it, some sitting on chairs, others lying on a yoga mat. Alice is on a chair, like me. She's glowing.

The days after the funeral all blend into one. There I was, back at my parents' house, spending the majority of each day in bed. For some reason, I found it easy to sleep during the day and then, at night, I was wide awake, pacing around the room like a madman, looking out into the garden and imagining shapes in the trees. I suppose it was a kind of jet lag: a cycle that left me dazed and groggy during the day and wired at night.

I knew that if I was ever going to get out of this rut, I needed to do something. It was a Monday morning when I had this epiphany. It was time to get my shit together. So I left the house and cycled over to the school to chat with the headmistress. Cycling was progress in itself. Even if I couldn't bring myself to get behind the wheel of a car, at least I was back on the road.

As I approached the school gates, I went a little weak at the knees. Each parked car reminded me of a person, a colleague who may or may not have known about what happened to me, or rather what I did to someone else. Luckily, the headmistress' office is slightly apart from the main school building, so I could slip in there without the risk of being noticed and interrogated. It's funny that even I, a teacher, a man in my thirties, shake a little before knocking on a door that says 'Headmistress' Office' on the outside.

'Come in, come in!'

Mrs Teasdale was at her desk, surrounded by stacks of paper and at least eight mugs. For a lady in her position of authority, she's remarkably scatty: her hair in a makeshift bun, the shirt to her trouser suit untucked, and always looking a bit overwhelmed and out of her depth.

'Ben, Ben. Great to see you! We've all missed you, you know.'

And I found myself limping slightly as I walked to take a chair, grabbing the top of my back and wincing.

'Hello, Mrs Teasdale. It's nice to see you.'

'Oh, you really have hurt yourself, haven't you? Is it your back?'

My back was totally fine, but it was so much easier to explain my absence if I feigned a physical injury. I didn't want my colleagues thinking that it was just stress and anxiety that had kept me off work. And what if the kids found out? The parents?

'Yeah, it's an extreme form of whiplash. I'm all dosed up on paracetamol, though. I'm ready to come back, I think.'

'Great, so you can start again next Monday?'

I hadn't made up my mind about when I was coming back. But maybe this was what I needed – someone decisive, someone to push me into action.

BONG.

The sound of the gong pulls me back into the room. Shit, I'm supposed to be focusing on my breath.

'OK, so how was that for everyone?'

If I look down, she won't pick on me.

'Ben, how was your practice?'

'Oh, really good, yeah. I was really in the zone that time.'

It's so hard to tell the truth. It's just easier to say that it went well. Otherwise, I might have to go into detail about what it was that prevented me from staying focused on the meditation and then I'd get sanctimonious nods from the more experienced members of the group.

'OK, folks, so let's do one more mindful movement meditation and then we'll call it a day. Close your eyes and when you hear the bell, we'll begin.'

I love the instructor's calmness. I reckon that even if the most horrible thing happened to her, even if she were defending herself against an armed terrorist, her tone would still be soft and measured.

BONG.

BONG.

I open my eyes, and look around me. Good session – I really managed to focus that time. I feel good.

As I roll up the yoga mat and grab my socks and shoes, I feel quietly content: calm and present. I like how slowly everyone moves here: no one is in a rush, there's no urgency – I get the impression that for these few moments as I step back into the world, nothing matters and everything can wait.

I pluck up the courage to ask Alice if she fancies going for a drink and then immediately regret it when she rejects me. I should have thought that she'd be in a rush to get back to Max. Maybe another time.

BEN

The journey to work this morning felt truly exhilarating. Not because I was going fast, or because I was in a sports car with a punchy engine, but because just being behind the wheel was a real achievement for me. In fact, I drove very, very slowly, like a learner who doesn't know how far the pedal goes, or an elderly person who's in no particular rush to get to the shops. I pulled my seat belt so tight it cut at my waist and I looked in the wing mirror so frequently that I felt dizzy by the time I arrived. But I did it: I drove to work.

I'd already mentioned to the headmistress that I wanted my return to be as unremarkable as possible. I didn't want a fanfare; I didn't want it to be a big deal. In an ideal world, no one would even acknowledge that I'd been gone. I wanted it to be just like coming back to work on a Monday morning after the weekend. I didn't want to answer questions, least of all from the children. There's an innocence and naivety to children that means they would ask questions that would pierce me right where it hurts.

'It is true, Mr Anderson? Is it true that you knocked someone over and killed them?'

And what would I reply to that?

In the end, the kids got it just right. They were warm, clearly happy to see me, but not over the top. It turns out the supply teacher had been a bit of a flop, which helped – 'Mrs Taylor didn't even know her twelve times table' – and at the end of the day a little girl called Evie, who I have a real soft spot for, came up to me and said, 'I'm really glad you're back, Mr Anderson.'

It's funny how a comment as simple as that can have such an impact on me. It felt like returning back to work after a stint in hospital, as if I had been the one injured in a car crash. I was so glad to be back: I had spent a whole day focused on something else, a whole day when I wasn't alone with my own guilt. And as I walked out of the old Victorian building to my car, I had the distinct feeling that everything was going to be OK.

But then, on the way home, as I was pulling out of the main gates, a couple of drops of rain fell on the windscreen, so I turned on the wipers. I was suddenly mesmerised by the back and forth of the rubber and plastic, grey and wet. It was like everything was happening again, in sequence: the zip, the thunder, the mist, the dial, the stain – and I knew what would happen next.

My hands were shaking and I could feel the warm trickle of sweat tracing down the back of my head, onto my neck and down my back. At the mindfulness course they went on about having 'strategies in your toolbox', to help in moments of stress, but I was blank; the only thing I could focus on was the road in front of me. My vision started to blur and I felt light-headed. I was totally out of control and if I didn't get off the road soon, I'd kill again, either another innocent passer-by or myself.

Just in the nick of time, I indicated right into a pub car park and managed to park, despite my legs shaking. I turned the engine off, opened the window and broke down in tears.

And now, on a dark Monday evening, I am in the front of my car with my seat belt still fastened, rubbing my eyes and blowing my nose with the remnants of a tissue that I've found in the glove compartment.

Another car pulls up beside me, and I hear the crunch of the brakes and the slam of a door as an elderly man stumbles out and heads towards the pub. It's still pouring and he doesn't seem to be in any particular rush to save himself from getting wet. I'll wait in the car for ten more minutes and see if the rain stops. I'm not going to try driving again until it stops, because clearly it's not safe.

Half an hour later, it's still raining, so I decide to stay for a drink in the pub. It's a pub that I've driven past for years but never been inside. When I walk in, it's almost empty: there's a woman serving behind the bar who looks like she hasn't moved from that spot for half a century and the man I saw limping from his car is now slouched at the bar with what looks like a triple whisky on the rocks. I look around and opt for a seat at the back by the window: far enough that I can keep myself to myself, but near the door in case I want to make a quick escape.

'You ain't even going to order a drink then, young man?'

The words 'young man' surprise me. I certainly don't feel young. I feel like a man old beyond my years, a shadow of my former self.

'Sorry, sorry . . . can I have a tonic water, please?'

'What – just tonic?'

'Yes, please. I'm not a massive drinker.'

The barmaid raises her eyebrows and I wince at the sound as she scoops a mound of ice into a glass.

I get out my phone and flick through Facebook. I'm one of those people who scrolls a lot but doesn't post much. Most of the people on here I haven't seen since school or university, and when I see their photos, it usually makes me upset and jealous because they're married or have children.

I finish the tonic quickly, not because I'm particularly thirsty but because sipping it constantly keeps me occupied and helps me to avoid any further interaction with the barmaid. But then when I order another one, she takes the bait:

'You live around here, then?'

I've always felt a bit awkward talking to people in a scenario like this. My mum used to take me to the barber in the rougher part of town when I was little and it always made me feel self-conscious that I was too posh.

'Yes, well, I . . . I work just around the corner.'

'Not seen you in here before. Had a rough day, have you?'

I didn't realise that it was written so clearly on my forehead.

'No,' I lie, 'not at all. Just fancied a drink.'

I certainly wasn't about to tell this stranger my deepest, darkest secrets.

'Suit yerself, Mr Chatty.'

An hour later, I'm still in the same position, on my fifth tonic water. I'm searching through my latest WhatsApp conversations to see if there's anything I've yet to reply to, but it's row after row of double blue ticks – everything's been read and all conversations have come to a close. About halfway down the page is Alice and I click on her name, scrolling up to read back the conversation we had just after the mindfulness class. She was surprised to see me there but wrote 'nice to see you, anyway', which I reread four times. I put my phone down and order another drink.

'Another one of the same, please.'

'Bloody hell, mate. You must really love tonic water.'

'Can I have a packet of those salt and vinegar crisps as well, please?'

The barmaid hands me two packets.

'On the house, love.'

That's nice of her. I smile, look down and pick up my phone again. I open one of the packets of crisps and start stuffing them down – they are crinkly and the intense taste of vinegar stings the ulcer inside my left cheek. Fuck it, I'm going to text Alice.

BEN

I'm in the car again and it's pissing it down. That kind of rain that seems like it's never going to stop: tropical, apocalyptic. It's also freezing cold and I blast the heating up to full whack. The windscreen wipers are going so fast that it just looks like a blur of black, back and forth, back and forth, obstructing my view. I hear a crack and the windscreen splits, the rain gushing in and covering the dashboard. I can't even see my speed anymore and I feel a squidge in my right sock as the rainwater seeps through the leather of my shoe.

Nausea sweeps over me and I feel like this is going to go one of two ways from here: either I'm going to pass out at the wheel and I'll swerve into the central reservation. Or the car will finally give in to the elements and collapse mid flow, shattering into a thousand pieces, swept away into the cold English countryside to be buried among the leaves, conkers and cones of the previous season.

I sit up, my pillow drenched in sweat, and turn over to look at the time on my phone: 5.15 a.m.

ALICE

Sunday, 15 April

'Max, can you put this Lego away and tidy up the living room before our guests come round?'

I can't remember the last time I hosted a meal. As the years went on, Adam became progressively less tolerant of other people and, for the last couple of years, I've basically been on a ban from inviting anyone over. When Max first started school, some of the other mums would try to be friendly in the playground and invite us over for Sunday lunch. Adam didn't mind me going on my own as long as he knew the people, but he'd never come himself and it was always a bit awkward. The invitations quickly dwindled as I was unable to reciprocate and some of the mums who had previously been friendly to me started avoiding eye contact.

Last weekend, after Max had gone to bed, I sent emails to a few people who I knew were particularly hankering for an invitation and invited them round for a Sunday roast. In some ways, hosting a dinner party is the last thing I want to do at the moment. But I don't want to get stuck in a rut and find myself creaking around this big house on my own, feeling sorry for myself, like a widow in a black hood from a pension advert. I need to start putting myself out there.

Helen is the first to arrive, with her daughter, Ava. Ava is in Max's class and they seem to get on pretty well, even though she's not going to appear on *Child Genius* anytime soon. Helen and I first bonded over the fact that we're both trained accountants and she still works full-time at a firm in the City. Clearly, her wardrobe is not very extensive, because she's turned up in a frumpy black trouser suit that is more suited to the boardroom than a casual Sunday lunch. She's clutching a box of Celebrations – how imaginative – and shoves them in my face.

'Here you go, Alice. It's good to *see* you. How are you holding up?'

She's got her head cocked and I feel like slamming the door in her face. I don't need her sympathy. I control myself.

'Come in, Helen. Thanks for these. Ava, Max is upstairs. Can you take your shoes . . .'

But she's already leapt past me and up the stairs.

Next to arrive are Lisa and Gary. I've known Lisa since we were eight, when I was banished to boarding school by Aunt Lydia. I found it pretty hard to make friends there. Little girls can be such bitches and because I joined at an unusual time, all of their friendship groups were fully formed and closed for new members. It didn't help that I was overweight, or that I would turn scarlet and start sweating profusely as soon as any physical exercise was demanded of me. Lisa was the other outsider at the school – in the year below, ostracised because she had brittle bones and would break a limb quicker than anything. She once fractured her pelvis while using a skipping rope in the playground: I went with her in the ambulance to A & E and fed her strips of fizzy apple liquorice.

We spent most of our time together as teenagers, but then fell out after school. Lisa decided not to go to university – she was never particularly academic – and when I accepted my place at Durham, she seemed put out, affronted that I had made such a life decision without her permission. And then when I got to Durham and immediately met Adam, she started acting like a jealous lover, suspicious of him and doing her best to drive us apart. When I told her we were engaged, she hung up the phone and sent me a text message the following morning:

Alice, what are you doing? He's a headcase. What do you see in him?

And the truth is, no one ever saw in Adam what I saw in him. I'm not saying there weren't some hard times in our marriage, but if I reflect on our life together, we were, more often than not, happy. In the early years, anyway. To everyone else, he was aloof and then, at times, too confrontational – always seeing the worst in people and making sure they knew exactly what he thought of them. But no one ever saw the Adam I knew. Behind closed doors he was different. He would cook me dinner after work and then run me a bath, give me foot massages when I'd developed blisters because of the lethal stilettos I wore for work. He would tell me that I was beautiful, that I was the most beautiful woman in the world. I felt safe and I felt special, as if I'd cracked a code and reached Adam in a way no one else could – passed a test that everyone else had failed.

He was always such an amazing father. We had some challenges during my pregnancy with Max – I'm sure my hormones were at least in part to blame – but I'll never forget the look on Adam's face when he held little Max for the first time. He was transfixed in a state of glee – I can picture it now – and that love for Max, that unmatched and unconditional dedication, is one that never left him.

And, of course, then there was the physical connection between Adam and me: a sexual chemistry that raged furiously and that was like nothing else I'd ever experienced. He had this knack for making me feel desired. To him, everything about me was beautiful. Even when I was at my lowest, when I felt fat, or ugly, or ashamed to keep the light on for sex after giving birth to Max, he lifted me up, worshipping every scar and imperfection with each stroke. With Adam, I was a goddess.

And later, when times were harder, he still had a hold over me. We were inextricably linked, bound by our commitment to each other, and so it became impossible to walk out.

Lisa and I reconciled about five years ago. She had also got married, to a total slob called Gary, who says he's a freelance sports journalist, but I'm not sure he's ever had an article actually published.

When I open the door to them, I can't quite believe how Gary can turn up so casually dressed. He's wearing a Man United football hoodie and through his grey tracksuit trousers, which are riding far too low, I can see the outline of his penis. I flinch slightly as he goes to give me a kiss on the cheek; I'm not so comfortable with casual contact from men.

Lisa is chirpy.

'Hi, babe! How's it going? Here – we've bought you an orchid. Apparently, it barely needs watering.'

She shoves it towards me and, as I feel the petals, I realise that it will need very little water indeed, being artificial.

'Ha! Thanks, Lisa, nice to see you both.'

I lead them to the conservatory, where Helen is sat on a sofa, already helping herself to Pringles.

'Helen, this is Lisa and Gary. Old friends of mine. This is Helen; her daughter is at school with Max.'

I leave my guests in the conservatory and head into the kitchen to continue getting the food ready. The leek and potato soup that I've made is on the boil and I rush forwards to tend to it. I can hear it popping, and then notice the flashes of pale green spurting out of the pan and onto the wall. I turn the heat down, then open the oven to check on the roast chicken and veg. Helen wanders in.

'Oh my God, Alice, you've gone *mad*. It smells delicious!'

'Oh, it's nothing, Helen, really,' I reply, smiling as I stir the soup.

Helen doesn't need to know that all the food arrived about half an hour ago from an online caterer. All I've done is transferred it all into my own dishes and stirred.

It's twenty minutes before the doorbell rings again.

'Ben, hi! I thought you weren't . . .'

'Oh! Am I late? I thought you said 1.30 p.m!'

'Don't worry; food's not even remotely ready yet. Come in, let me take your coat.'

93

So, to complete this lunch of waifs and strays: Ben. We've been texting a bit over the last few weeks and I'm growing fond of him. He's funny, in a goofy kind of way, and there's something about his self-deprecation and lack of confidence that gives me a boost. He's suggested a couple of times going out for dinner and there's a limited number of times I can reasonably turn him down without causing offence. I'm not sure exactly what his intentions are and I don't want him thinking that something romantic might happen between the two of us. And yet, there's something about him that draws me in: something about the irony of the situation that I should strike up a friendship with the man responsible for Adam's death. It piques my interest. An invitation to lunch – with other people – strikes, I think, the appropriate balance.

I lead Ben into the conservatory and introduce him to everyone.

'Everyone, this is Ben. He's a . . .' I pause. How do I introduce him? This is the man who ran over my husband? This is a new friend of mine? This is a man I've been seeing? 'This is Ben. We met at the mindfulness course that I've just signed up to. Ben, this is everyone.'

Ben is staring at me, wide-eyed, amazed. I feel a chill run down my spine.

BEN

Sunday, 15 April

I don't go shopping very often and when I do, it's for a specific item. I have a pretty extensive wardrobe, but that's because it's not in my nature to throw anything away. There are jumpers in my drawers that I haven't worn in at least a decade, some because they are just plain horrible, others because they've become so frayed that I feel shabby wearing them. After turning my whole wardrobe upside down last night looking for a shirt/trouser combo for today, I decided that the best course of action would be to head to the shopping centre and find something new.

The idea of actually going to Alice's house is both exhilarating and terrifying. I've been trying for a while to set up a date with her, but she seems to be eternally busy. It's not that she's not up for seeing me – she's made it pretty clear that she doesn't hold any grudges – it's just that every time I've suggested something, she's had another arrangement. Either she's already made plans – she seems popular – or else it's been too late to find a suitable babysitter for Max.

I was about to give up asking, because there's only a certain number of times my dignity will allow rejection, when I got a text from Alice with the invitation.

It was the first time Alice had initiated a conversation. Scrolling back through all of our WhatsApp chats, I realised that up until then I'd always been the one to start the conversation. And it's understandable, because she's busier than me. Apart from all the stuff that she's dealing with at the moment getting Adam's affairs in order, she's got Max to look after – and she told me that she's not feeling 100 per cent, so she's sleeping more than usual.

So, when my phone lit up and I saw it was Alice – she's the only person in my phone book whose name begins 'Al' with five letters, so I knew it was her – my heart skipped a little beat.

ALICE: Hey Ben.

ALICE: How are you?

ALICE: Are you free this Sunday? Having a few friends round for lunch and wondered if you wanted to come along.

ALICE: Let me know, Alice X

One little 'X' and my mind was racing. Ever since we exchanged numbers that night in the hospital café and started sending each other messages, I've found it hard not to analyse every word she's sent. Over time her messages have got longer, asking me questions and including detail beyond the polite minimum. But this was the first time I'd had a kiss from her.

I didn't reply immediately – didn't want to come across as too keen. I got into the shower, flung some clothes on, raced down the stairs and went out for a walk round the block. It was a crisp and dry morning, and bluebells had sprung up around the trees that line the pavement on the way to the high street. I felt amazing, adrenaline pumping through my veins, and I had to stop myself from mumbling as I strode along the road, rehearsing how I would greet Alice.

I should get my hair cut, I thought. I hadn't had it cut since the crash – somehow, it seemed too vain to worry about my own appearance – and this seemed liked a good opportunity. I'd left my phone in the flat but remembered the messages clearly: 'having a few friends round for lunch', she'd said. I wondered who else had been invited. I didn't speak to anyone at the funeral other than Alice and the only person she'd talked to me about in detail was Helen, who is the mother of one of Maxy's friends. It'd be nice to meet her.

Before I knew it, an hour had passed and I'd walked the circumference of the local park three times. On the last loop past the café, I picked up a tea and then headed back to the flat, ready to reply. I found my fingers quivering as I typed, deleted, typed and then finally sent:

> *ME: Hey Alice! I'm great, thanks, how are you? How is Max? How are you sleeping? I'd love to come, thanks. What time? Can I bring anything? Ben X*

That all-important 'X' to reciprocate hers.

Later, in a queue at Zara, I was waiting to pay for three different shirts and two pairs of trousers, to keep my options open. It's difficult to know the dress code, so

I went for something middle of the road – my navy-blue blazer, a smartish shirt and a pair of slim-fit jeans. I did think about messaging Alice to ask, but it's not the end of the world if I'm a bit too smart, is it? It's better to err on the side of too smart than turn up looking like I've just rolled out of bed.

I decided to get an early night – I didn't want to turn up to meet her friends with massive bags under my eyes.

This morning I woke at six and went to my computer to work out the best route to Alice's house. The last thing I wanted was to be late, so I consulted Google Maps to find the most reliable journey that didn't involve getting in a car. I left myself two hours just in case but ended up getting there in just over forty minutes, so I found a local café and waited. It's not a good look to turn up early.

I've known for a while where Alice and Max live and have checked their road out on Street View a few times. But as I walk down the road towards the address, I'm blown away by the size of the houses. Some of them look like they could be embassies, synagogues, private boarding schools, and I wonder how and when Alice found herself with such wealth. Adam, maybe. Or maybe her family are well off. As I approach number 99, my stomach churns, so I stop outside, take a deep breath and brace myself.

The house itself is imposing and grand. There are two marble pillars either side of a large oak front door and garages either side, draped in thick ivy. The front driveway and garden alone are bigger than my entire flat. I find myself checking that my shirt is properly tucked in and approach the great front door.

I ring the bell and wait. My heart is pounding and I'm breathing heavily. I swallow, hard, and blow a long, deep exhale as the door opens.

'Ben, hi! I was worried about you – I said 1 p.m.!'

'Oh, did you? I'm sorry; I thought it was 1.30 p.m. I'm so sorry!'

She definitely, *definitely* said 1.30 p.m. – God knows, I've read those texts enough times. Good to hear that she was worried, though. She looks sensational, in a gorgeous teal dress, and has made a real effort, maybe for my benefit.

'Well, are you going to come in, then?'

Alice leads me through a wide hallway to the back of the house, where a few people are gathered in the conservatory. I don't recognise anyone. Suddenly, I feel bad for not having brought a gift – how did I forget that? – and I am about to apologise for this, when Alice introduces me.

'This is Ben – we're friends from the mindfulness course.'

Are we? Is that what we are? Do these people not know the full story? Could I start afresh in this house, just a friend from a mindfulness course, nothing more and nothing less?

I catch Alice's eye from across the room and realise that with our secret about how we met, we are bound together now more than ever before.

ALICE

Sunday, 15 April

'Listen, Alice, I still think you should consider it. The pay's really good, you know, and we're gasping for someone with your experience.'

Helen's helped herself to another serving of roast potatoes. She's smashed through the majority of them: no one else has even had a look-in. Every time I speak to Helen, she tries to convince me to come and work with her. I told her once in the playground that I had trained as an accountant and spent a few years working at PwC and Deloitte before Max was born. But the truth is, I've got absolutely no desire to go back. There's no mortgage on the house and with the regular income that we get from Roger, there's just no need for me to work.

I used to be driven, ambitious, but I had all of that beaten out of me by Adam, who didn't like me coming home from work late and got angry when my boss started calling me late at night. When Max was born, I took my maternity leave and never went back, and now I feel so detached from it all that it would be too hard to get back into it. Helen's clearly just after some kind of referral bonus.

'Thanks, Helen. I've been out of the game for too long, I think – wouldn't know where to start!'

'Oh, I think it's a good idea, Alice. Good for you to get out of the house.'

That's Ben. There's an uncomfortable silence, because everyone's a bit taken aback by his input in this conversation. Who is this man who's giving me life advice, having known me for five minutes? I briskly change the subject.

'Anyone been watching anything good on Netflix?'

'There's some great true crime documentaries on there at the moment,' says Gary. 'I saw a great one about this guy who throws himself off a crane on a building site.'

Lisa kicks Gary under the table and she thinks I don't see.

'Well, that's all a bit morbid, isn't it? I've been watching *Queer Eye* – amazing some of the makeovers they do. Shall I nominate you, Gary?'

And everyone laughs, including Gary. The conversation has been a bit stilted, but it's only to be expected when you bring together a group of misfits like this.

'Does anyone want a coffee?' I offer, gathering some of the plates.

'No dessert then, Alice?'

Awkward. I haven't made dessert, no, but thanks for bringing it up, Ben. There's a moment of silence. Gary is smirking.

'Only joking! I'm absolutely stuffed.'

Helen and Lisa both help me to clear up the plates and we head into the kitchen. I'm conscious of not leaving Ben for too long on his own with Gary. Conversation with Gary can barely stretch beyond football and Ben doesn't strike me as the most ardent fan.

'Honestly, ladies, just leave all the stuff on the worktop. I'll clear it all up when you're gone.'

And when I say 'I'll clean it up', what I really mean is that my cleaner, Paola, is booked for first thing tomorrow.

This seems to satisfy Helen, who fills her glass with Merlot and heads back into the conservatory.

But Lisa hangs back, waits for Helen to be out of the room and then says in a hushed tone, 'What's going on with this Ben, then, Alice? Are you sleeping together? He seems pretty full-on!'

'Oh, God, no, Lisa, it's nothing like that. The truth is . . . well, he was there when Adam . . . He was the one driving the car.'

'Shit, really? Fuck, that's a bit heavy, isn't it?'

'It's all good, Lisa. I think he's a bit lost, to be honest. And he's a nice guy, as it happens.'

'Oh yeah? No, don't get me wrong; he seems lovely. Just a bit . . .'

I push out a half-smile and head towards the conservatory. Ava is slumped on the sofa, her arms folded and her back strategically turned away from Max.

'I don't want to play Lego. It's boring. I want to do drawing.'

Max continues regardless, tipping a whole crate of Lego on the floor around his feet.

'I want to play Lego and it's my house so it's my choice.'

Ben stands, heads over towards where Ava is sitting and crouches down.

'How about this, Ava? Why don't you let Max do his Lego and you draw whatever he ends up building? How about that?'

Ben takes a folded piece of paper out of his pocket and hands it to Ava, along with a blue biro that he's got in his blazer pocket. Ava looks up, grabs the pen and paper and joins Max on the floor.

Peace is restored five minutes later and Ben is down on the floor himself, helping Max with the Lego.

'I'll tell you what. Why don't we try to build Hogwarts? Max and I can build it, and then, Ava, you can draw it. What do you think?'

'Hogwarts? That's too hard!'

Ben ruffles Max's hair and rolls up his sleeves.

'What you don't know about me yet, Maxy, is that I'm a Lego ninja.'

Well done, Ben.

I sit down on the sofa next to Lisa and she whispers in my ear, 'Well, that's magic if I ever saw it. I take it back, Alice. This one's a keeper. Can I swap him with Gary?'

ALICE

Wednesday, 2 May

The only time previously we'd been called in to see the headmistress, Mrs Lacey, was when Max took it upon himself to give one of his classmates a haircut. He'd only just started at the school and they were doing some kind of craft activity with scissors and glue. It turns out the mother of this little girl, whose name was Mary-Rose, like the ill-fated ship, was horrified when her blessed princess came home from school with a fringe. Adam and I tried our hardest to keep a straight face as we were reprimanded for our son's prank, but we couldn't help but feel a bit proud. As we walked out of Mrs Lacey's pokey office, I couldn't resist a little gag.

'I mean, with a name like Mary-Rose, she'd better get used to the odd setback.'

When I got the phone call this morning from Brenda, the school receptionist, to ask that I come in to chat about Max's behaviour, I expected something similar. Maybe he'd gone for a full-on perm this time.

'Can you tell me what it's about?' I asked Brenda as I cleared up the plates from Max's breakfast.

He'd only been at school for about forty-five minutes, so he couldn't have done anything too serious in such a short space of time.

'I'm afraid I'm just the messenger, Mrs Selby, but I don't believe it's an emergency. Are you able to make it in for eleven thirty?' she offered in a tone of voice that was irritatingly smug, as if she knew exactly what was on the agenda and relished the small power that she held for this short period, knowing something about my son that I didn't.

'I suppose I can make it work – I'll have to move things around – eleven thirty it is.'

That was a lie – I had no plans – but I played along with the facade and performed my role as the busy housewife. I didn't want the school to know that my only plans had been to sit in front of the telly watching two teams of obese pensioners fight for victory on *Bargain Hunt*, eating cold leftovers from last night, maybe having a nap mid-afternoon, finally showering and then rushing to the playground to pick up Max.

Max goes to a private school called Woodland Green Primary about ten minutes' drive from where we live. When I was in my late teens and early twenties, I would have been horrified at the thought of sending my child to a paying independent school. Even though I, myself, had been privately schooled, the idea of choosing that for my own children seemed inconsistent with the identity I had established for myself at university: Labour-voting, Quorn-eating liberal with aspirations to save the world, one starving child at a time. But I soon lost the idealism of youth when

I married into wealth. Still, I was taken aback when Adam told me that he'd already signed Max up to Woodland Green just a month after he was born.

'Honestly, Al, half the intake for each year is already filled by people who put their kid's name down before the mums are out of the labour ward. It's one of the best primary schools in the country,' he explained as he showed me the letter confirming Max's place.

'The boy can't even hold his own head up, yet – how on earth can we make decisions about his education at this stage?' I'd replied.

It had all seemed preposterous and it annoyed me that Adam was faffing with speculative application forms for four years' time, having not once taken it upon himself to change a dirty nappy.

I'm driving from our house to Woodland Green Primary on the edge of town seven years after that confrontation and I'm quietly pleased that Adam had that foresight as I pass groups of children loitering outside the neighbouring state schools. Why aren't they in class? The reputations of these schools are abysmal – the two nearest ones have both recently been downgraded to 'Requires Improvement' by Ofsted and at the school on the high street there were allegations of child molestation by one of the PE teachers. I guess you get what you pay for.

Adam used to drive Max to school every day and then we'd share the duties of picking him up in the afternoon. Since the age of four, he's been going to the homework club three days a week, which means that he's often out at school for most of the day – from 8 a.m. to 6 p.m. I'm aware that most of the other parents who send their kids to this club have busier lives than me: bankers, solicitors, who battle through the evening commute, rushing to get back from Central London in time to pick up their darlings for supper and a bit of reading before bedtime. But Adam and I decided that there was nothing to lose in keeping him there for a couple more hours.

Usually when I pick him up from school, Max runs down the path and meets me at the gate, so I don't have to face the inane conversations with the other mothers − conversations that inevitably descend into expressions of pity and invitations for dinner, which they offer through duty and I decline with apathy.

I park and as I step out of the car, I can see that Mrs Lacey is at the front door, waiting to greet me.

'Hello, Mrs Selby. Thanks for coming in. Please, follow me.'

Mrs Lacey is a stout, matronly woman who must be fast approaching her sixties. She's wearing a frumpy grey skirt that is too short for someone of her age and her jumper creates a muffin top that would win awards.

She guides me up the stairs and towards an office that seems to double as a lounge, and I get the distinct sensation that I'm being prepared for a sensitive conversation.

'Here, let me take this.'

I flinch as Mrs Lacey starts peeling my jacket off my shoulders. If I'd known she was going to do that, I wouldn't have worn such a scatty T-shirt underneath. She places my jacket on a hook, and pulls out a chair for me. I sit, and she takes the chair opposite me.

'It's been a while since we've seen you, Mrs Selby. Must have been almost a year − since the last parents' evening, perhaps.'

'Ah, yes, well, with everything that's being going on with Max's father, the funeral and so on, it's been hard to stay on top of things.'

I didn't realise that my attendance was being tracked as well as my son's.

'Yes, Mrs Selby. This is why I asked you to come in. We were devastated to hear about Mr Selby's accident. It must be a very hard time for you, indeed.'

That word again: *accident*.

'Er, you know, it hasn't been easy. But we're getting on with it,' I retort, searching for something in my handbag to avoid eye contact.

'When something like this happens to a family,' Mrs Lacey continues gingerly, 'it can have quite the impact. Particularly on a young boy as sensitive and emotionally alert as Max.'

Emotionally alert? What does that mean?

'Has something happened? What do you mean?'

'No no, nothing serious, Mrs Selby. It's just . . . well, we're all a bit worried about Max, you see. When he first came back to school after it all happened, we couldn't quite believe how resilient he seemed to be. He was getting on with his work as usual, playing with the other children and behaving as if nothing had changed. But in the last few weeks, Mrs Selby, well, his behaviour seems to have shifted somewhat.'

'Shifted?'

'Well, yes. It's his temper, Mrs Selby. It's not something I've really experienced before.'

'Well, we all lose our temper from time to time, Mrs Lacey.'

As I say this I realise that maybe Mrs Lacey doesn't even

have a temper to lose – her manner is so calm that even an impending tsunami wouldn't faze her.

'Of course that's true, Mrs Selby. It's just that . . . well, it's got a bit out of control over the last few weeks. Just the slightest thing and he flies off the handle. The other day he screamed at one of his fellow classmates when she asked to borrow his ruler. A simple, polite request, it was.'

Is this why she's called me in? To tell me that Max got a bit pissed off with a child who was nicking his stationery?

'I'll have a word with him. Is there anything else?'

'His concentration is a bit of a worry, too. As you'll remember from previous parents' evenings, Max has the potential to be one of the brightest children in the school. But over the last month or so, his work has been deteriorating. He used to score top marks in the weekly arithmetic test, but now we see him daydreaming and chewing the end of his pencil as the teacher calls out the questions. Often, he only attempts to answer just some of the questions. And his reading – I'm worried that he's falling behind the others. It's just such a shame, is all, and I'm wondering what we can be doing at home to support him better.'

What *we* can be doing at home to support him better? I won't be patronised by her choice of pronoun.

'Well, that's precisely the issue, I'm afraid. There is no "we" at home anymore: it's just me. Me on my own, trying my very hardest to keep things going, to keep him happy. And I'm sorry if it seems to you that I'm failing in that regard, but . . .'

I stand and put my coat on, ready to storm out and demonstrate who he inherited his temper from.

'Please, Mrs Selby. Please stay for a little longer. I'm sure it must be very hard, indeed. Here at Woodland Green we just want to do what we can to provide support. It's all part of the school's ethos.'

She points to a slogan on the wall – 'Supporting Children in the Classroom and Beyond' – and the cheesiness of it all makes me let out a little chuckle.

'Look,' Mrs Lacey continues, 'why don't we tackle one thing at a time?' She reaches over and hands me a shabby book. 'Narnia. *The Silver Chair*. Read to him. Just a few pages every night. It's actually quite an engaging story for adults, too.'

Reading's never been my strong suit and while I've never officially been diagnosed with dyslexia, there have been signs: I've always found spelling difficult and I remember Adam once laughing at me when I misspelt 'pepper' on a shopping list. When I'm reading a book, some words are bigger on the page than others and letters disappear, and then I get flustered. I'm convinced that the reason I got a 2:2 in my accountancy degree is that I couldn't write as quickly as everyone else. I would ace all the numeric stuff – financial modelling, statistics, forecasting – but when it came to writing essays, I fell short. Adam once suggested that I apply for extra time for exams, but my pride wouldn't let me go for an assessment. How funny that it is here, in the office of my son's primary school, that I finally embrace this and come out with it.

'I'm a bit dyslexic myself, actually, but we'll give it a go. Thanks for the book, Mrs Lacey, it's really kind of you.'

It's not that I can't read at all, obviously, but the whole scenario just stresses me out and the experience becomes as stressful for Maxy as it does for me. If I'm polite and gracious, maybe we can bring this meeting to a close before it forces me to come to any more realisations about my own weaknesses. Besides, I haven't had any breakfast and if I don't eat something soon, I'm going to get even more edgy and may end up saying something to this woman that I'll really regret. I pull the chair back, stand and reach for my coat for a second time.

'Well, if that's everything, Mrs Lacey, I'll leave you to get back to your day and I'll—'

'Well, there was just one other thing I wanted to chat to you about if you've got another moment, Mrs Selby. It's a bit of a sensitive one.'

She whispers these last few words as if the rest of the conversation might have been overheard. I give a forced smile, sit back down and open my eyes wide in an invitation for her to continue.

'Mrs Selby, I've been working with children Max's age for the last thirty-five years and I've seen just about everything there is to see. All kinds of unconventional and unusual behaviour.'

Unconventional and unusual behaviour? Makes it sound like she's been teaching a coven of child witches.

'And,' she continues, 'if there's one thing I know for sure, it's that a young man needs as much stability as possible. Particularly a young man like Max who has lost a parent at such a tender age. I also believe that every young man needs someone they can look up to – a man, I mean. Someone who can teach them the ropes and ease their path into adulthood.'

'I'm not sure what you're saying, Mrs Lacey,' I reply, the volume and pitch of my voice raised.

There are other single-parent families at this school, other scenarios where the father has fucked off, leaving the mother to raise a child on their own. It's a good school, full of privileged families, but this doesn't make them exempt from family breakdowns.

'I know Max is an only child, too, isn't he? Perhaps there's someone else in the family: a cousin, a grandfather, an uncle, who could take Max under his wing a bit. A male role model who can step in.'

At this, I feel a sudden surge of anger pulse through my veins and I stand with a start.

'You don't think I'm capable of bringing up Max on my own? You don't think I'm fucking capable of that?' I bellow, putting my jacket on and picking up my handbag as I edge towards the door. But I'm not done yet. 'You know, maybe it's possible, just possible, that Max is better off without his father anyway. Have you thought about that? Have you thought about the example that my wonderful husband may have set him, by running out in front of a car and killing himself? Is that a role model for you, Mrs Lacey? Is it?'

I don't give her the chance to respond, because I'm out of the door before I've finished yelling. I'm rushing down the corridor and, to my surprise, I can feel my cheeks burning and tears streaming uncontrollably.

I'm running towards my car, my heart still racing, livid that I've been called out for things that are completely beyond my control. I start the engine and head off in a hurry, the gearbox groaning as I shift too quickly. I can feel the salty taste of my tears as they trickle into my mouth and I don't stop crying for the whole journey home: tears of anger, I think, but also of sadness.

I hate the idea of Max having trouble at school. The reading is one thing, but the idea of Max struggling to concentrate, that he's playing up and getting angry because of something that's going on at home, makes me feel terrible. My display of anger in Mrs Lacey's office was nothing but a front, a shield for parental guilt.

An hour later, I'm lying on the couch in the living room, with a chilled glass of Sauvignon Blanc and a bag of Wotsits, in a spot that has now become a haven for me, staring out into the garden and towards the tree house that Max and Adam started together but never finished. I feel sad for Max. Maybe he does need someone other than me. Maybe he does need a male role model in his life. Maybe he needs someone to help him finish that tree house, because God knows I don't know where to start.

I go over to the kitchen counter, pick up my phone and text the only man who comes to mind:

> ME: *Hey, how's it going? Want to come round for dinner tonight?*

> BEN: *Hey, Alice, how are you? Sure, I'd love that. What time?*

> ME: *Whenever. Come whenever. Nothing fancy. Will make some pasta or something.*

> BEN: *Sounds yum. Looking forward to sampling some more Alice specialities! I'll be round at about seven?*

> ME: *Great. Oh, and have you ever read* The Silver Chair?

> BEN: *Are you kidding? It's one of my faves xx*

BEN

It's funny how things go, isn't it? When the year began, something happened to me that turned my whole world upside down. Or rather, I did something to someone else that turned their world upside down. When I ran Adam over, I was a total stranger to Alice and Maxy. If we were to pass each other in the street, we wouldn't even have registered each other. And then one horrible coincidence happened, followed by a series of events that led me to an evening like tonight. Who would have guessed that, as a result, I would be spending a Wednesday evening, not on my own bingeing a Netflix series and eating an M&S Meal Deal for one, but with a beautiful woman and her son? Who would have guessed, after such a tragic start, that I would turn up at their front door, ring the doorbell and be welcomed in with open arms?

It was a last-minute arrangement. Alice texted me at one forty this afternoon, just after lunch break as the kids were settling down for afternoon lessons. I don't get texts that often – and when I do they are usually from Domino's, offering me two stuffed-crust pizzas for the price of one – but I like to read them as soon as I receive them and reply quickly to stay on top of things. I'd been thinking about Alice a lot, resisting the urge to text her every day. So when I picked up my phone and saw a message from her, I felt a wave of relief.

I changed my plan for the rest of the afternoon, giving the kids a drawing exercise so that I could sit at my desk and have the text conversation with Alice immediately. It wouldn't be nice to keep her waiting, particularly as she'd made the effort to contact me. Anyway, she asked me over for a slap-up Italian meal, and I decided that I could easily freeze what I had planned to eat and save it for another day, so I accepted.

I found it hard to concentrate after that little text conversation. I spent twenty minutes trying to decide whether or not to take round a bottle of wine. It wasn't clear from her text whether or not Max would be eating with us, so I wasn't sure whether this would be a quick meal for three or a romantic dinner for two.

After school I decided to head down to the barber over the road. I don't usually go to the barber twice in one month, but it's pretty cheap and I thought it was worth making the effort. I had an awkward conversation with him, actually, because he asked me if I had 'a hot date' this evening and I panicked. I've never liked engaging in conversations with the person cutting my hair, not because I'm particularly antisocial, but because I always feel under pressure to make my life sound more exciting and glamorous than it is, ending up descending into lies and exaggerations. And that particular question about my evening plans was far too complicated to try to explain to him in a short amount of time.

By the time I arrived outside Alice and Max's house, I felt exhausted. It's tiring enough to get up early in the morning and spend the day in front of a class of misbehaving eight-year-olds. But today was particularly gruelling as I'd had this spanner thrown in the works, this change in my usual routine, and I found myself downing a can of Red Bull before I got out of the car and headed to their grand front door. I rang the bell and was taken off guard when it was Max who opened the door.

'Hi, Ben. Mummy said you were coming round.'

'Oh, hi, little man. Do you know what we're having for dinner?'

'There's some fishy pasta for you and then just the same but with a plain pasta sauce for me. And there's grated cheese. Do you like grated cheese?'

'I love grated cheese. In fact, I like all types of cheese. Even the really smelly, yucky blue ones . . .'

Maxy screwed up his face and held his nose as he ran into the house. I followed him in and heard Alice call through from the kitchen.

'Hi, Ben! Come in. Sorry, having a total nightmare in the kitchen. Come on through.'

It smelt delicious and I was excited about the chance to see a new side to Alice. I've always thought you can tell a lot about a person when they cook for you: which dish they opt for, whether they overdo it with the salt or leave it bland, whether they make so much food that you feel stuffed afterwards, or whether they make just enough for each individual portion and then leave you yearning for more. More than anything, it's interesting to ascertain how much effort has gone into the whole process, as an indicator of where you stand in their general estimation: how long has it taken for the meal to be prepared? What is the quality of the ingredients and how much money would it have all cost? How much am I worth to you, Alice?

'Max, can you *please* lay the table? How many times do I have to ask?'

I still hadn't seen Alice yet but could hear her shouting demands from the kitchen. She didn't hold back with Max, often asking him to do things that I wouldn't have done at his age. I suppose now that it's just the two of them, he's had to take on more responsibilities. He's been forced into early maturity and has to assume some of the roles of a partner. How sad.

'I can help you out, buddy,' I offered, going into the conservatory to find Maxy riffling through the drawers of the side cabinet for cutlery and place mats.

He'd obviously changed out of his school uniform since getting home and was wearing a pair of shorts and a Green Day T-shirt that, being far too big for him, reached his knees.

'Are you a Green Day fan, Maxy? That's very grown-up of you.'

He looked at me in surprise, then down at the T-shirt, then back at me.

'Yeah, they were Dad's favourite band. And mine, as well. Do you like them?'

'Love them,' I lied. 'Although not their latest album.'

The truth is, I had no idea what their music was like, although judging by their general look, I would assume too explicit for a boy of Max's age! I didn't feel bad about this, though. It was a white lie – nothing serious or malicious. I don't think I need to try too hard to win Max over – he seems to be pretty keen on me – but if there's one thing I've learned from my time as a teacher, it's that kids respond best when they can identify themselves in an adult, when they can sense similar interests or mutual understanding. I'd better buy a Green Day CD and swot up.

I helped Max to get the table ready for dinner: just three places on a massive table that could probably fit fifteen. As we were doing so, I couldn't help but daydream about large dinner parties that Alice and Adam must have thrown in the past. I pictured the table crowded with wine glasses and side plates, big salad bowls in the middle, and plat-ters of meat and fish. Alice and Adam at the heads of the table, holding court and telling their guests stories about their university days, their first date, the time that they got caught having sex in the back of her parents' Honda. A whole group of similarly happy young couples, pouring each other glasses of wine, comparing notes on babysitters and nannies, gossiping about the latest scandal at work. I wonder how long it has been since there was so much laughter in this house.

With the table laid, I made my way into the kitchen to see if I could help Alice with the final preparations. I counted three ovens and more stacks of plates on display than you could expect to see in a small restaurant.

'You could cook on an industrial scale in here, Alice,' I joked as she took her head out of one of the ovens.

She stood and walked towards me, greeting me with a warm hug.

'Ugh, tell me about it. It's ridiculous, isn't it? Good to see you, lovely. Dinner will be ready in about fifteen – I hope you like prawns!'

I was so taken aback by the 'lovely' that I froze.

'Oh, God, you don't, do you? It's OK, I'll make something else,' she offered.

'No no, prawns are perfect. Perfect.'

Shellfish does actually tend to give me an upset stomach – I'll ask for a small portion.

Alice looked sensational. Not in a made-up, ready-for-a-night-out kind of way, but radiant and maternal. She was wearing an apron with little penguins on it and had her hair up tight in a bun – it was the first time I'd seen it like that. She had a bit of eyeliner on and subtle pink lipstick, although it could have just been lip balm. It struck me that she might have made this effort just for me. I imagined lifting her up onto the island in the middle of the kitchen and kissing her hard, with her legs around my hips.

'I brought some wine,' I said. 'It's a Saint-Émilion, 2015. Should be pretty good.'

Alice took the bottle and riffled in a drawer just beside me for a corkscrew.

'Very sweet of you, Ben. I could really do with a glass tonight. Max, can you get down a couple of glasses, please? You can climb the stepladder, but slowly. And careful not to drop the glasses, please!'

And so we sat down to dinner, Alice at the head of the table, and Maxy and me on either side of her. I actually really didn't like the prawn pasta, but I don't think Alice caught on to that, and for dessert there was a delicious tiramisu that made up for it. It was just the right balance of bitter from the coffee and sweet from the cream, and I was happy to conclude that the effort that it must have taken Alice indicated a fair amount of affection.

I was worried before that the conversation at the dinner table might be a little stilted – I have been known to clam up in situations like these – but, thankfully, there was lots of energy and few pauses, as Max told us the ins and outs of the politics of his classroom, chirpily recounting the drama that had ensued at lunchtime that day. Alice and I also discussed the mindfulness silent retreat that we're both attending on Sunday and Maxy laughed at the prospect of his mum keeping her mouth shut for a whole day.

By the time we'd all had our second serving of dessert, and all that remained on the table was the empty bottle of wine that Alice and I had devoured, it felt like this had been the most natural meal of my life: like it was something we'd done a hundred times before, like we'd known each other for decades. Alice then looked over at the grandfather clock on the other side of the dining room and put a stop to the proceedings.

'Blimey, Max, it's nearly nine o'clock. Well past your bedtime. Head upstairs, sweetheart.'

'Oh, but Ben is still here, can't I stay down here with you?'

'Ben hasn't got to get up first thing and go to school, has he?'

'He has, actually. The teachers always get to school before we do!'

'Enough, you. Go upstairs, get your PJs on, brush your teeth and get into bed. Maybe Ben will come up and read you a bedtime story.'

This seemed to satisfy Max, and he leapt off his chair and ran upstairs.

'Well, he's certainly taken a shine to you,' Alice said.

I felt blood rushing to my face and, if I wasn't already bright red from all the wine, Alice must have seen me blushing.

'He's a great kid, you know. You're very lucky to have him.'

It's true: he is a special kid. I've seen plenty of seven-year-olds in my time, and few have the maturity and sense of humour of this one.

Alice then told me about a meeting she'd had earlier that day with Max's teacher, who had expressed some concerns about his behaviour. I reassured her that it was always the brightest children, the kids with most potential, who played up and, if anything, it was a sign of great promise. She said the teacher had suggested that his reading level might not be as high as some of his peers, which surprised me given his apparent intellect.

'That's why I asked you about the Narnia book,' she continued. 'I was hoping you could read it to him. I'm . . . well, Adam used to read to him, you see. Reading's not my forte.'

I had noticed previously that Alice might be dyslexic. When we were at the mindfulness class, we all had to write down an anecdote about a time when we felt like things were getting on top of us and then read out someone else's story to the rest of the group. Alice seemed reluctant to participate and when she agreed to have a go, she read very slowly. I found it endearing at the time: when I see weaknesses in others, I feel a pull towards them. A demonstration of fallibility is an invitation to come closer.

While Alice cleared the plates and started washing up, I headed upstairs with a battered copy of *The Silver Chair* and called out for Maxy. It was the first time that I had been invited upstairs and I had no idea where I was going. There was door after door – four on either side of a long corridor – and only when I heard Maxy calling back was I sure where he was.

'Hey, buddy. I think your teacher at school has given you a new book to read.'

'Oh, is it the one about the lion and the witch and the wardrobe? Will you read some to me? Here, you can sit on Dad's rocking chair next to my bed.'

Of course, I felt a bit funny taking the seat for the first time. I was sitting where Adam would have sat, performing the role that he would have been performing. I felt that familiar wave of guilt but let it subside when I saw Max's expectant face. It struck me that he probably didn't know the role that I played in all of this. I took my seat, opened the book and started reading out loud.

ALICE

'Goodnight then, Ben. And thanks again for your help with Max tonight. I really appreciate it.'

He's lingering. He has this way of looking at me, of looking straight into my eyes, as if he can see right through to the back of my head and out the other side. It's easy to get lost in a moment with him and it's as if he is aware of his eyes as a weapon, his special power to draw you closer. There's a moment of awkwardness, a silence that is just that bit too enduring. Is he expecting a kiss?

I shut the door and head straight to the toilet. As I sit down, I realise that my head is spinning and that I've probably overdone the wine. When I wash my hands, I look in the mirror and see the stain of red wine on my bottom lip. I know that Adam wouldn't have approved of how much I've been drinking recently. After washing my hands, I head into the dining room to clear the last few things from the table. The dishwasher is broken, so I stand at the sink, hand-washing everything with a scatty sponge that I really need to replace.

I look out to the coat hooks by the front door and see that Ben has left his jacket. I reach into my pocket for my phone. It's a vile jacket – one of those gilets that Prince Harry might wear on the ski slopes of Val d'Isère – but I should probably get it back to him. In fact, he's already texted me:

BEN: *Left my jacket at yours! Sorry, I'm a forgetful penguin. Can I come and pick it up tomorrow? Ben xx*

I start typing. Ben is online:

ME: *Or I could just bring it to the mindfulness retreat at the weekend?*

Ben is typing . . .

BEN: *I'll come round in the morning. Need my wallet back, you thief ;) It's in the pocket. I'll bring breakfast. What time?*

ME: *I'll be here – come whenever. Bring a croissant or something for Max, too!*

BEN: *It's a date xx*

I could have done without this, but I suppose at least now I won't have Max nagging me for something to eat for breakfast.

I fetch his jacket and drape it on the back of one of the kitchen chairs, heading over to the sink for a glass of water. I down two full pints of water and pop three ibuprofen out of a packet that I find in the cupboard under the sink.

'Did you drink too many wines again, Mummy?'

Max has crept up behind me, with just pyjama bottoms on, holding his empty cup.

'How did you . . . Why are you . . . why aren't you in bed?'

'I was in bed, but then I got out of bed because I'm not tired yet. There's no point in just *lying* there, Mummy.'

Max takes a seat at the kitchen table and puts his thumb in his mouth. I sit down to join him, ruffling his hair.

'Well, the thing is, if you don't get to sleep soon, you're going to miss breakfast with Ben.'

His face lights up.

'Can I make pancakes for him?'

The last time Max made pancakes, the kitchen was transformed into what can only be described as a winter war zone – the floor covered in more than a light dusting of flour, broken appliances scattering the worktop and water overflowing on the ground after he clogged up the sink with clumps of dough that he said were 'for the rats in the sewers'.

'No, darling, we're not doing that. If you're a good boy and go to bed, maybe Ben will bring you something yummy from the bakery.'

I'm only mildly worried that my son is turning into one of those Channel 5 case studies on obese children. He definitely has a large appetite and I often have to smack his hand at birthday parties when he isn't letting the other kids get a look-in with the Haribo sweets. I got a call from the school nurse recently to advise me that he had been swapping the apple in his packed lunch for Mars bars and that he was already 'far from the normal BMI for a seven-year-old'. She then proceeded to ask me if there was anything at home that might be unsettling him and causing him to overeat. This struck me as a bit of a liberty considering she, herself, is at least a size 18.

ALICE

I wake up to the buzz of the doorbell, still in my bra and knickers.
I don't even think I brushed my teeth last night, because I can
still taste the booze on my lips, and I definitely didn't remove
my make-up. I rush out of bed, chuck on my dressing gown and
head downstairs. Max is obviously already up, because there are
toys strewn all over the landing. I'm still half asleep and trying to
work out who could be calling on us so early as I open the door.

'Alice, hi. I went to Costa on my way here. Got you a
flat white, hope that's OK?'

Fuck. I only have a vague memory of making the breakfast arrangement and raise my hand to my face – partly to
shield my eyes from the early morning sun, partly to spare
Ben from the mess that is my face.

'Jesus, Ben. What time is it? Come in, come on through.'

As I lead Ben through the hallway into the kitchen, he
carries on talking.

'I've got coffee, some smoked salmon bagels and also
some pastries. Where's Maxy? I got him a hot chocolate.'

126

I feel affronted when I hear him refer to Max as Maxy. It establishes an intimacy between Ben and Max that seems premature. I let it slide, realising that I need to focus on making myself more presentable for our visitor.

'You head on inside. I think Max is still working on that Hogwarts Castle. I'm just going to go up and, erm, brush my hair.'

Ben goes into the conservatory and, as I rush up the stairs, I can hear Max chirping away, thanking Ben for the hot chocolate and singing the *Harry Potter* theme tune.

I fling off my dressing gown and put on the same clothes from last night. I wet my finger and try to scrub the stain off my dress. I check the time on my phone – eight fifty. Fuck, need to get Max to school. I run down the stairs and see that Max is already getting his coat on.

'I'm going to be late for school, Mummy. Ben says he'll take me in his car.'

Just behind Max is Ben, looking up at me, his eyebrows raised, as if to say, 'What do you think?'

'No, Max, don't be silly.'

I can't just let him get in Ben's car. You hear too many stories about kids going missing with people you think you know. And what do I actually know about this guy?

'I don't mind, Alice. I can drop him off on the way to work.'

'Please, Mummy.'

On the other hand, it's such a short drive and I don't want to be one of those uptight mothers who don't know where to draw the line. What's he going to do? School would call me pretty swiftly if Max didn't turn up. I'm a total mess, I've got no idea where my own car keys are and I could really do with a few more minutes in bed. And he's a primary school teacher, for God's sake. He'll have had all the checks.

'Go on, then. I'll have to ring the school and add you to the drop-off list, Ben. If you're sure you don't mind?'

'It'll be my pleasure. You go and take it easy. Have some me time for a change.'

Max is already outside, trying to open the door of Ben's Volkswagen Passat. I wave them goodbye, make the phone call and then pass out on the sofa.

ALICE

'The silent retreat is an integral part of the mindfulness course. We are now halfway through the course and this is an opportunity to put a whole day aside to deepen your practice.'

This is an aspect of the course that had almost put me off altogether and I had to drag myself out of bed this morning to make it here on time. If there's one thing I know about myself, it's that silence isn't my thing. The idea of six solid hours, in this room, with this group of strangers, not saying a word, seems like an impossible feat. Shirley's voice is softer than usual, not much more than a whisper, as if she's gradually readjusting our ears, slowly bringing us to a state of calm.

'You may find some parts of the day easier than others, drifting in and out of clarity, but the important thing is that you recognise your experience, whatever it is, and embrace it. You may even find that sleep is a temptation at some points in the day. If you do find yourself asleep, accept this, as it is your body telling you that this is what it needs.'

That's all very well, Shirley, I think to myself, but if I fall asleep, the silence will be broken by my elephant-like snoring. I look round the room and some of the participants have already closed their eyes. Premature, I think, and cringeworthy: overeager students looking to impress, as if Shirley is grading us and will give us a verdict at the end of the day as to how well we've performed.

I look over to Ben and he's already looking at me, smiling. I roll my eyes, as if to suggest that he and I are above this. He's looking good today – he's got a polo shirt on and I can see a tuft of chest hair poking through the top. I allow myself to imagine that chest hair, continuing down past his chest, to his little belly, creating a little trail down to . . . Whoa – where did that come from? I'm blushing, I'm sure, so I divert his attention from my face by bending down and reaching for the bottle of water I've got by my side, taking a sip and then placing it back down.

'And so if everyone is feeling comfortable,' Shirley continues, 'we'll begin.'

BONG.

BONG.

'OK, we're now going to take a break to eat some lunch. If you've brought something with you, feel free to eat it in here, and if you do need to pop out to buy something, try and maintain the silence if you can.'

Well, I was asleep for a lot of that, but it seems outside of the spirit of the exercise to dwell on it too much. Whether or not I was asleep, I feel calm, which is why I've come here in the first place.

As my fellow meditators gather their things, put their shoes back on and fold the blankets they've been using, I look over for Ben and catch his eye. He tilts his head towards the exit as if to invite me to walk out with him, so I smile and follow. Does he want to break the silence? I'm not sure that I want to talk. If I sign up for something, I do it properly.

It turns out that Ben doesn't want to talk, either, and he seems content just walking along with me towards the parade of cafés and restaurants on Finchley Road. It feels funny and we both giggle silently when we catch eyes. Here we are, sharing a moment together, not having to interrupt it with trivial chatter.

It's become warmer over the last week – about 18 degrees most days – the sun is shining and the sky is untouched by clouds. We walk down the high street and there's a stall selling peonies in cream and pale pink. In this state of silence, every sound is amplified so that distant birds tweet like sopranos over distorted traffic. The world seems alive.

We walk into Pret a Manger together. Ben opts for a baguette and I go for a salad, kidding myself that this will be enough to keep me going until supper. Ben puts his hand out for my salad in what I assume is an offer to pay for mine, and I shake my head and get behind him in the queue. I reach into my handbag for my purse and wonder how this wordless transaction is going to work.

'Good afternoon, madam. Thank you. Do you want any coffee or pastries?'

The server has terrible acne and I feel slightly sick focusing on one particularly gruesome boulder on his left cheek. I simply shake my head and offer a meek smile, and he must think me rude, but I don't give a shit.

'Would you like to pay contactless?' he tries again.

This time I smile and nod, before placing my card on the reader, grabbing my salad and heading towards the exit. Ben is waiting; he opens the door for me and we walk back out onto Finchley Road. As we stroll back towards the mindfulness centre, we stand closer together and, at one point, my hand brushes his and I feel a shiver that runs straight up my arm to the top of my spine.

Back in the room, Shirley breaks the silence.

'Well, I hope everyone's had a nice lunch break. We will now slowly enter back into a state of stillness, starting with a simple sitting exercise before moving on to some more compassion-based practice. So, if you get into a comfortable position once more, we will begin.'

BONG.

It's harder to focus this time round. Even though I only had a salad, I feel bloated after lunch and I find my mind racing with conflicted thoughts. I break the rules quite early on and open my eyes, looking at Ben and wondering if it's possible that I could have feelings for this man. It's easy to forget, but he killed my husband, even if it wasn't his fault. It all feels a bit *Daily Star*. Am I confusing feelings of loneliness with desire? Is this my grief manifesting itself in an unusual way and, if it is, would it be wrong for me to act upon it? Should I even be thinking, just months after the death of my husband, about what my next move might be? Have I just got the wrong end of the stick?

I feel a sudden urge to shout out, to break the rules that have been established in this little room. There are so many things on the tip of my tongue and yet, at the same time, nothing at all: what do I want to say to him? What do I want him to know?

I stand and take myself out of the room, heading to the bathroom and locking the door. If I'm going to shout, I'd best do it on my own and somewhere no one will hear me.

I can feel wet hair on my forehead. I sit on the toilet and put my head between my knees, breathing heavily and gathering my composure.

After a few minutes, I head back to the room and take my place. Everyone else still has their eyes closed, apart from Ben, who looks at me with concern, checking that I'm OK. I smile and nod, then I close my eyes and fall asleep.

BONG.

'OK, we're now coming to the end of the day and so if you want to start gathering your things, I'd just like to say a few words before we leave.'

I would feel embarrassed that I must have been snoring, but I'm so keen to get out of the room that I brush it aside. I stretch a little, clean my eyes with my finger and reach for my handbag.

'I hope you've found today to be valuable and that it's been a good way to deepen your practice. I would like to recommend to everyone that, as we step into our ordinary lives and start speaking again, we try to maintain a sense of calm. It might be quite overwhelming as we return to our families, and to the hustle and bustle of our everyday. So I wouldn't recommend going to a rave right now!'

There are flutters of laughter and the people around me start whispering to each other. I'm first out of the door and, as I head down the stairs, I try to decide whether to take the Tube or call an Uber to get home. I'm almost out of the door, when I hear Ben behind me.

'Alice, Alice. Wait! Wondered if you wanted to grab some dinner?'

And I want to.

BEN

'I used to come here all the time with my ex. Literally can't get enough of their ravioli.'

Alice and I are in Lecce, a family-run Italian restaurant just around the corner from my flat. It's formal, without being too stuffy, and the food is delicious: freshly made pasta, deep, garlicky sauces and the creamiest burrata cheese. This is the perfect place to take Alice on our first official date: tried and tested, a safe option.

'I'm absolutely starving,' Alice admits. 'Who was I kidding that a little salad would be enough for lunch?'

I like a woman with an appetite. It's no fun when you're having dinner with someone who picks at a few vegetables and then doesn't want to order dessert.

'Yeah, my ex particularly loved it here because she was a vegetarian, so you know, lots of options.'

Is it too early to be talking about past relationships? She doesn't seem to be taking the bait.

'Oh, God, I just couldn't live without meat. I mean

135

red meat I can do without, but chicken is a real staple, isn't it?'

The conversation needs to get better than this if I'm going to secure a second date.

'Let's order some wine,' I suggest.

'Oh yes, please. Would love some red.'

'Red it is. Any preference?'

I know nothing about wine and my dad helped me to pick the one I took to Alice's house. Judging by the collections and wine racks there, she's in a much better position to pick. I don't mind what she goes for, even if it's the most expensive one on the menu.

She chooses a bottle that she describes as 'middle of the road' and at fifty-five pounds, I can't help but worry that I may struggle to cater for her expensive tastes in the long run.

Once we're drinking, conversation flows more freely and she does most of the talking. I think this is a good thing for a man to do on a date: let the woman set the agenda, and ask as many questions about her and her life as possible.

She tells me about how she'd found the afternoon part of the silent retreat more difficult than the morning, but that she was glad she'd signed up for the course because it was teaching her ways to deal with stress. She tells me more about the meeting she had at Maxy's school, where the teacher had told her that he was struggling. I volunteer to help him where I can, particularly with reading. She seems to respond well to this and appears not to be taken aback by the prospect of us all spending more time together. There are no awkward silences, and everything feels natural, like we've known each other for years.

I allow myself to imagine this restaurant becoming a regular for us, a restaurant that we'll always remember as the location of our first official date.

After we've finished the main course, I excuse myself and head towards the gents. As I'm standing at the urinal, my heart is pounding with excitement and I replay in my head the conversations we've had. I lean my head back and say, out loud, 'Nailed it, Ben. Well done.'

I head over to the taps and hear the toilet flush in one of the cubicles. Out comes a man of a similar age to me, with a smirk on his face. Bit embarrassing, but I don't care. I wash my hands thoroughly – water, soap, water, soap, water, soap – tuck my shirt in and head back out to Alice.

As I approach the table, I allow myself to take in her beauty; she's got a glow about her this evening and I dare to give myself credit for making her happier.

We order dessert – I eat most of Alice's as well as my own – and after the waiter takes our order there is an extended moment of silence. I want her to take the lead. I want her to ask me about my feelings, about where I see our relationship going, but after what seems like a couple of minutes, I take a different tack. It's a risky one.

'So, I want to hear more about Adam. I wish I had known him.'

And Alice tells me more about Adam than I expect. How, when they got together, on that first night at a university social, she had actually been after one of his mates, only pulling him because the mate went off with someone else and she wanted to make him jealous. How they'd slept together on that very first night, fumbling around in the single bed of her dormitory. How Adam had studied philosophy at university. How from the outset he was intense and booky, which had its pluses and minuses. Alice tells me that Adam helped her to 'raise her own intellectual game' and to see the world with more maturity than she had previously. They would spend hours over dinner debating utilitarianism and Adam would offer piercing insights into current affairs. The downside of this, Alice explained, was that Adam always found it hard to have fun. Everything was serious, everything was planned, everything was either morally corrupt or highly commendable. She added that, on reflection, for all Alice gained in intellectual maturity with Adam, she sacrificed levity and triviality.

I chip in that it is important to find a balance between the two and tell her that I got a first-class degree in English while also managing to get off my face most nights, and this seems to impress her.

She tells me that a key thing that she and Adam had in common was a lack of clear parent figures. Adam's dad left when he was a child and his mum killed herself when he was fourteen. She doesn't go into the details of why her parents were absent, but I let it be. I say that I am so sorry to hear about the ongoing theme of tragedy in this family.

It's like we are in our own little world, on a private island, vaguely aware of those around us but too focused to take notice. We're only interrupted when a timid waiter comes over and offers us the bill without us having requested it. Only then do I look around and realise that we're the only people left in the restaurant, the lights now raised and the staff clearly itching to go home.

'God, look at that,' I say as casually as I can. 'This is far too late for a Sunday night for me!'

'Yeah, we'd better get back and relieve Mrs Turner. I bloody hope Max is in bed by now.'

We'd better get back? Is that an invitation to go back with her? It wouldn't be such a big deal usually – I've been there a few times now – but in the context of tonight and the dinner we've just had, my heart pounds. I feel the need to clarify, just to make sure.

'Shall we get an Uber back to yours together, then?' I ask, struggling to look her straight in the eye.

'Yeah, let's have a nightcap.'

Is that a euphemism?

ALICE

'Better keep our voices down. Max is such a light sleeper.'

I open the door slowly and am glad to see that all the lights in the house are off apart from one in the conservatory. We walk through the front door, across the corridor and into the back of the house. Mrs Turner is slumped on the couch, watching something vaguely erotic on TV. She straightens with a start.

'Alice, hi. I must have drifted off.'

'Sorry it's so late, Mrs Turner. Did you get my text? Ended up going for an impromptu dinner. This is my friend, Ben.'

It's clear that we've both had a bit too much to drink and I can see her judging me, but I don't give a fuck. I'm sure she thinks it's too soon for me to be moving on, but she's a lonely old spinster, so I'm sure she'll get off on it later, imagining us together.

'Hello, Ben. Nice to meet you. I think I remember you from Adam's . . .'

140

Ben goes bright red and rushes over to shake her hand. I'd completely forgotten that Ben had been at Adam's funeral. I put the thought to the very back of my mind.

'Hey there. Is little Maxy in bed?' Ben enquires as he walks over to shake Mrs Turner's hand.

'Oh yes, dear, of course. He's been in bed since about nine thirty. We had a nice chat about the planets before he went to sleep. He's been learning about them in school.'

That's lovely, Mrs Turner, I think, wondering how long I have to indulge this conversation before she heads back to her house. I rustle in my bag for my purse and hand her a fifty-pound note.

'Oh that's far too much, dear. Let me give you some change,' she offers.

'Don't be silly; you've been so good. It's late! You go and head off home.'

Ben is still standing there with his coat on and I can see he's feeling as uncomfortable as I am.

'I'll leave you two to it, then,' Mrs Turner chuckles and I look straight to the floor.

I walk with Mrs Turner towards the front door, desperate to expedite the situation before anything else awkward happens.

When I come back to the living room, Ben has taken his coat off and has helped himself to some Highland Park whisky, which is on the counter.

'Adam's favourite, that one. Used to drink it by the gallon. Let me go and get some ice. Pour me one, will you?' I smile and head into the kitchen.

As I open the freezer and reach for the bag of ice, I keep the door open a bit longer than needed, composing myself before heading back to Ben. Do I really want this? What, exactly, do I want? If I'm honest with myself, I'm just keen to get laid. It's been such a long time and what's the harm in having a bit of fun with someone who has shown so much kindness towards me? Or maybe I'm getting the wrong end of the stick. It occurs to me that he's barely talked at all about his own personal life, largely because I haven't asked him. How do I know he wants to fuck me? Well, I think, there's only one way to find out.

By the time I head back into the living room, Ben has taken a seat on one of the leather sofas and it looks like he's undone another button on his shirt. I can see that tuft of chest hair again.

'Here you go, Ben. Some ice to cool you down.'

I sit next to him and I'm aware of this scene being like the three minutes of preamble at the beginning of a porn film. Does that make me the sultry blonde, preying on the younger man, ready to pounce? I haven't got the tits.

'I really shouldn't stay for very long, Alice,' Ben mumbles as he shuffles in the seat next to me.

'Oh, I thought you were going to stay the night.'

What do I sound like?

'I don't know. I've had a lovely time, it's just that we don't want to rush things.'

Rush things? Oh, God, he's gay, isn't he?

'Don't you find me attractive, Ben?'

And then he kisses me, as if suddenly overtaken by an urge to prove that he is a lothario. He's not the best kisser – a lot of tongue and his teeth seem too far forwards – but I go with it and start unbuttoning his shirt.

This is his cue to reciprocate, but he seems too focused on eating my face to worry about my clothes, so I remove my top. He stops suddenly, staring as if he's never seen a pair of tits before. He dives straight in and reaches round clumsily to unclasp my bra. I help him while he rips off his shirt. His body is better than I'd imagined – broad and slim, in shape without being gym chiselled.

'I've wanted this for so long,' whispers Ben.

I stop for a second and look at him to see if he's joking. He has his eyes closed tight and there's no sense of irony. As he draws me down towards him on the sofa, I do a quick mental calculation of how long we've known each other. When do we start the clock? I feel a lump in my throat. While Ben kisses my neck, I look over to the mantelpiece at a photo of Adam, holding Max on the beach in Brighton. I remember that day well. He had decided that he'd take a day's break from writing, so we'd got in the car on a whim and driven to the coast. It was a Sunday morning and the roads were clear. We whizzed down the motorway and Adam told me excitedly about the latest developments in his screenplay as Max sat in the back, listening to some music on his headphones.

We stopped at a service station about half an hour outside Brighton and picked up a few things for a picnic, then parked by the beach. I think it was March or April and it probably wasn't warm enough for us to be there, but we had the beach to ourselves, apart from the occasional smug jogger. Max would have been about four, I reckon, and he was totally baffled by the pebbles and kept asking who had stolen the sand. I have a distinct memory of Adam rolling around with his son, tickling him and yelping as the stones bruised his back. For all his faults, Adam was a great dad.

'Shall we move to the bedroom?' Ben sighs and suddenly I'm back here with him.

He stands and is totally naked now, but I don't allow myself to look directly at it. I'm still wearing my knickers and I'll keep it like that for the time being.

'Hang on a sec; I'll be right back. Come and join me in two minutes,' I offer and gather my clothes, using my top to cover my chest as I head upstairs.

I tidy the bedroom, make sure there isn't anything incriminating on the sheets and bundle the dirty laundry into a cupboard to give the impression of having my life in order.

'Are you ready? I want you, Alice.'

Ben appears at the door and this time there's no avoiding him in all his glory. Wholly unimpressive.

'Turn the light off, will you?' I ask. Adam always preferred it with the lights off.

'I want to see you. You're beautiful, Alice. You're more beautiful than you know.'

And who doesn't like to hear that? So the light stays on and we have sex, because he wants it and, for a moment, I want it, too.

But then as soon as it's over, I head into the bathroom, sit on the toilet and stare at the tiles on the wall. I place my head between my knees and sob.

ALICE

Monday, 21 May

I keep my eyes closed and do my very best not to stir. I haven't slept all night, and I mean that. When Adam used to say that, I was always dubious. How could he not have slept, even for just a moment? I always insisted that he must have had some rest, that he must have drifted in and out of sleep without even realising. But I can say with full confidence this morning that it *is* possible to spend a whole night without a single moment of sleep.

And there, in the darkness, with nothing to stimulate your eyes and only soft, regular breathing next to you to disturb the silence, time is expanded, so that a minute turns into ten, an hour into two. I've been desperate, for hours, to go to the toilet, but I'm scared that if I get up I'll wake him and then we'll have to talk. Talk about what happened, about how I let it happen. Or maybe he'd even want it to happen again, and then I'd have to put my foot down this time and say no. No, that's not going to happen again, Ben. Never.

When the alarm on his phone goes off and I hear him groan then turn over to the bedside table to silence it, I make an extra effort not to move. The birds have been awake for hours now, chirping away, so I've been on alert, waiting for the alarm to sound. I'm relieved when it finally does. I'm so glad that it's a Monday morning and I know Ben will have to get going for work. Imagine if this had happened on a Friday or Saturday night . . . He might have wanted to sleep in, to spend the whole morning in bed, to read the papers together, him reading one supplement while I read another.

I decided hours ago that when the alarm went off I'd let him believe that I was still asleep. It seems to work. I feel him roll over towards me and I can feel the proximity of his breath as his face comes up close. He stinks of booze – not beer, or wine, or any drink in particular, just booze – that chemical smell of alcohol that reminds me of Adam after a heavy night. I drank a fair amount myself last night, but besides a dry mouth and a chapped bottom lip, it hasn't hit me too hard – after all, I've had the whole night to sweat it out.

So I lie there, consciously gentle in my breathing as I feel Ben close to me, watching me sleep. He uses a finger to stroke a strand of my hair and I twitch, willing for this moment to pass as quickly as possible. He kisses me on the forehead with a tenderness that makes me feel sick and I fight an urge to break my silence, to open my eyes and shout, to ask him to leave my bed and leave my house and never contact me again. I hold my poise, then I hear Ben let out a long sigh and get out of bed.

He heads to the bathroom and I place my fingers in my ears, pressing tight. Listening to him pissing is not an intimacy that I want to experience. When I hear the faint sound of the flushing, I release my fingers and reach over for the large glass of water on the bedside table. The door to the shower closes and the water starts.

I run my hand down my body and am disgusted by myself. I need to get in that bathroom and wash – I need to remove every trace of him from my body. What kind of a wife am I? How could I throw myself at another man, someone I barely know, so soon after the death of my husband? And not any man. *Him.*

Where would I have been without Adam? An orphan from the age of eight, he was the only man who truly loved me. And now at the first opportunity, I have betrayed him. The second I felt Ben inside me, I felt like a cheat, like a whore. And then he said that he *loved* me and, instantly, I went cold. How on earth have I allowed him to get anywhere near to thinking that?

That was the turning point; that was the moment when I knew I'd made a mistake. On the one hand, I felt sorry for him – how damaged and vulnerable he must be to have confused his own loneliness with love. And on the other hand, I felt vulnerable myself – violated by those empty words.

The water stops, then the shower door opens and shuts. I close my eyes again and pull up the covers. He's in the bathroom for another few minutes and I imagine him drying himself with one of Adam's towels, wiping the remaining suds off his crotch with the very same piece of material that, just a few months ago, would have been draped around my husband's shoulders.

It seems like minutes before the door opens and he's back in the room, and I'm determined not to stir, not to give him any encouragement to speak, to think that I might be awake enough to engage. He seems to respect the fact that I don't want to be disturbed and moves around quietly, presumably putting back on the same clothes as yesterday.

I hear the zip of trousers and feel a dip in the bed as he sits on the end. I picture him pulling up his socks and tying his shoelaces, smiling with the smugness of having just got laid. He stands and I can sense him coming round the side of the bed, leaning into me. His breath is now minty, and I'm sickened by that. He's either used my toothbrush or brought his own, both of which are totally unacceptable.

He kisses my forehead again, a slow, considered kiss that lingers, and I know that he wants me to wake, to open my eyes and reciprocate affection. He wants a little conversation, a sign-off, an 'I had a great night', or a 'let's do this again soon', but I won't give him that.

He gets the message when my eyes remain closed and he finally leaves me in peace, walking quietly out of the bedroom, across the long corridor and down the stairs. It's not until I hear the front door shut, not until the house is fully still, that I feel safe enough to open my eyes.

BEN

The first time is always the best. It's the moment when all barriers come down and two people meet properly in the most intimate way. It's not necessarily the most pleasurable time, or the most satisfying, but it is special because it is the watershed moment. No matter how long it lasts or how good it feels, for being the first time, it is the best time.

I just wish that it hadn't been a Sunday night. When I woke up, my mouth felt so dry that when I swallowed, the back of my throat felt tender. Usually when I have drunk as much as that – which, I have to admit, hasn't happened in years – I make a point of downing at least two pints of water before going to sleep. And then there's usually at least one visit to the kitchen during the night for a little more. But last night was too passionate, too rushed and spontaneous, for us to have had time to think about the consequences of our actions.

When I woke for the first time next to Alice, there was such a discrepancy between how I felt in my mind and

149

how I felt in my body. My head was banging with two conflicting forces: waves of physical pain as my body fought last night's poison, and a swelling of emotional pleasure, endorphins pushing through my blood and congratulating me on my achievement. My life with Alice had entered the next phase.

It feels like I have spent the last few months working on our relationship and things have moved slowly. I knew that it was a step in the right direction for her to have dinner with me in a restaurant, but I didn't expect that we would move straight from that milestone to another. After all, Alice is not the type of woman to do this kind of thing very often. She is a woman with integrity, a proper grown-up, with adult responsibilities.

But then it was definitely Alice who initiated it. We were sitting on the sofa and she made the first move. I find this thought comforting and it's led me to replay all of our interactions over the past couple of months in my mind, cranking up my impression of her interest in me. Because this sexual desire, this need to be with me that encouraged an otherwise circumspect woman to act on such impulse, can't have come out of the blue.

On reflection, I allow myself to believe that my desire for Alice, which has been growing since the first day I met her at the hospital, has always been reciprocated. Swelling gradually on her side as well as mine, like two fledgling sparrows, getting stronger in their separate nests, then finally daring to rear their heads and face each other.

Lying in my own bed tonight, I'm still there. I'm still in the bed with Alice, reliving each kiss, each touch, each time that I experience a part of her body for the first time. The first time I kiss her neck, on the right-hand side and then on the left, smelling the scent of her perfume stronger on one side than the other. The first time I run my foot down her leg, feeling the slight tickle of hair where she hasn't shaved for a few days. The first time I take her earlobe in my mouth and bite it ever so gently, but hard enough so that she calls out and asks me to stop. The first time I feel the scar above her right eyebrow, making a mental note to ask her about it and then another note not to until she volunteers the information. The first time I am inside her. And us making love, gently at first, and then, at her command, with increasing vigour.

My instinct is to keep it tender, to cherish every touch and brush of our skin together, but she wants more. She orgasms twice, screaming with such intensity that it's as if she wants everyone to hear and to know that we are finally together. When I come, it is straight inside her. I feel a swell of pressure and find myself bellowing.

'I love you, Alice. I fucking love you.'

It just came out and it surprised her as much as it surprised me, I'm sure. But it was true, of course. These feelings of tenderness and warmth, now consummated after all this time, had become fully formed and certain. I can still see the look on Alice's face as our breathing regulated. She was shaking as she looked deep into my eyes, and though she didn't say the words herself, I felt the connection and saw in her gaze reciprocation.

She got up, headed to the bathroom, shut the door. And as I reached for the covers to wipe the sweat off my chest,

I took a deep breath, rolled over and laughed straight into the pillow.

It's taken me all day to get over the hangover. When I was in my early twenties, I could drink as much as that, and more, and not feel a single thing the morning after. But I struggled at work, trying to keep inconspicuous, dosing myself on paracetamol at the appropriate intervals.

The trouble is that it's pretty hard to keep a low profile when you're a teacher at a primary school. I think of some of my old uni mates, the ones still getting trashed midweek, and decide that it must be a lot easier if you're in an office job, because you can just choose not to do too much on a particular day, stick your headphones on and keep your head down. For me, there's no such opportunity. Every day as a teacher is a performance in front of a very unforgiving audience and it's just not worth the risk to come in at 50 per cent capacity after a night out. Not to say that I regret it in this case.

The kids were actually pretty nonchalant and I seemed to get away with it. It was my fellow teachers who cottoned on to a change in my routine. I was in the staffroom at break time, pouring myself my third coffee of the morning, and Lesley, one of the older teachers who was already working here when I was at primary school myself, made a characteristically catty remark.

'Late night was it, Mr Anderson? You look bloody knackered.'

I'd been desperate to talk to someone about last night, so I took the bait.

'I've just starting seeing someone actually, Lesley. So last night was, well, later than expected.'

This made Lesley blush and I was glad to have planted the kernel of gossip in her mind, hoping it would be sown across the staffroom and beyond. Having previously squirmed at the idea of people talking about what happened on the motorway, now I liked the idea of there being idle chatter about me. I liked the idea that people would think that my life had taken a turn for the better. I liked the idea that they could move on from the speculation about why I was off work for a while.

Equally, though, I knew I should be careful not to divulge *too* much of my personal life at work. It is, after all, only the very beginning of our relationship and, with Alice being a discreet person, it doesn't seem fair to share any major details about what's going on. Not that Alice knows any of these people at work, of course, but in the future she may well come to meet them. Knowing Alice, she wouldn't be delighted with the idea of me having indulged in kiss and tell.

I love the idea of taking her to the staff Christmas party this year. I haven't minded, in the past, going without a plus-one, but for various reasons it would be advantageous to be able to go this year with Alice. First, it would get Louisa, the teaching assistant, off my case. For the last couple of years, she's been all over me at work dos, telling me how much I remind her of her ex, which is definitely not a compliment, because I've overheard her tell colleagues at other points about how he was violent. She's not attractive, and even if she were, it would be too awkward to get into a relationship with someone at work.

Secondly, I like the idea of taking a girlfriend as an indication of my own achievement. I'm always impressed when I hear that a colleague is in a significant relationship. It indicates a stamp of approval, that there is at least one person in the world who vouches for that person, and I can't help but judge others who don't have that endorsement.

And, besides, Alice is impressive. I like the idea of Alice and my boss comparing notes about their time at Durham – I think maybe they even went to the same college – and I'm sure everyone will be entertained with her stories of the Christmas parties that she went to when she was still working in the City.

Obviously, I'm getting ahead of myself. The Christmas party is still six months away and everything could change by then. But it's fine to think ahead and, for the time being, I don't mind a bit of gossip.

I left work at 4.30 p.m. I'd got a taxi from Alice's to school in the morning – a treat – but my phone had run out of battery during the day because it hadn't been charged since the Saturday evening, so I had no means by which to order an Uber back to my flat. I got the bus and took the opportunity to have a little nap. I can't have had more than four hours' sleep last night and those hours weren't of the best quality. I would have missed my stop if it hadn't been for the old lady who woke me up to ask for my seat at just the right moment.

As I got off the bus, I reached into my pockets to check that I had everything – wallet, keys – and when I felt the lump of my phone, my pace quickened. I was almost home, where I could plug it into the charger and see what Alice had texted me back. I'd sent her a couple of messages in the morning, but before I got a chance to see her replies, the phone switched itself off.

When I walked into my flat, my hands were shaking and I ran to the bedroom to find my charger. I plugged the phone in and sat on the floor beside it, waiting for it to have enough juice for the white Apple logo to appear. When it finally did, I was so eager to enter the pin code that I got it wrong a couple of times – first one too many zeros, then one too many fives. Finally, I got the right one and waited.

There were three texts – three! Alice was probably worried. Worried because I hadn't replied. I felt terrible – I didn't want her to think I was one of those guys who would sleep with her and then ghost her. Would she think that I had not had a good time? That I had been disappointed by her performance in the bedroom? That couldn't be further from the truth. Before reading the texts, I scrolled through my contacts and gave her a ring, waiting once more for her to pick up the phone.

I smiled as I heard her voice.

'Hey, this is Alice. Leave me a message.'

'Hi, Alice, it's me. Just wanted to let you know that my phone ran out of battery at school today, so sorry if I haven't been available. I probably could have borrowed a charger from the technician's office; that would have been sensible. Anyway, just calling to say that and, well, to say hi. So hi!'

Ugh! what an idiot. How many times had I said 'hi' in one short message? As I put the phone down, I opened the text messages and saw that I needn't have worried, after all. One text from Vodafone – about a deal for international roaming – and another two from my mum:

MUM: Hi, sweetheart. Haven't heard from you in a few days. All OK? xMumx

And then the second:

MUM: ?? xMumx

I thought I'd better call Mum and let her know that everything was OK, that I had just been a bit busy, but I didn't because I realised that Alice would be trying to call me back and I didn't want to have the awkwardness of voicemail tennis. Instead, I decided to send Mum an email, so I picked up my phone, put it on loud and headed downstairs to my computer.

Compose email:

Hey, Mum, sorry I missed your call and your texts. Been a busy couple of weeks at work. Been driving myself mad preparing for the mid-year tests for the kids and there's one little girl called Ella who's really struggling, so spending a bit of extra time figuring out a special plan for her. How's everything with you and Dad?

New paragraph.

Do you want to come round for dinner after work on Thursday? It's been a while since I've cooked for you – will be nice. What do you fancy? Maybe I'll make some salmon or something – nothing too fattening, I know what the rules are! Anyway, yeah, come round. Look forward to catching up – got lots to tell you. Let me know if dinner works? Love from Ben xx

Send.

Lots to tell her. Am I ready to tell her about Alice? I know it's probably premature, but even though we've only just officially got together, we have known each other for quite a while. She'll be so pleased to know that I've met someone. It will get her off my back with those awkward questions and her false open-mindedness.

'Is there anyone, Ben? You know you can bring anyone home? Woman, man, whoever it is. Your dad and I just want you to be happy.'

I don't have to tell her everything. I'm not going to tell her about Maxy just yet, because she'll freak out at the idea of me being in a relationship with a woman who already has a child. And then, if I bring up the subject of Max, I'll have to tell her about Adam, and then if I bring up Adam, it will lead to the story of how we met. And I don't want to go there again. Not with Mum and not with anyone.

BEN

Thursday, 24 May

I've always really enjoyed cooking, but it's so much more gratifying when you're doing it for others. I managed to get out of work early again today, early enough to head to Waitrose to buy some food in time for Mum and Dad to come round. I wasn't going to go crazy with the menu, but I wanted to demonstrate to them that I was back to normal, that I was no longer depressed and that I could look after myself. The fact that I could cook had always been a source of pride for them, particularly for my mother, who saw it as a marker of my being an independent adult.

'I don't think your father could even boil an egg, if he ever tried! I'm very impressed, you know. You'll make a good husband,' she would say, as if marriage is the only achievement worthy of note.

Mum and Dad met when they were sixteen and were married by nineteen, so the idea of me still being single at thirty-two is excruciating, the cause of much pillow talk between them and, I'm sure, one of the contributing factors to my mother's increasingly nervous disposition. The woman won't be content until the day she finally sees me walk down the aisle, because that will be the day when she will consider her job done as a mother, the day when she can hand over the mantle to a caring wife, as if I couldn't possibly look after myself.

I get back to my flat with the shopping at about five thirty and do some last-minute tidying before they arrive. I've always been a bit obsessed with keeping the flat tidy, but over the past few months I've let things slip. There was that period straight after the crash when I moved back in with my parents, and when I returned to my flat after the funeral, it was freezing and some of the plants had wilted. I still didn't water them. I didn't have the energy. Keeping the flat tidy and ordered felt petty, so unimportant. It's only in the last few weeks that I've got things back in order – washing the floors, dusting, buying flowers. And today as I plump the fat red cushions on my three-seater, I look around in satisfaction to see my little empire returned to its former glory.

The buzzer goes at six. I'd invited them round for seven-ish and should have known from experience that the 'ish' would mean an hour early rather than fifteen minutes late. When I open the door, it's just Mum, dressed in a green dress as if she's been invited to the Queen's garden party. She's got a new necklace, spelling out Amanda, just in case she ever forgets her name and needs a little reminder. She lunges forwards, the overwhelming waft of floral perfume tickling me at the back of my throat.

'Hello, darling. Sorry, you're going to have to make do with just little old me in the end. Your father is stuck with some clients in Leighton Buzzard – he sends his love.'

'Come in, come in. There'll be loads of food for the two of us, then,' I offer cheerily.

Mum bounds straight past me, throws her coat on one of the hooks and, as if by impulse, adjusts a photograph from my graduation on the wall that wasn't askew.

'Got any red?' she calls from the kitchen and when I walk in to join her, I see that she's already found a glass and is in the process of uncorking a bottle that I had put aside for a special occasion with Alice.

'I'm making salmon, actually, Mum, so maybe white would be . . .' I offer, but I can see that it's too late.

'Oh, well, we can always move on to white, can't we, darling? So, what's new? How's work? I see you still haven't replaced those ghastly curtains.'

No matter how many times I tell her that I actually rather like the curtains that were in place when I first bought the flat, she doesn't seem to be comfortable with me having an independent creative opinion on the decor of my own living quarters. It's as if by not sharing her taste in curtains I'm somehow disrespecting her, that my refusal to update the decor is a teenage defiance, an eschewing of her authority.

'Work's good, thanks. Nothing too exciting to report, really.'

'What about that new teacher? The young, pretty one who started teaching Reception. What's her name?'

Here we go. She's talking about Debbie Ross, a supply teacher who worked at the school a couple of years ago. She's pretending not to remember her name, but really I know very well that her name is on the tip of her tongue, because it's a name that she's asked me about before.

We went on a couple of dates over a few weeks and for a while it looked like it was getting pretty serious, so I told Mum about her and she got all excited, because she's Jewish like us and Mum knows her mum, Diane. Neither of my parents are particularly observant, but still, the prospect of my meeting someone Jewish to take as a bride seems to be more important to them than most things in life. I made the mistake of telling Mum about Debbie because I was pretty certain that it was shaping up to be an important relationship and I didn't want it to progress too far without keeping her in the loop.

'If you're talking about Debbie Ross again, Mum, I've told you before; we're not in contact anymore. We only dated for a few weeks and she's moved schools now, anyway.'

Mum raises an eyebrow, smirks and helps herself to another glass of wine.

'OK, well, there's no need to be like that, Benjy. You know, I just want you to meet someone and have a nice life together.'

I hate it when she calls me Benjy. It makes me feel like I'm five years old again and gives her a feeling of superiority, like she can control me in the same way she did when I was a child. And if she does have any influence over me, it certainly doesn't extend to my love life. I'm having second thoughts, now, about my plan to tell her about Alice. I don't want to get into the same situation again, where she puts pressure on and it becomes something that it isn't.

On the other hand, I can hardly compare Alice to Debbie Ross. With Debbie, we just had a couple of drinks – I'm not sure if we even ever had a meal together. We just didn't have a connection. That's not to say that we didn't have things to talk about. In fact, we probably had more in common with each other than Alice and I do. We were both teachers, for a start, and having both grown up in north-west London, we had mutual friends from school and university, so lots of stories to share.

But there's something about Alice, something about when we are together, that transcends anything I ever experienced with Debbie or, indeed, in any previous relationship, so I think the risk is low. And, of course, there's the other key difference: my relationship with Debbie was never consummated.

'There is actually someone, Mum. It's early days, but I have started seeing someone.' There we go – it's out there. No going back.

'Oh, sweetheart, how exciting!'

She's so thrilled she almost falls off her stool and, as she comes towards me, I feel an overwhelming sense of glee. I can finally share this excitement that's been bubbling up inside of me with someone else. She reaches over the counter, sprawling her arms towards me for a big hug.

'I'm so proud of you, darling. You must tell me all about her.'

And so I do. Well, I don't tell her everything, but I tell her as much as I feel comfortable with her knowing. About how intelligent Alice is, about her former career in the City and her gorgeous house in Rickmansworth. I find myself having to fill in some details, because Mum has so many questions and I simply don't have all the answers yet. But I make some good assumptions on her professional qualifications and interests based on what I already know about her.

She's obviously good with numbers, and when we were at the Italian restaurant, Lecce, she told me about the portfolios of billionaire property tycoons that she used to manage. I've surmised from this that she has a particular expertise in tax planning. Mum comments that maybe she can provide some advice on a current dispute she has with HMRC and I suggest that while Alice might be willing to help, she might be a bit rusty.

I'm conscious not to spend the whole evening talking about Alice – I don't want Mum to think that this is any more serious than it is – so as we sit down for dinner, I manage to swerve the conversation to other topics. We talk about Mother's floaters – the small black blobs that have been appearing in front of her eyes over the last few months – and Dad's gardening: 'He's getting obsessed! The other day I caught him talking to a palm tree!' And I'm not sure if she's joking or not.

I am, of course, thinking about Alice throughout, wondering how she'd be chipping into the conversation. I find myself imagining what she'd have to say about Mum's latest ailment and about all the gardening tips that Dad could share with her – God knows, she needs some expertise to help her manage that beast of a garden.

I think the salmon goes down well, because Mum asks for a second piece and, before we know it, it's past ten o'clock.

'Thanks for that, Mum. I've had a nice time – it's good to have a bit of a natter.'

I show Mum to the front door and pass her the handbag she's left on the sofa.

'Thank you, darling. Salmon was absolutely divine. It's good to see you back on track after, well, you know, all that horrible stuff on the motorway and . . .'

I go bright red and she stops herself short, sensing that she's hit a nerve.

'Anyway, darling, off I trot. And, you know, no pressure, but Dad and I would love to meet this new girlfriend of yours. When you're ready.'

As I close the front door behind her, I reach into my pocket for my phone. Alice still hasn't texted me back and I know that, strictly speaking, it's her turn to get in touch with me, but I can't resist.

BEN

Friday, 25 May

I wake to the sound of a WhatsApp notification. I look over to the clock on my bedside table: 3.35 a.m. I used to leave my phone on airplane mode overnight – I read something in the *Guardian* about it being important to switch off all devices at least thirty minutes before going to sleep – but for the last few weeks I haven't bothered. It's not like I get many phone calls or text messages anyway, particularly not in the middle of the night. And I've come to realise that if someone does go to the effort of getting in touch with me, then it's only polite that I should respond straight away. As a compromise, I don't leave my phone on the bedside table but instead on the floor next to the window at the other side of the room, where it is charging. This way I limit the radiation, at the very least.

My first thought when I hear the beep of the notification is, of course, that it must be Alice. It's been a few days since I've heard from her and, having sent her a message just before I went to bed last night, it would only be logical that she should text me back.

As I climb out of bed and head towards the edge of the room, a wave of panic comes over me, a warmth in my chest and gut, as I wonder why on earth she would be replying at this time. Is something wrong? Is there an emergency? Has something happened to Maxy? What if someone has broken into their house in the middle of the night? It is one of the biggest houses on their street and, if I put myself in the shoes of a burglar, I can imagine that it would be an obvious target. What if a burglar has been tracking the house for the last few weeks, watching Alice and Maxy come in and out, on their own, realising that they are alone?

I realise that I'm catastrophising but, as I grab my phone, I allow my fears to be confirmed for a brief moment as I see that it is Alice who has sent me a message and the message is so long that it takes up the whole of my iPhone screen:

Hey Ben,

Sorry for the radio silence the last few days – I haven't been ignoring you. It's just been a case of working out exactly what I wanted to say and how I wanted to say it.

The first thing I want you to know is that it's not anything you've done, or haven't done, or haven't done well, or anything like that. I've really enjoyed getting to know you over the last few months – I really do think you're a great guy. I'm not sure there are many other men who would have been so kind and thoughtful, in light of what happened, and you've been there for me when no one else was. And I know that Max has really enjoyed spending time with you, as well.

I think we both just had a bit too much to drink the other night and we probably ended up getting a bit confused about what our relationship is. I don't want you to think that I didn't enjoy it, but something just didn't feel right, you know?

I thought I was ready to move on from Adam, in that way, but the truth is I'm not. And what with the particular circumstances and everything! Anyway, thought I'd get it all down in a text for you, because honesty is the best policy and all that.

Hope this is not all disappointing, Ben, and it doesn't come as too much of a shock? Hopefully we're on the same page? I'll leave it in your hands now — I'd still really like to be friends, if you're up for that. Such a cliché, I know, but I mean it.

Take care,

Alice x

BEN

Friday, 25 May

OK, let me read the text again. It's never good to respond quickly to things like this – always better to give yourself a few minutes to reflect, really think about it – otherwise, you end up saying something you regret. It was such an extensive block of text and I was so eager to take it all in straight away that I didn't start at the beginning. Instead, I skipped to the middle of the first paragraph, scanning up and down, looking for the key words in each sentence to try to catch the gist of the message as a whole within the first few seconds.

I remember a similar feeling when I got a letter from Cambridge University, containing the verdict as to whether or not I had been accepted to study there as an under-graduate. I was desperate to be accepted and I ripped open the envelope, unfolding the letter, my hands shaking, only seeing the word 'delighted' before throwing the letter down and screaming in jubilation. In that case, the result had been as I had hoped: the head of admissions was 'delighted to let me know' that I had been accepted on the course.

When I opened the text message from Alice, the first words I saw were 'kind', 'thoughtful' and 'relationship', so in those first few instants, my heart raced and I felt a wave of relief, from my head right down my body. But then on second reading, some other words appeared. 'Disappointing' was first and then 'friends', and my heart picked up even more pace, my hands started to shake and I felt light-headed. I threw my phone down on the bed and took three deep breaths, focusing on the inhale and exhale, trying to get things in perspective. And then I must have fallen back to sleep, because my alarm's only just gone off.

I feel calmer now. I pick up the phone again and read the text properly, this time from start to finish. As I read, I can feel my eyes welling, my mind racing with questions and indignations. What had brought on this sudden change of heart? Why did this coincide with the first time we made love? What is really behind this message? Has someone made her write this?

There's no way I can go into school today. I have to get to the bottom of this. I ring the school reception.

'Hey, Linda, it's Ben Anderson. Just to let you know that I'm feeling a bit under the weather and so I won't be coming into school today.'

Linda sighs and then concedes. 'Well, I suppose it's for the best. We don't want you infecting all the children.'

And then I cough, a pathetic, superficial bleat that comes out without thought.

'Thanks, Linda. I think there's probably something going around. Hopefully, I will be back in tomorrow.'

'OK, Mr Anderson. Well, you have a nice rest then and get yourself better.'

I put the phone down and head across to the study, switching my computer on to try to figure out an action plan. I open Google Chrome, go into favourites and click on Alice's Facebook profile. I've thought several times about adding her as a friend, but every time I've looked at her profile, I've hovered on the button and resisted. It's always felt to me like our relationship is bigger than an online friendship, which are for work colleagues and people who you went to primary school with – relationships that are casual and non-committal. I don't want to signal any of this to Alice. Whether we're going to be friends or lovers, our relationship will never be so superficial – there's no need for an online tie to validate our connection. I suppose I'd have been more tempted to add her as a friend if she'd had a more hidden profile. As it is, the privacy settings are pretty minimal.

I can't find anything incriminating. No status updates referring to a terrible experience in the bedroom, no new friends recently added that might indicate that she's met someone else.

While at the computer, I spend some time scrolling through her old photos, all of which I've seen before: from university days, to those first months and years after gradu-ation, when everyone moves to London and has enough energy to go out three times a week as well as juggling a full-time job. When she first graduated, Alice moved into a small flat in Camden with a couple of girls who were both called Lucy. I know that it's Camden because there's a photo of them in the garden, with Camden Lock just about visible in the background.

Adam is in a lot of the early photos and, although I can see his name, when I hover over his face, I can't click on his profile. I'm not sure whether this is because he was never on Facebook, or whether his profile has been removed since his passing. Either way, it's nice to have these photos of Alice's to look through – it feels like I can get to know Adam a bit, so now he's not just a flash of white on the motorway, a comatose body in a hospital bed, but a living, breathing man.

There's a particularly nice one dated 15 September 2007, where it looks like Alice and Adam are at a fancy dress party. Adam is dressed as a superhero, with a red cape and a mask over the left-hand side of his face. He's got a drink in one hand – the colour of Coke, but I assume there was also rum in it – and his other arm is draped around Alice. She's dressed as some kind of cat, all in black, with little triangular ears attached to her own and some quite severe make-up. She's got a leotard on, which makes me think that she was either into ballet when she was younger or else she bought this especially for the costume. It's a little bit low-cut for my liking. My knowledge of superheroes is not great, but it doesn't take an expert to surmise that she's dressed as Catwoman who, I gather, is Batman's girlfriend.

Looking at this photo again today, I consider commenting on it but resist. I right-click and save the photo on my desktop, then carry on looking through the photos, but they seem to tail off from about 2009. Unfortunately, there are no wedding photos on her profile, no snaps from family holidays, not even any albums from when Max was little. It goes suddenly from those photos of Alice as Catwoman

– slimmer, fresher – to some photos from earlier this year. The years have taken their toll on her, but she's still the same person inside.

My eyes are starting to sting, so I leave the computer and head back into bed. I check my phone to see if anything else has come through. Nothing. I decide to bite the bullet and give her a ring. I could spend ages composing a text to her, but I think in situations like this, it's better just to speak directly.

I grab my phone and, instead of searching in my phone book, just dial the numbers. I count the rings. It goes to voicemail, so I hang up and ring again. When it goes to voicemail again, I try one more time and then leave a message, which is a little rambling. I send her a text message as well, because, knowing her, she won't check her voice-mails. I set a timer on my phone for two hours' time and decide that if I haven't heard from her by the time the alarm goes off, then I'll give her another try.

After twenty-five minutes, I decide I can't wait any longer. I've come to the conclusion that speaking on the phone is not enough, that I need to see her face-to-face so we can be really honest with one another. It's not that I want to try to convince her to change her mind but that part of me is hoping that by speaking in person, by looking each other straight in the eye, she might be reminded of our connection enough to reconsider.

I stop at the Primark on the high street and buy myself a new shirt before picking up some Percy Pigs from Marks & Spencer and getting back in the car. I get stuck in a traffic jam on the high street, so I pull down the mirror on the sun visor and rehearse my opening line.

'Alice, hi. Thought it would be easiest just to pop over and talk in person.'

'Alice, it's me. Hi. Just thought I'd say hello.'

'Hey, Alice, I've bought some Percy Pigs for Maxy.'

Nothing's quite right. Apart from anything else, isn't she going to wonder why I'm not at work? I don't have an explanation that I can reasonably offer without coming across as a total lunatic.

As I enter their road, I drive slowly, deciding what to do. I pull up just opposite their house, on the other side of the road.

I get out of the car at 2 p.m. on the dot and check my reflection in the car window. The shirt looks good, but my hair's a total mess. I probably should have had a shower before heading out.

I cross the road and make my way up the path towards the front door. The bed of roses on the left of the drive looks dry – a tangle of stems and deadheads. I assume that Adam was in charge of the gardening, so I do Alice a favour and prune them. I detach one of the flagging roses from the bunch and stuff it in my pocket. Then I walk to the front door, before changing my mind, retreating back down the path and into the comfort of my car.

I check my phone to see if she's called me back yet and it's only the disappointment that she hasn't that gives me the courage to get back out, striding forwards with conviction and choosing the knocker rather than the bell. I feel nervous but resolute: proud that I'm being proactive, facing the issue head-on, with maturity.

When no one comes to the door, I try knocking again. I take a few steps back and look up to see if any of the bedroom windows are open and when I see that everything is shut, I come to the conclusion that Alice is out. She'll obviously be back at some point, so I wait in the car.

It's 4 p.m. now and I can see two figures in the distance walking up the hill. My eyesight is pretty sharp, but at first they're just that bit too far away to identify. As they come closer, I wind the window down and put my ear out, straining to hear their conversation. I would recognise Max's voice in a stadium full of people and, as they approach, I see that he is with Mrs Turner.

I get out calmly, give them both a big wave and Maxy runs towards me.

'Hi, Ben. You'll never guess what happened at school today!'

He's holding a giant model made out of papier mâché and smiling with such force that dimples appear on either cheek.

'What's that, buddy?'

'This is Terry the Pterodactyl. We made dinosaurs out of papier mâché and the teacher said that the person who made the scariest one would win a prize. And guess what? I won, even though mine wasn't as big as Trudy's. What do you think?'

Max lifts Terry the Pterodactyl high up in the sky and makes a menacing roaring noise.

'That is seriously impressive, buddy. You'd better keep it away from me – you're scaring the living daylights out of me!'

Max giggles. 'You're just saying that. I know *grown-ups* don't get scared, silly!'

'Oh! Is that so?' I reply. 'Hey, say cheese!'

I get out my phone and take a photo of Terry and Max. Mrs Turner is in the background: I'll crop her out when I get home.

She turns to me.

'Hello, Ben. How are you doing? Are you here to see Alice? She's been at an appointment this afternoon, but she should be back soon. I'm going to wait with Max until then.'

'Oh no, I was just in the area seeing another friend. I need to head off now.'

I don't know why that comes out, but it does, and so I have to be true to my word.

'See you soon, Maxy,' I shout as I climb back into the car and whizz off into the distance.

I'm only round the corner, on the road adjacent to Alice's, when I pull up again. An appointment? Is Alice ill? Obviously, my mind races to the worst possible scenario: cancer? Surely this little family has had enough to contend with. My mind's all over the place now, because on the one hand, I'm horrified at the thought of Alice dying and leaving Max all alone, an orphan. But on the other hand, I'm relieved because a hospital appointment would explain why she'd not been able to take my calls or reply to my texts. Clearly, I'm jumping to conclusions, but the possibility of something so horrific only reinforces my desire to see her, so I make a three-point turn and head back in the direction of her house.

I park a bit further up the road this time. Not directly outside the house but near enough that I can see everything in the rear-view mirror.

I see a taxi pull up, then Alice step out and hand the driver a note. She looks dishevelled, but that's not out of the ordinary for her. She heads up the drive and, I presume, into the house. About five minutes later, Mrs Turner leaves, stepping into the road and then next door into her own front garden. I decide not to go to the front door straight away. I should leave Alice a few minutes to get in the house, I think, maybe go to the loo, spend some time with Maxy.

I put the radio on and calm myself listening to the news. I look at the clock – 5.27 p.m. – and decide that enough time has passed for me to go in and speak to Alice. I undo my seat belt and look back in the rear-view mirror. To my surprise, I see Alice and Maxy heading out, hand in hand, towards me. Where are they going?

I put my seat belt back on, start the engine, watch them pass until they are almost at the end of the road, then drive slowly in their direction.

The high street is a hive of activity. The shops are starting to close, workers leaving their offices, and I almost lose them. Then I spot Maxy and his orange T-shirt as they head into Bubbles and Burger, and I park as close as I can get. I grab my wallet from the front passenger seat, get out of the car, lock the door behind me and head towards the restaurant. If I walk in now, it could just be a happy coincidence that we happened to be in the same restaurant at the same time. I could walk in, take a seat on my own in a different area of the restaurant and then wait until they notice me sitting there, alone. And then Alice would have no choice but to invite me to join them and we could eat together. I obviously wouldn't bring anything up in front of Max, but perhaps after the meal we could go back to the house together and Alice and I could have a chat.

As I approach the restaurant, I tuck my shirt in, adjust my collar and start rehearsing how that first exchange might go.

'Oh, fancy seeing you guys here!'

'Now, isn't this a coincidence?'

I get a funny look from a young woman as we pass each other in the street and I think she even brings her small child closer to her as if to shield him from the man who's talking to himself.

I walk past the restaurant and then, when I turn back again, I look through the window to see that Alice and Maxy are sitting in a booth on the far right-hand side. I stop for a moment, hoping that one of them might notice me and beckon me inside. But they're lost in their own world, Maxy jumping around and gesticulating wildly with Terry the Pterodactyl, and Alice throwing her head back in glee. All of a sudden, I feel like an intruder. I find myself beaming, delighted to see that in spite of everything these two have been through – in spite of the great loss that they've suffered at my hands – things are returning to normal.

I head back towards my car and I feel a tightness in the back of my throat. I dive into my car just in time and then find myself with my head against the steering wheel, hiding my face, uncertain as to why that particular snapshot has knocked me over the edge again. I don't want Alice and Maxy to come out and see me like this. I need to be strong for them. That's my duty, after all that I've done.

Alice and Max leave the restaurant at 7.17 p.m. and as I see them walking down the high street, away from my car and in the direction of their house, I consider turning round, driving past them, winding the window down and offering them a lift. But I resist and instead let them walk. It's good for them both to get some exercise.

And then I get out of the car and pop into Bubbles and Burger for a bite to eat myself. It's pretty packed, so I head to the booth in the right-hand corner, where the staff are yet to clear away Alice and Max's empty dishes. I start stacking the plates, and a waitress, whose name badge says 'Gabby', comes to greet me.

'Table for one, is it?'

I stay in the booth and, as Gabby clears away the remnants of Alice and Maxy's meal, I pick up the receipt.

'I'll have exactly what they had, please.'

Gabby raises an eyebrow, scribbles down my order and strides away towards the kitchen.

I end up with two burgers and three portions of chips.

ALICE

I got a call from the coroner's office this morning. Some perky bimbo called Stacey reminding me that the hearing was soon approaching and asking if I had any questions about what would happen. I asked her to remind me of the date and how long I can expect it to go on for, then I put the phone down and made a note in the calendar on the fridge.

When I first heard about the need for an inquest into Adam's death, I found the idea preposterous. In my mind, an inquest was something that happened in cases where there had been evidence of foul play. They happened after horrible crimes, or when celebrities like Amy Winehouse or Prince died as a result of an apparent drugs overdose. I don't think anyone doubted, at any point, that Adam had stepped in front of that car. It wasn't the first time that Adam had attempted suicide, and medical records would show that he had suffered with depression and anxiety for many years.

The advice I was given at the time was to 'leave it to the experts' and to 'focus on the grieving process'. As it turned out, there was so much else to think about with the funeral arrangements that I did put it to one side. If there's one thing I've learned in the last few months, it's that the brain is not limitless in its capacity to deal with things beyond the everyday: one thing at a time, Alice, it tells me, one new thing at a time.

The inquest hearing has been scheduled for 4 July, which gives me plenty of time to get my head around the next stage in this saga. I am to report to the court at 9.30 a.m., ready for the hearing to start around thirty minutes later. I am to wear 'whatever I feel comfortable in', but I'm sure it wouldn't be appropriate for me to turn up in bra and knickers, so I'll have to dig out one of my old work suits, to make sure to give the right impression.

Of course, none of the suits are going to fit properly. I haven't worked since Max was born, and if there are any women who can fit into their clothes after having a child stuffed inside them for nine months then they must either have extremely malleable skin or else have starved themselves silly during maternity leave. It's challenging enough to be stuck at home with what can only be described as an alien on the tit – to have to deprive oneself of basic needs such as chocolate and Coke is a step too far. Anyway, I will turn up in a work suit that is too small for me, ready to hear a stranger decree that my husband did, indeed, jump in front of a car in order to end his life.

I'm to be called as a witness, even though I insisted on the phone that I didn't actually witness Adam stepping out into the road. It is, apparently, a necessary part of the proce-dure that the deceased's next of kin be called as a witness – not necessarily to provide specifics about the nature of the incident, but to give information about any relevant circumstances leading up to the day in question. And, of course, I'm happy to fill them in on the details. Happy to let them know that Adam had been suffering from anxiety and depression since he was a teenager. Happy to tell them that this wasn't the first time that he'd tried to kill himself.

Adam's major issue, as we were told once in a counsel-ling session that I was asked to join, was 'a constant feeling of inadequacy'. Not rocket science, that's for sure. His first suicide attempt was after his first exam in the final year at Durham. For his entire time on the course, the professors had reassured him that he was top of the class, that he had the potential to go on to study for a master's degree and then a PhD. He could have walked into those exams without having looked at a single book and smashed it.

He was, of course, more prepared than anyone else. He had read every critical analysis of each text on the syllabus. He had read so far and wide that he was known, in tutorials, to reference obscure texts that even the professors had to pretend to recognise. And yet, as I walked with him from our flat to the exam hall that day, I knew that something bad was going to happen. He had spent the previous night tossing and turning, and in the brief moments when he was asleep, I could hear him moaning in distress. And I was right: just five minutes after the bell rang, Adam had a panic attack in the middle of the exam hall, hyperventilating and shouting, and was removed by an invigilator.

I had walked home after dropping him off for the exam and when I came back to collect him three hours later, I was told that he had been taken to hospital. He'd cut his wrist with a pair of scissors in the toilets just outside the exam hall.

I suppose I should probably tell the coroner that story, shouldn't I? And there are plenty of others I could tell them while I'm at it, but I don't want to say too much. Adam hated being talked about. No one ever knew the full extent. As complicated as Adam was, I loved him and he needed me. As close as I came to leaving him, I knew that if I ever went through with it, he'd take his own life. That lingering threat, and the thought that by sticking with him I might be able to save him, was enough to make me stay.

Receiving that phone call this morning came as a shock. It's not that I'd forgotten that the inquest would be happening, but I'd managed to isolate it, to put it into a box for later. Now, it's a screaming reminder of a trauma passed but not yet quite resolved. I just don't know how much more energy I have to deal with all this and I feel so conscious that I need to keep Max away from the drama. It had been so important to me, over the years, to shield Max from what Adam and I were going through, to explain away Adam's marks, each new bruise or scar he had made. I owe it to Max now to draw a line under the tragedy and give him a new beginning.

It's easy to assume that Max is coping fine. He just carries on, seemingly immune to grief, playing with his Lego, whinging about going to bed, jumping into bed for a cuddle in the night, just being Max. But every so often he makes a comment that is like a kick in the shin, a reminder that he is hurting, too. And every so often I remember my meeting with Mrs Lacey, the headmistress, and picture poor Maxy sitting miserably at his desk at school. This afternoon, he came home proudly clutching a model dinosaur. It looked more like a cow than a dinosaur, but I tried my best to be encouraging.

'Oh, darling, that's lovely. Is it a stegosaurus?'

And he looked so disappointed.

'No, Mummy, it's a pterodactyl. Daddy knew the difference.'

I felt terrible, caught out, inadequate.

'Why don't we go out for a burger?'

Fast food is such a lazy trump card, but Max's face immediately lit up. We walked to Bubbles and Burger, hand in hand, and when Max didn't touch his burger and instead asked for a second portion of chips, I couldn't bring myself to say no.

Now, we're back at home and Max has just gone upstairs to play in his room before going to bed. He's always been good like that – happy to entertain himself and then climb into bed when he's tired. It's a warm but breezy night, so I decide to open the back door and head into the garden with a glass of wine in one hand and the bottle in the other. The grass is so overgrown that I have to tread as if on a cross trainer in the gym, kicking up twigs with every step. The remnants of leaves from last autumn add a dark brown tinge to the flower beds. The pond, which last year was a feature, with beautiful blue irises punctuating its clear waters, is now a shocking green carpet of algae. The garden was Adam's pride and joy, and while it's tragic to see it descend into disarray, there is also something beautiful about this scene: something wilder, more natural and untouched about how it's been left to the whims of the elements.

I take a seat on the bench at the far end of the garden and down the wine in one, tossing the empty glass over the fence into the next-door neighbour's garden, in a small act of rebellion – against what or whom, I couldn't say. I look over to the outhouse that I haven't been in since that windy day in January, that day when I brought Adam buttered crumpets and expected to find him writing but instead found mayhem. I couldn't bring myself to open that door since and through the window I can see a few items that remind me of him: that small, quirky writing desk that I bought him as a present on our honeymoon in Hong Kong, the fountain pen with green ink that would forever leak onto his fingers, and mounds and mounds of paper. I feel my face contort and tears trickle down my left cheek. I take a large swig of Chenin Blanc, straight from the bottle.

I wake with a start and feel the chill. It's fully dark now and I'm out here in just a summer dress. God knows how long I've been asleep. I stumble to my feet, leaving the empty bottle at the side of the bench, and head back into the house. I'm feeling a bit sick and headachy, with one of those mini hangovers that you get post-nap after a boozy pub lunch, so I reach for a couple of ibuprofen and down a glass of water.

When I head up to the bedroom, I realise that I haven't checked my phone all day. I can see that I've got three missed calls from Ben and a string of WhatsApp messages. I can't deal with that right now, so I just switch my phone off and throw it on the bed. Then I head into the bathroom to brush my teeth, making an effort to keep my head down, not to look at my own reflection in the mirror, because I don't want to see the state that my face is in.

I reach for make-up wipes and catch a glimpse – my face is so bloated that I look like I've been on steroids. Is this the woman you're so keen to woo, Ben? Somehow, my own sorry state of affairs makes his insistence on developing a romance with me all the more pathetic. I shouldn't have led him on – this, I accept – but now enough's enough. And I couldn't have been clearer in my message to him: my stance is simple and I think I delivered it in a sympathetic, magnanimous way.

Imagine if I'd told him how I really feel . . . Imagine if I'd told him that a single touch of his hand on my skin sent a shock of guilt throughout my body. Imagine if I'd told him about the wave of nausea that came over me as he whispered in my ear. What if I had been direct, straightforward and clear, and I told him that the moment I felt his dick go in, and heard his whispered declaration of love, I saw a glint in his eye that made my skin crawl?

ALICE

Saturday, 30 June

I can't remember the last time I felt this horrific. I spent the whole night dragging myself to and from the bathroom, only conjuring up the strength to leave the warmth of my duvet when the cramps in my stomach were too much to bear. My face is soaking wet, and there's a dampness at the back of my head and on the top of my neck, the fever desperately urging the toxins out of my body. I've always had a bit of dodgy stomach, but my otherwise clean health record is punctuated every couple of years with a bout of gastroenteritis. It usually passes quickly, if I rest and drink lots of fluid. But I know that today, staying in bed isn't an option.

It was a bit of an annual tradition of Adam's to take Max to Hamleys toyshop the Saturday before his birthday to pick out a few toys. It's one that I have thus far managed to avoid. I love buying presents for Max, don't get me wrong. There's nothing that makes me happier than seeing his little face light up as he tears open the wrapping paper, flings it to one side and shakes the box close to his ear before ripping it open. But the idea of spending hours with him in one of the world's largest toyshops, wrestling with crowds of other people's overindulged children, is, for me, the parental equivalent of going to Glastonbury in the pouring rain when the headline act is Ellie Goulding. Crowded, overhyped and so physically inconvenient as to counteract any ounce of enjoyment that such an occasion might otherwise offer.

For Adam, on the other hand, it was the one fixture in a calendar of children's birthday parties and parents' evenings that he wouldn't miss. He was, after all, a big child, more content browsing through aisles of Meccano and Star Wars paraphernalia than in the company of adults. They'd start in the basement with the 'Interactive Zone', where young adults of questionable motive would demonstrate the latest and greatest gadgets that would almost certainly be out of fashion within three months. Then they would head up to the first floor, where they'd spend the majority of the day geeking out over the latest additions to the Meccano and Lego franchises, before having a bite to eat and coming home with bags full of shit that Max would never touch.

And now, on top of the general dread of the occasion, it happens to have fallen on a day when I feel like death. I thought about cancelling it, suggesting to Max that instead we sit at the computer together and order some things on Amazon. But I knew that I had to muster up the strength, because the fear of Max feeling let down trumped any anxiety that I might shit myself or vomit in the middle of a toyshop. So, I took some Imodium – quite a few – put on my thickest coat and bundled Max into an Uber, because the idea of braving the underground was just too much to bear.

The driver is irritating. Perky.

'So, Hamleys, is it? What are you going to buy?'

I feel like replying, 'I'm paying you to take us there, not to interrogate us,' but bite my tongue and opt for a more conventional response.

'I suppose we'll just have a browse and see what takes our fancy.'

I reach into my handbag for something to do, something to signal that I'm busy and I'd rather not talk, and the only thing I can find is my make-up bag, so I grab a lipstick and start applying it. The driver takes the hint and turns up the volume on the radio. But my head is banging, so I snap at him to turn it off and crack open the window, breathing in the London fumes in all their carcinogenic glory.

It takes us over an hour to get there, and when we finally pull up on Regent Street, I'm relieved to get out of the car.

I surrender two hours, three floors and about seven instances of having a child step on my toes later. I've done well so far, traipsing after Max, keeping up with him as he runs from display to display, but I really need a break now. My legs are aching and if I don't sit down, I might collapse on the floor, falling in a heap among a bundle of Eeyores and Olafs.

'Max, Mummy's not feeling so well. Do you mind if we have a sit down now? You can have a Frappuccino in the café.'

'But, Mummy, they're just about to start the Lego challenge!'

'What's the Lego challenge?'

'It's where you get in teams and have to build the biggest tower in thirty minutes. Please, Mummy, they only do it once a day!'

I look around and see that there's a red sofa by the escalators, just behind where the Lego display is. I reckon it'll be OK if I take a seat there, won't it? Just for a few minutes, while Max does his Lego thing. It's near enough and there'll be a clear line of sight from there over to the Lego section. Besides, Max is wearing his orange anorak, so he's hard to miss.

'OK, Max, you stay here and do the challenge. I'm going to be just over there, sitting on that sofa. Do *not* walk off from this area, please, and when it's finished . . .'

But he's already run off and put himself in a queue behind a bunch of other children. I draw a deep sigh, unzip my jacket, throw it over my shoulder and lay down on the sofa. I kick my shoes off and put my feet up. Max has got to the front of the queue now, and I can see him laughing and chirping away with another kid about his age. The mother of that child is with them, so he's safe.

I reach into my handbag and take out a blister pack of paracetamol. I know it's not time for the next dose yet, but I also know that an extra couple of tablets a bit early isn't going to do me any harm. I swallow the tablets, without water, tasting the bitterness of them as they hit the back of my throat, and I sit back.

'Excuse me, madam. Madam, please can you take your feet off the sofa?'

My eyes are sticky and my stomach is aching. I open my eyes and a spotty teenager with a black Hamleys polo-neck T-shirt is leaning over me.

'I'm sorry, I must have . . .'

I leap up. Suddenly, any pain in my head or in my stomach is gone. Where's the orange? Where the fuck is Max?

I rush over to where the demonstration is, barging past hordes of children and their parents, smashing them with my handbag as I go. The Lego demonstration is still going and I edge right to the front, waving my arms manically.

'Stop! Stop! Have you seen my son? He's seven, about the same height as that boy, wearing an orange anorak. Did you see where he went?'

Nothing. Just gormless stares.

I start racing around the surrounding areas. I end up stuck behind a man with a stick, walking with great trepidation in front of me, and as I overtake him, I hit him with my bag and hear a pathetic squeal. Don't come to fucking Hamleys at the weekend if you're worried about being shoved a bit, mate.

I make it to the other end of the floor and get on the escalator. There's a load of Chinese tourists standing on the left-hand side, so I shove past them and run down the first flight. I can feel a huge bead of sweat on the back of my dress and I reach into my bag for my inhaler, taking three big puffs as I make my way down the next escalator. By the time I've reached the basement, I'm in a complete state: I can feel a dampness in my crotch and I'm panting like an obese child after the egg-and-spoon race on sports day.

I run through each aisle, calling his name, looking left, right, left, right, with sharp head movements and sudden turns that must be disconcerting to the other parents and children around me. I'm shouting now, yelling his name in desperation. What if a paedophile has grabbed him and he's locked up in a dungeon somewhere underground? What if he's wandered out into the street and got run over by a double decker bus?

I resist the temptation to ask for help at first, because I can't bear the idea of admitting to a stranger that I have been so lax, that I have lost my son while taking a nap on a sofa in a toyshop. Besides, isn't it the case in scenarios like this that the simplest explanation is the most likely one? The most logical explanation is that Max has wandered off on his own to explore a different part of the shop. It's just a question of trying to second-guess where he might be browsing.

Where do I even start? This is a child's dream: a labyrinth of toys and games, a world of fidget spinners, nerf guns, walkie-talkies and motion-controlled drones – a place where even the most shy, clinging child would be compelled to run free like a headless chicken. I'm in the basement now, so I'll just have to make my way up gradually, floor by floor, until I find him.

It's not until I've searched the third level unsuccessfully that I decide to change tack. This place is too big to cover everywhere and if I go on for much longer, I'll have a heart attack or a stroke and then when Max does finally turn up, he'll be left completely parentless. Where would he go then? Would Mrs Turner take him full-time?

I find the nearest staff member – an obese, red-faced man – and have no time for his pleasantries.

'Listen, I'm looking for my son. He was at the Lego thing and then he was gone . . . can you please help me to find him?'

The man's expression turns in an instant to one of great concern and then it's all action stations. It's funny how that one question from me – can you please help me to find him – is enough to trigger a chain of events. That by uttering certain words in the right order, I've hit a red button, raised an alarm and set in motion a process often rehearsed but rarely executed.

I detach myself from this and allow myself to be swept along, taken from one place to the next like a child myself, dependent on the action of others.

I'm in a small room off the main shop floor ten minutes later. Some kind of control room that reveals what a military operation it must be to keep this shop running efficiently. There must be thirty security cameras, and an army of staff watching them closely and talking into mouthpieces. It's how one imagines a NASA control room, an image established by the numerous, indistinguishable space films of the nineties. I can't help but think that these staff must have a bloated sense of grandeur, seeing themselves as the brains of an important mission to save the planet rather than as administrative bodies in place to prevent toys from being stolen. The fat shop assistant is doing his best to distract me with small talk, while also asking for as many details as possible about Max.

'Oh, I don't know how tall he is,' I say. 'The normal height for a seven-year-old – four foot two?'

'He's got brown hair, green eyes and I suppose he's a bit chubbier than he should be. Runs in the family!'

'I was just sat on the sofa near him. Can't have been more than twenty, maybe thirty minutes.'

'No, it's nothing like that. He'll definitely be here some-where, in the shop.'

'Yes, it was just the two of us. His father . . . his father's not around.'

And then I watch as a stout, acne-ridden young woman takes her moment, presses a red button and speaks into a microphone. Her voice is crisp and clear, in a tone that is reserved only for shop tannoy systems.

'Will Max Selby, that's Max Selby, please identify himself to a member of staff. That's Max Selby. If you hear this, please speak to a member of Hamleys staff. Thank you.'

And then we sit and wait, and my mind wanders. If that announcement has been made throughout the shop floor, why hasn't there been a response yet? Max isn't stupid or particularly disobedient: if he'd heard that announcement, he'd have done as he was told and reported himself to a staff member.

I get out my phone to see if anyone's been in touch with me directly. Nothing. And then the pain comes back. The ache in my temple, the throbbing in the core of my stomach. And I feel sick now, imagining Adam shouting at me for letting this happen.

'He's been found, Mrs Selby! He's been found!'

I feel a kick in my throat, warmness in my chest and tingles in my toes.

'Oh! I knew he'd be around here somewhere. Thank you so much – and sorry for all the bother. Is he on his way here, then?'

'Yes, he's heading down now. He's with a friend of yours. A family friend, he says, who he bumped into on the shop floor.'

I don't have any family friends. I don't really have any friends or family now. I don't have too much time to think about this, as I hear Max's voice as he runs towards me, giving me a hug and chuckling to himself.

'Don't worry, Mummy, I'm here! So cool that they called out my name – did you hear?'

'Yes, Max. I heard, I heard. But you know you shouldn't run off like that on your own. And you mustn't, you just mustn't, talk to strangers. We're going home now and you're going straight to your room.'

'But I didn't run off on my own, Mummy, silly. And I swear I didn't speak to one stranger! Not one!'

And lurking behind him, smiling away and holding three large bags of shopping: Ben.

BEN

I love going on the Tube these days. Before the accident, I drove everywhere. Even if it was a question of driving into Central London, paying the congestion charge, then circling around the side streets of the West End, endlessly searching for an available parking spot, before giving up and paying an extortionate amount in a car park, it would always be my preference. But in the last year I've been forced to reconsider my modes of transport. It's not that I don't drive at all anymore, but where there's a viable alternative, where there's an option that doesn't involve too many crowds or too much of a detour, I go for that.

It's not like I'm worried that someone is going to jump in front of my car every time. I'm honestly not crazy enough to believe that there's something about me, something about my little red car, that attracts tragedy. But there are certain triggers that set me off: like rain that is just that bit too torrential, or a road that is just that bit too fast and straight. I'd say one time out of three, something like that happens and sends me right back there, to the flash of white.

On the Tube, there are no risks. Well, none that has me as the key player, anyway. Sure, someone might jump in front of a train – which, one presumes, would be even more gruesome. Apparently, if you see that happening, you can see limbs flying in all directions: a leg might fall on the platform, an arm might be caught between the tracks, being gnawed at by rats until some sorry soul has the thankless task of clearing up the remains. But from what I understand, train drivers are prepared for this. Apparently, as part of their training, they are taught how to deal with such a scenario and are given therapy in anticipation of such a disaster. I had no such luck.

I haven't been into a toyshop in years and never to one of this size. To call Hamleys a toyshop is, in fact, to underplay it: it's more like a theme park, a whole world in itself. And I knew that if I was going to buy Maxy the best present, it would have to be from here. On our date in the Italian restaurant, Alice told me about Adam's tradition of taking Maxy to Hamleys on the Saturday before his birthday, and the idea of him missing out on this, of not having the latest gadgets and toys, makes me feel unbearably sad. I did actually text Alice and suggest that I could take him up for the day, but she didn't get back to me.

I don't know for sure that they'll come today, but there's a good chance and, if I spend the whole day here and make sure I go to the areas of the shop that Maxy is most interested in, it's possible that I'll bump into them. I start at the Wizarding World section, which is the majority of an entire floor dedicated to the various franchises of J.K.

Rowling: figurines of Harry, Hermione and Ron, flying beasts, giant Sniffles and so on.

I have to admit that I'm a new fan: when the books first came out, I got about halfway through *Harry Potter and the Philosopher's Stone* and gave up. I've never been one to believe in magic, even as a kid, and I remember feeling a bit above it. But I've got into it all recently because of Max and I've binged the whole series of books in the space of a couple of months. I spend ages trying to decide what Maxy would most like from this section and, in the end, opt for a wooden sign for his bedroom door that reads 'Wizards Welcome, Muggles Tolerated'. I chuckle to myself.

Moving on to the board games section, it's harder to figure out what's best. I feel strongly that Maxy should have a variety of toys and games, not just ones that involve him sitting in front of a screen. I remember what Alice told me about Max's probable dyslexia, so anything that involves writing or reading is out. It's surprising how many board games actually require this. Scrabble is an obvious no-no, but I imagine that Maxy would find something like Monopoly stressful too, having to read all those cards with property names and prices. It's not that I don't want him to get better at reading and writing, but I don't think it's healthy to encourage such developments in the guise of play. We can work on that together separately.

I go for a game called Risk, which I used to play with my dad back in the day. Max's probably a bit young for it at the moment, but it's a game that involves strategic thinking and one that – hopefully – he, Alice and I can play together at some point. I'm good at it but can give them a head start.

When I reach the Lego area, I have to pick up a second basket. I've already filled the first and I know that this is the section that I need to focus on most. I imagine how much all of this is going to cost, totting up approximate amounts based on everything I've picked. I consider going back and replacing some of the pricier items. And then I feel guilty that I've had this thought, reminding myself that this is a good cause and that there's nothing better for me to spend my money on. After everything that's happened, after everything Maxy and Alice have been through, it's hardly likely that I'll be lying on my deathbed, regretting having spent a few hundred quid to make their lives just a little better.

I'm a bit frazzled by the selection, so I decide to enlist the help of an expert and approach a staff member.

'Excuse me. I'm looking for something that's suitable for a seven-year-old, almost eight. He's into magic at the moment. What can you suggest that's at the right level for him?'

The shop assistant frowns at me as if appalled by such narrow criteria.

'Oh, I don't know. There's just so much to choose from. Is your son into cars?'

Do I correct him? I should. But how do I do that without it sounding too convoluted, too unlikely, too strange? It's not an easy relationship to describe in such a brief interaction and it doesn't seem relevant. It doesn't matter who I'm buying this for, does it? In fact, it's none of this guy's business.

'Not particularly. When he was younger, we used to go plane spotting, though. Have you got any model planes that are suitable for his age?'

'Oh, I used to go plane spotting all the time with my dad, too.'

'Yes, well, unfortunately our Max has a health issue, which means that he can't really travel. Building a model plane is about as close as he can get to the real thing.'

I don't know where this comes from, but I feel exhilarated. I am constructing a new history for Maxy and myself that is exclusive to us: in this moment, Maxy and I are inextricably linked by an alternate reality.

'Oh! Gosh, that's terribly sad. I think I know the perfect thing. Follow me.'

I pick up my two baskets and follow the guy to an aisle on the far side of the floor labelled 'Aeronautical'. I'm not sure if it's fate, or just a question of being in the right place at the right time, but there's the little man himself. I can only see the back of him, but I recognise the scar on his right calf. I tap him on the shoulder and he turns round. He's delighted to see me, as always.

'Ben! Hi! Check out this Lego pirate ship – I want it, but Mum will never let me have it!'

Maxy seems unsurprised at the coincidence, as if it's the most natural thing in the world that he and I should be browsing in the same area of Hamleys. I guess he sees me as a peer, an ally on his level, which is nice.

'Where's your mum, buddy? You shouldn't be wandering around on your own like this.'

'It's fine. She's just having a rest over there. I'm not allowed to leave this area.'

Max gestures towards a couch on the other side of the shop floor and I can see the blue-and-green of Alice's Adidas trainers, dangling over the edge.

'Come on, let's go and find her.'

What on earth is she doing, lying down on a sofa in the middle of Hamleys? How can she possibly be keeping an eye on Maxy from all the way over there?

'Wait, Ben. You haven't looked at this pirate ship yet. I *really, really* want this one.'

I pick up the ship that Maxy is coveting, look on the back for a price tag and gasp in disbelief.

'A hundred and fifty pounds? Bloody hell, Maxy! You could buy a cruise on a ship like this for that price!'

'What's a cruise?' he asks, and he looks so crestfallen that I can't resist and I place the Lego ship in my basket.

'Well, I suppose you only turn eight once, don't you?'

And at this, Maxy jumps up and gives me a hug. It's so sudden, so sweet, and I have to steel myself so I don't get emotional.

'Let's pay for all of this and then go and collect your mum, shall we? Maybe we can have something to eat together.'

I feel a rush between my ribs, a surge of adrenaline at the thought of seeing Alice. I wonder what she's wearing. Knowing her, it will be pretty low-key – maybe some jeans and one of her strappy tops. How should I greet her? I know I'll feel an urge to kiss her, but that will be too much. A hug will be fine – our faces will brush against one another and I'll be able to inhale her perfume: that warm, summery, soothing aroma that will take me straight back to that night in her bed.

I place Maxy on my shoulders and grab hold of one of his legs, feeling a responsibility not to let him slip. I try to put him down as we join the queue for the tills, reaching into my pocket for my wallet, but he's not having any of it.

'No, no – I want to stay up here!'

After we've paid – I don't look at the amount on the display, I just hand my card over and enter the pin – we head back towards where Alice is waiting. It takes us a good few minutes to get across the shop floor and I feel a flutter in my tummy. I'm nervous to see her. We haven't been in the same room, at the same time, since that first night we spent together. That night is marked in the timeline of my memory with a green flag and, in the same way as my first day at school, or the day I received my final results at university, most other past and future events will for ever be viewed in relation to that moment.

I'm not expecting her to take one look at me and go weak at the knees, regretting the text message she sent me and asking me to take her back. But, equally, this could be a key moment in our reconciliation. Maybe, just maybe, seeing me here with Maxy on my shoulders will remind her that life is just that bit sweeter with me in it. So even though my shoulders are aching, and I'm dying for Maxy to jump down and walk on his own, together we roam the length and breadth of the Lego section, looking for Alice, searching for the missing piece to make our little family complete.

As we approach the other side of the shop floor, the crowds clear a bit and I see that the sofa's empty. Where the hell has she gone? I'm immediately angry. Angry that Alice has been so damned irresponsible, not only leaving Max on his own in a huge crowd of strangers, but also then failing to stay in the place where she said she'd be. It's like she's a child herself, unleashed and unreachable, and I'm left here mopping up her mess. Still, I mustn't show Maxy that I am angry – the last thing he needs to see now is disunity among the troops – and instead I suggest that we sit down on the sofa and wait for her. It's for the best that we stay here and, hopefully, Alice will come back and find us.

I try to keep Maxy entertained, but with every minute that goes by, I feel more indignant. How can Alice be so utterly hopeless? Has she not heard enough stories of kids who go missing on the news? How many more examples does she need of parents leaving their children for just a few moments, never to see them again, to know that it's not safe? And, of course, I can't help but wonder what Adam would make of all this. Adam wouldn't abandon his son in the middle of a massive toyshop, would he?

Then we hear an announcement on the overhead speakers and Maxy jumps up.

'That's so cool! How do they know my name?'

'Come on, mate, let's go and find your mum.'

Maxy leaps off his chair, and I gather the shopping bags and run after him. We speak to a member of staff, as instructed, and head down to the basement, where Alice is waiting. I'm so happy to see her that any residual anger gives way. Seeing her again, in the flesh, is a physical relief, like downing a bottle of freezing-cold water after a cross-country run. She hasn't seen me yet and I deliberately hold back to give the two of them a moment together. So that she realises how much she needs what she nearly lost. She's shouting at him, as if it's his fault, and I feel angry again.

'Max! Don't ever, ever run off like that again!'

And then I step forwards, the valiant prince. Locking eyes with her again is like taking a drag of a drug that I have resisted. I've seen her, from afar, but this is the first time in a while that we've looked each other directly in the eye and the feeling is electric. My skin tingles and I think hers does, too, because the stare between us is extended and intense, and she rubs her arms. She is looking deep inside me, her wide emerald eyes reaching for something far beyond the surface.

'What the hell are you *doing* here, Ben?' she snaps, yanking Maxy away from me and storming towards the exit.

'Wait!' I shout, because I'm still standing here with the three bags full of Maxy's toys.

He looks back and gives me a big grin, but Alice pushes him forwards and, within just a few seconds, they have blended into the crowd and I'm standing here alone.

I leave Hamleys and head back to the Tube station. That was a bit unfair of her. Even if Alice doesn't love me anymore, there's no denying there's a connection between Maxy and me. It's his birthday on Thursday, so I'll take everything round then. That gives me a chance to get all the presents wrapped.

When I get home, the door to my flat is stiff and I have to kick it to get it to open. There's a letter on the mat that I almost tread on as I rush to turn off the alarm. It's unusual for me to get anything in the post and my first thought, ridiculously, is that it must already be a letter from Barclays advising me that I've gone into my overdraft after spending so much at Hamleys. I take the letter and slump down on my bed, ripping it open and reading it slowly:

Dear Mr Anderson,

REMINDER

Inquest into the Death of Adam James Selby

We are writing to remind you that your presence is requested at an inquest into the death of Adam James Selby, deceased 15 February at Watford General Hospital. You are kindly requested to report to Watford Magistrates' Court on 4 July at 9.30 a.m., where you will be called as a witness.

Should you have any questions about the proceedings, please call the coroner's office on 0208 836 6555.

Kind regards,
Jane MacPherson

Senior Coroner, Watford Borough Council

Reminder? I didn't get the first letter. How did I miss that? I remember the police officer telling me in the station that this might be happening, but they could have given me more notice! I need more time to prepare for this. What am I going to say? Who else is going to be there? Poor Alice to be put through all this – she'll need my support.

I throw the letter to the floor, undress, get under the covers and do my best not to fall asleep. Because I know full well, with the trigger of this letter, which dream awaits me.

ALICE

Wednesday, 4 July

When the doors are unlocked and I head into the room, I'm underwhelmed. It's much smaller than I'd imagined – no bigger than our own living room – and the furnishings are rudimentary: three rows of brown wooden benches on either side, a line of twelve flimsy metal chairs with black plastic backs and a trestle table at the front that looks like it's been borrowed from a village hall. On the table rests a jug of water and two small cups, and behind is a chair that looks like the last one standing at an antiques fair: slightly raised, wooden, with a latticed back, vile rusted gold detail on the arms and three wheels at the base that allow it to spin.

I'm guided to the front bench on the left-hand side and stare directly at the clock on the wall across from me: if clocks had personality, this one would be a lonely old bachelor, dressed in simple shirt and trousers, no frills and no fancy; a melancholy man. It's just gone 9.25 a.m. and, with only five minutes to go until the proceedings begin, the room is remarkably empty.

The lady who let me inside is still here, taking out some papers from a large ring binder and placing them on the trestle table in front of the antique chair. She's wearing a ghastly, poorly fitted pinstripe skirt, and I can't help but smirk when she leans over the desk and I notice the lining of her thong: this woman with her little council job, officious and uptight, unwittingly showing off her saucy drawers.

Next to join us is Mr Al-Shawawi, the brainy consultant with shitty social skills, who strides straight to me and shakes my hand far too vigorously.

'Hello, Mrs Selby. Good to see you again. You look nice.'

Don't comment on my appearance, you pervert.

I can't think of anything appropriate to respond, so I just smile and nod, then quickly take my seat again, signalling, I hope, that I have no desire for a conversation.

Next to enter the room is a man I don't recognise, in his twenties, dressed in a suit with a bright red tie. He scurries in with a messenger bag and waves to the council worker in the tight skirt, who smiles and blushes as if it's the first time a man has ever noticed her. He takes a seat on one of the plastic chairs at the back and gets out a notepad and pen. I try not to make eye contact with him but feel him looking me up and down. When I see that he's taking notes already – before anything has even started – I turn to him and give him a stare that makes him turn away in an instant.

A few more people file in, some of whom I recognise and acknowledge: the police officer with the mole on his face – he's still not got that removed; a nurse who was with us when the life support machines were turned off; and then

Lisa, who has, as usual, got the dress code slightly wrong and looks like she's about to go to the gym.

I told her that I didn't need her to come, but she insisted that I should have moral support. When she sits down next to me and squeezes my hand, I'm glad that I'm not doing this alone. I don't really know what to expect. I had the opportunity a few times to speak to support workers, the coroner's office, therapists even, but this whole thing has seemed so unnecessary to me, so inconsequential, that I've allowed it to creep up without much consideration.

I'm so unprepared for the inquest, so unaware of the procedure and the players, that when I see Ben burst through the door just before 9.30 a.m., panting and sweating with his shirt untucked, it doesn't even occur to me that he should have been invited. So much has happened between Ben and me, so many awkward moments, so many avoided interactions and so much unwanted attention of late, that in my mind he is totally dissociated from the original circumstance of our meeting. And this is the first time that I can actually say I feel a bit afraid when I see him.

I haven't really allowed myself to think too much about what he was doing in Hamleys that day, because whenever I do, it goes to a dark place and I start asking questions that don't bear answering. What on earth was he doing there? Who was he buying presents for? How did he know we were going to be there? What does he want? Is he following us? I've got this image of him standing there, with bags full of toys, larking around with Max, and I feel sick. And here he is again, walking through the courtroom and taking a seat in the row behind me as if it's the most natural thing in the world.

Then I remember that Ben is as key to this process as I am, that if there's any point at all in an inquest it is to confirm, once and for all, that Adam did jump in front of Ben's car. I stay seated, looking straight ahead, avoiding any acknowledgement, but then I feel a hand touch my shoulder and I turn round to see him behind me.

'Stay strong, Alice,' he says, 'we'll get through this together.'

And before I get a chance to respond, before I can correct him and insist that I don't need his help, don't want it, and would rather he never spoke to me, or touched my shoulder, or looked me in the eye ever again, let alone anything else, everyone around me stands. And so I do too.

I've never met a coroner before, but if you'd asked me what I expected a coroner to look like, it wouldn't be this. The great authority for whom everyone has stood is a mouse of a woman, no taller than five feet two, and so skinny that, in keeping with her rodent-like qualities, she's grown fur on her chin to keep her warm. She scurries in, pushing her glasses higher up her nose and barely looking up as she heads for the coroner's chair. Her voice is shrill and she clears her throat in the most pathetic way before she begins.

'Good morning, ladies and gentlemen. My name is Jane MacPherson and I am Senior Coroner at Watford Borough Council. Now, before we get started, some housekeeping notes. If everyone can ensure that their mobile telephones are switched off for the entirety of the proceedings, or at least turned to silent mode. And may I remind any members of the press present that any photos or recordings are strictly forbidden; although, of course, note-taking is permitted.'

I look over and see the guy in the bright red tie give the coroner a smile of acknowledgement. Why on earth a local newspaper has considered it a good use of resources to send a reporter to this inquest is beyond me – it must be a very slow news day.

The coroner continues.

'The purpose of this morning's session is to establish the cause of death in the case of Mr Adam James Selby, who was certified dead in hospital on 15 February of this year. This is not an investigation to identify if any parties are guilty or innocent but instead a mere fact-finding exercise, whereupon I am called upon to establish, to the best of my abilities, the circumstances of death.

'Before we proceed, I'd like to take a moment to express my deepest sympathy to the deceased's widow, Mrs Alice Selby, who is with us this morning.'

I close my eyes to avoid any eye contact, but I can feel everyone turn towards me. I don't want sympathy – I just want to get this over and done with. I feel a hand on my left shoulder from the row behind me again and I shuffle forwards. He needs to keep his hands off me.

I'm the first to be called to the stand and, as I approach the designated space opposite the coroner, I feel a crick in my neck. I tilt my head back and forth, as if readying myself for the shot-put. My blouse is a little too tight and I pull it down at the back as I head across the room.

'Mrs Selby, thank you very much for attending this morning. If I can start by asking you to confirm that you were married to the deceased until his death?'

'Yes, that's right.'

'Wonderful, thank you, Mrs Selby. And during your marriage, were you aware of any mental health issues that may be relevant to today's inquest?'

'Yes. My husband suffered from clinical anxiety and depression, and had attempted suicide before.'

'I'm sorry to hear that. Now, can you please walk me through the morning of 9 January from your perspective?'

And so I do. I don't hold back – I tell her the story as best as I can remember and it comes out with surprising fluency, as if it's a story that I've told many times before. The truth is that no one has really asked me these questions, apart from on the day itself, and there's something about getting it out there, revisiting it after everything that has happened, that feels cathartic.

I'm only up there for a few minutes – fifteen at most – and then the coroner signals that she has finished with me.

I shuffle back to my seat and, as I approach the bench, I lock eyes with Mr Al-Shawawi, who smiles at me and flutters his eyes in a condescending manner. I can see Ben in the corner of my eye, desperate for acknowledgement, but I don't give him that satisfaction.

Next to be called up is Alan Reid – a man I don't recognise and who I don't remember seeing enter the room. He's about fifty, stout and with one of those bulbous red noses that indicates years of alcohol abuse.

'Hello, Mr Reid. I believe you were present on the M1 on the morning of 9 January and you decided to call the emergency services. Can you describe, as best you can, what happened and what you saw that led you to make that call?'

Mr Reid clears his throat, and as he speaks, in an almost comic Cockney accent, I feel detached, as if I'm watching a film.

'It ain't for the faint-hearted. I was driving along the motorway, on my way back from a night shift. I live up Luton way. Anyway, there I was, driving along, minding my own business. I wouldn't say there was traffic, per se, but we was moving relatively slowly. Probably about forty?

'Anyway, all of a sudden this car in front of me stopped, suddenly, and I had to swerve past him and onto the hard shoulder to avoid crashing. I got out of my car and walked back, and that's when I first saw matey lying there. He was covered in blood. I remember seeing this massive gash on his forehead, all the way down from here to here, and I thought he must be dead. Of course you would, wouldn't you? Anyway, that's when I called 999 and they turned up just after.

'Was all very quick. Took down some details and made my way home. That's the be-all and end-all of it from my end.'

Mr Reid looks around the room, as if waiting for some applause, and seems taken aback when the coroner asks him a follow-up question.

'And what did you notice about the car in front of you? Do you remember that at all?'

'Sure, it was an old red Volkswagen. Looked pretty intact, as far as I can remember.'

'And the driver of the car – do you remember him?'

'Nah, sorry, I don't remember. As I said, I was in and out.'

'Thank you very much, Mr Reid. That's all for now.'

Mr Reid returns to his seat and next to be called is Mr Al-Shawawi.

'Mr Al-Shawawi, thank you for being here. I know you were one of the specialists who treated Mr Selby when he was admitted to Watford General Hospital. Would you be able to confirm, as per your statement, that the symptoms you first encountered were consistent with what one might expect after the impact of a car?'

'Yes, certainly. Mr Selby had sustained multiple injuries and of most pertinence to this case was that he had immediate damage to the frontal lobe, such that would only usually be seen as a result of significant trauma to the front of the head.'

The questioning of Mr Al-Shawawi is far more in-depth and I switch off for a few minutes. Occasionally, I perk up when I hear a few words that hit a nerve – 'minimally conscious', 'life support machine', 'next of kin' – words that conjure up images of Adam in his final moments, traumatic experiences that I'm being forced to revisit. But so much of Al-Shawawi's interrogation is technical that I allow my mind to wander.

I look over at Lisa and contemplate whether or not to mention to her that I've noticed she's put on a bit of weight on the face. I look over to the journalist in the red tie, blushing as we lock eyes, and I allow myself to imagine myself leaving the court and meeting him in the toilets, letting him fuck me over the bank of sinks.

'OK, and now on to our next and final witness.'

I dread to think that I've dropped off, but it does seem like a few minutes have passed, because I can see that Mr Al-Shawawi has now returned to his bench and the coroner is moving on.

She's staring over in my direction. For a moment I forget that I have already been up there and wonder if it's me who she's looking for. In fact, she's looking just past me.

I turn round. Ben's face is drenched in sweat and his eyes are red raw. He's breathing heavily and looking from one side of the room to the other, as if searching for something, or someone.

'Mr Anderson, before we hear from you, perhaps you'd like a glass of water?'

BEN

There's something so cold about Mr Al-Shawawi, so unfeeling in his delivery, that I want to go over and shake him. I want to ask him to be less clinical about it, to show a bit more empathy. I hate the idea that he's done this countless times before, that this is just part of his job, that occasionally he's late to the hospital in the morning because he has to go and give evidence at an inquest. His life just goes on, doesn't it? Meanwhile, Alice, Max and I have to live, every day, with the consequences of what has happened. I wish Mr Al-Shawawi would show more respect.

It doesn't take much to knock me off-kilter these days and when I received the letter inviting me to participate in the inquest, I freaked out. Having spent so long coming to terms with Adam's death and making peace with my role in it, it crushed me that there was now going to be an investigation into the cause of his death.

I spent that first night after I received the letter going over it all again in my memory, rewriting what had happened, implicating myself further and further. I allowed myself, at one point, to imagine that I had *wanted* to run Adam over, that I'd woken that morning with the specific intention of finding him on the motorway and ending his life. In one dream sequence, I saw myself being handcuffed in a courtroom and led down to prison, where other inmates, dressed in lurid yellow-and-green jumpsuits, hurled stones at me, shouting, 'Paedo! Paedo!' The morning after that dream, I called the school, told them I had food poisoning and stayed in bed.

I thought last night would be difficult as well, like the night before an exam or job interview, but I was so tired after preparing what I was going to say until late in the evening that I slept like a baby. When the alarm woke me, I was relieved that I'd properly rested and would be fully alert today.

I thought I'd left more than enough time to get to Watford, but I hadn't factored in the rush-hour traffic and, in the end, I parked at 9.28 a.m., leaving myself two minutes to get to where I needed to be. In a way, I was glad that I didn't have ages to sit about and wait; it would only have made me more anxious. As I locked my car, I thought about the irony of the fact that I'd driven to this hearing in the very car that had caused all of this to happen and it occurred to me that I should probably think about exchanging it.

I got into the courtroom just in time. I was in such a fluster that I didn't have a chance to look around and clock who else was there. I was glad that there were enough seats left and I managed to get one close enough to Alice. I had thought that maybe we'd sit together, but as I was so late, I didn't want to draw any more attention to myself by shuffling across to the row where she was seated. The seat directly behind Alice was unoccupied, so I went for that one instead.

And so I've sat and listened as each person has taken their moment and replayed their part in this tragedy. Alice is, as usual, admirably brave. So many people in her shoes would crumble, but she took to the stand with poise and control, calmly answering the questions and helping the coroner to understand what happened. And, of course, it isn't just the coroner learning new things today. For me, it has been an opportunity for many of my unanswered questions to be addressed.

It is a relief to be reminded that Adam had a history of anxiety and depression. Too many times I have allowed myself to believe that this was a freak incident, that his jumping was out of the blue. I feel comforted to hear confirmation that this was not Adam's first suicide attempt. It has also been fascinating to hear the details of Adam's diagnosis directly from Mr Al-Shawawi. If his delivery was clinical, it was also thorough. And to hear details about the specific injuries and their consequences has filled in some gaps that I have felt too afraid to ask Alice about for fear of upsetting her.

I feel privileged to be in the room – one of a select few who are privy to this final investigation, the closing chapter in the life of a man I never met but whose existence has become so inextricably linked with my own.

The coroner has just called my name – the time has come for me to step up and tell my version of events. I'm ready

– ready to share the story that I've replayed in my head, time and time again. Ready to play my part, to recite my lines. Spotlight on little old me.

'Mr Anderson, thank you for your time. Would you like a glass of water before we begin?'

Nice of her to offer, but I'm fine. I glance at Alice and she's looking right back at me with a warmth that spurs me on. Her eyes are wonderful – emerald and perfectly round – and I give her a quick wink with my own left eye and a smile with the right side of my mouth.

'No, thanks.'

'OK, so if you can just give me a quick account of what you saw that day on the motorway please, Mr Anderson.'

'Well, for me, that day started like any other. I left my house at 6.15 a.m. on the dot – I was a man of great habit and routine back then! – and joined the M1. I'm sure everyone else remembers that it was horrible weather that morning – it was absolutely pouring and I can clearly remember seeing the rain hit my windscreen at such a rate that even the fastest setting on my windscreen wipers was not quick enough to clear it efficiently. There was something apocalyptic about it, like this was the storm to end all storms, and I remember feeling a distinct sense of foreboding as I headed along the motorway.

'I couldn't see more than a short distance ahead of myself and I felt like I could be anywhere, driving at an unspecified speed towards an unknown destination. I felt out of control, at the whim of the elements, powerless to stop whatever was coming in my direction. And then it happened – a flash of white that appeared in front of me, so quick that if I had blinked, I would have missed it a second later. I have tried over and over again to remember more detail, but I'm afraid that's all I've got. Just a flash of white, before my eyes, and then I swerved to the side. It was as quick and as straightforward as that. And all I can say is that I'm sorry. Terribly sorry for being the one who . . . Just awfully sorry for being there and then being the one to cause such terrible injuries.'

I shoot a glance straight at Alice, but she's looking down now. I wonder what she's thinking. Is she crying? Is she shocked by my confession? I've never spoken so frankly to her about all this before, mainly because she's never asked. How does it feel for her now to hear it from my perspective? I don't blame her for looking away.

I look towards the coroner and see that she's writing something down. I'm desperate to see what it is, but I don't have the right angle. I wonder if there is anyone who can tell what someone is writing by analysing the movement of the pen. She is noting, on that piece of paper of hers, a verdict, some sort of judgement in relation to my involvement in this case. And now that it's written, now that it is inscribed in black and white, the deed is truly done. My fate is sealed.

'That'll be all, Mr Anderson. Thank you.'

I step down and avoid eye contact with Alice as I take my seat behind her again. I feel exposed now, like I've revealed a deep, dark secret that I can never retract. As I take my seat, a drip of water falls on the bench in front of me and I realise that I have been sweating like a pig. I take the handkerchief out of my jacket pocket, wipe my brow and then fold it again before putting it back.

The coroner continues.

'Thank you very much to all witnesses, doctors and family members for your assistance in this inquiry. We will now take a short recess while I consider all the evidence that has been presented, both in my pre-inquiry investigations and in light of what I have heard this morning. I ask you all to remain seated – I will return shortly.'

I can't believe that this whole process has been so quick. I look over to the clock on the wall and see that barely an hour has elapsed since the session started. On the one hand, I am glad for Alice's sake that the morning has been relatively painless and swift, but on the other, I feel affronted on Adam's behalf that the council couldn't spare a few more of their precious minutes to consider his case with more scrutiny. I lean forwards and offer a word of support to Alice.

'We can all move on after this, Alice,' I say, 'and finally put this to rest.'

And I'm so taken aback by Alice's response that when I hear it, my stomach muscles clench of their own accord and I feel a tightness in my bladder that could make me lose control of it.

'Ben, please, just don't. Just . . . *back* off, OK?'

I'm so stunned by this, so confused and shaken, that I don't notice the coroner returning to her seat. The 'b' of 'back' is ringing like an echo, as if she's just clanged a bell right by my ear. Everything around me is a blur. Faces have no features; the clock on the wall has no hands. I take a deep breath and focus on the coroner's words.

'Thank you for your patience. I've decided to deliver a narrative verdict, because although suicide seems to be the most likely cause of death, as is often the case in scenarios such as this, I cannot say without reasonable doubt that this was the deceased's intention on the day in question. Thus, I rule that Mr Adam James Selby died in Watford General Hospital on 15 February of this year as a result of injuries sustained in a road incident on 9 January.

'No further investigation is necessary and, at this point, I would like to reiterate my deepest sympathies to all friends, family members and associates in their bereavement. Thank you and good morning.'

I stay seated for a few moments, feeling dizzy. It's amazing how quickly everyone else moves into action: gathering their papers, picking up their bags, stepping out from the benches and heading towards the door. The coroner will now move on to the next in her list of cases. Mr Al-Shawawi will hail a cab and travel back to Watford General, where he will see countless patients before the day ends. Maybe he'll pop out for lunch and buy a sandwich, or maybe he'll have something in the hospital canteen. Then he'll go home, watch some television and perhaps he'll mention to his wife that he went to an inquest that morning. But then maybe he won't. For me, and for Alice, it's different. This is not part of the usual beat of everyday life. This is a verdict on which we will reflect for years. And it was all over in under an hour.

Alice stands up in front of me and, as she walks across the bank of benches, I look in her direction, in the hope that she'll look back and offer me a smile. I want a gesture, an indication that she regrets what she said to me. And I'm not the only person looking for a reaction from her. There's a chap with a pad and paper who clearly wants to speak to her, to get a scoop on the first reaction from the grieving widow. But she walks out with her head bowed, avoiding eye contact with everyone and, I fear, me most of all. For all the support I've offered her and Maxy, for all the effort I have made, don't I deserve acknowledgement?

ALICE

Waitrose on a Thursday afternoon attracts a very specific type. I watch a woman, in her early seventies, creaking down the aisles with a trolley, picking up a packet of organic chicken and studying the label with intensity. In the dairy aisle, two mothers with babies are chatting, discussing the benefits of breast milk over formula. They stop talking as I pass them as if their conversation is top secret. One of them looks me up and down before giving a half-smile, condescending and sympathetic.

After gathering a few things – including a double-decker chocolate birthday cake for Max – I head towards the checkout. When it's my turn, I stand there and wait as the gormless woman, Elaine, does all the work: she beeps, she packs, she beeps, she packs.

'Anything else for you, my love? Lottery ticket? Cigarettes?'

'Oh, go on, then. Do you have Vogue Menthols?'

I've no idea where this comes from. I haven't smoked for years – it's one of the many pleasures I agreed to give up when I fell pregnant with Max. But Adam is not here anymore to tell me what to do. He's not here to pass judgement, to lecture me on the environment or vegetarianism or the potential impact that smoking may have on our child.

I feel rebellious, alive, and so while I'm at it: 'And a bottle of Hendrick's as well, if you have it.'

Elaine loves it.

'Oh, why not, my love. Partial to a G & T myself!'

I bet you are, Elaine, I think as she chuckles with her rosy cheeks and her overconfident bosom, placing the bottle of Hendrick's in a bag and announcing the total.

'That'll be £66.25, love. Do you have a myWaitrose card?'

I shake my head and bend down to take my purse out of my handbag, which is on the floor by my side. As I do, I stop, because I can't believe what I've just seen.

'Are you OK, my love? Do you need a hand?'

But I don't speak. I'm transfixed, focused on a pile of newspapers in a stack under the checkout. There, looking straight at me, posed in front of the courthouse and with a grin on his face: Ben.

THE WATFORD GAZETTE

I'M IN LOVE WITH THE WIFE OF THE MAN I KILLED

Driver ran over suicidal playwright
– then promised to protect his family

BY RYAN COLE

A driver who accidentally killed a suicidal pedestrian has vowed to look after the man's widow and son, saying, 'I love them like they're my own family.'

Primary school teacher, Ben Anderson, 32, was driving to work in January when troubled Adam Selby, an award-winning playwright, also aged 32, jumped in front of his red Volkswagen Passat.

The collision led to Mr Selby's death in hospital a month later – but also resulted in the most unlikely of relationships forming between his inadvertent killer and the loved ones he left behind.

Mr Anderson told the *Watford Gazette* how he met Mr Selby's distraught wife, Alice, 32, in hospital when he visited to leave flowers.

'We were instantly united by this incredibly traumatic experience,' he said. 'We consoled each other and started meeting regularly. No one could understand what we were going through apart from each other.

'I like to think I have also been able to fill in to help look after her son, Maxy, who turns eight this week. We want to make sure he still has a male role model. I really do love them like they're my own family now.'

Asked if the relationship is romantic, Mr Anderson smiled and said, 'We'd rather not go into intimate details, but everything is going really well.'

Mr Selby won a Laurence Olivier Award for Best New Play in 2009 for *The Girlfriend*, which later had a short run off-Broadway. Yesterday, the inquest into his death concluded, with the coroner giving a narrative verdict describing how Mr Selby threw himself in front of Mr

Anderson's car in the slow lane of the M1 just after 6.42 a.m. on 9 January. There was heavy rainfall that morning and Mr Anderson did not see him before the collision.

Mr Anderson told the inquest that he screeched to a halt on the hard shoulder after a man hit his windscreen. Police arrived at the scene within four minutes. Mr Selby was treated in hospital for severe injuries to his brain and various body parts, remaining alive for five weeks before life support was stopped at 2.34 p.m. on 15 February.

Mr Selby was known to have serious mental health problems and had attempted suicide before.

Mr Anderson, who lives in Cricklewood, north-west London, sat behind Mrs Selby, a stay-at-home mother from Rickmansworth, Hertfordshire, during the inquest. She could be seen leaning backwards and whispering to him during the hearing.

'We have done as much as we can to help the police and the coroner, but now it's time for us to try to move on with our lives and find some normality again,' said Mr Anderson, who spoke on behalf of the family outside the court.

'Yes, it has been very difficult for me to deal with running over someone and killing them. You think about why it happened and if you could have done anything differently. It has been traumatic. But the most important thing is making sure Alice and Maxy are OK. They are amazingly resilient and I'll do everything I can now to look after them.'

A narrative verdict records the factual circumstances of a death and can be chosen instead of verdicts such as accidental death, unlawful killing or suicide.

Senior Coroner, Jane MacPherson, said, 'It's always sad to preside over cases such as these. I'd like to extend my heartfelt sympathies to Mrs Selby and all friends and families involved.'

Samaritans operates a twenty-four-hour service all-year round and can be contacted at 116 123.

r.cole@watfordgazette.co.uk

BEN

Thursday, 5 July

I can feel my phone ringing in my pocket. It's probably just Mum. She knows I'm at school and I can't pick up my phone in the middle of the working day. She'll leave a voicemail or call again if it's urgent. We're in the middle of a session about the environment and it would be pretty remiss of me to whip out my mobile phone. Or maybe it's Max, calling me on his birthday. I'd love to hear his voice. When it rings for a second time, and immediately after for a third, I call the teaching assistant to cover for me.

'Miss Stone is going to carry on from here for a few minutes,' I tell the children. 'I'll be back soon.'

I know this means that when I return, the classroom will be upside down: some of the kids will be gathered at the back, no doubt throwing a football against the wall, and others will be at the front, begging Miss Stone to let them plait her hair.

I rush out of the classroom and into the staff toilets, relieved to see that there's no one else in here. I lock myself in one of the cubicles and sit on the toilet seat: three missed calls, but not from Mum. From Alice. It must be Max! My thumb is shaking as I go to dial back. I hope Alice doesn't pick up. I'm breathing heavily and tear off a piece of toilet roll to wipe my forehead as the phone rings just twice.

'What the hell do you think you are doing, Ben? What the fuck is wrong with you?'

Alice.

'What? What do you mean?'

'You're not fucking in love with me! You don't even know what love is!'

'I don't know what you're talking about, Alice. Please, stop shouting.'

'The newspaper article! It's on the front fucking page of the local paper. "I'm in love with the wife of the man I killed." What the hell is wrong with you?'

'I did not say that! They've misquoted me! I didn't say I was *in* love with you, Alice, honestly I didn't. That journalist has twisted my words!'

'Just leave us the fuck alone, Ben. Leave me alone, leave Max alone. I don't need you; you are absolutely nothing to me. Nothing! You are just a man who was driving a car. You've got a massive hole in your life and you're trying to fill it with something that is totally meaningless. I felt sorry for you at the start, because you're fucking pathetic, but enough is enough. Just stay out of my life. Do you understand me now? Have I been clear enough?'

'You sound drunk, Alice. You're slurring your words. Are you OK? It's not even lunchtime yet, for God's sake.

Is Maxy back from school yet? Is he with you? Put him on, please.'

'If you ever, ever mention my son's name again, or come anywhere near him, I swear to God I'll call the police. Do you know what Max said to me the other day? Do you want to know what he said? He said that he feels sorry for you. He pities you. How does it feel to be pitied by an eight-year-old boy?'

That's the bit that really stings and I lose my temper.

'And how does it feel to be the wife of someone who was so unhappy, so unloved, that he was driven to throw himself in front of a stranger's car? At least Max has empathy. At least he has a modicum of feeling, so that he can feel pity for someone like me, who is just trying to do the right thing.'

'Oh, trust me, Ben. You don't know the half of it. If only you knew what our relationship was really like.'

And with that there's a pause, a brief ceasefire, while I process what Alice has just said.

I hear the sound of running water and realise that someone is at the basin washing their hands. But I don't feel embarrassed, because nothing else, no one else, matters.

'Look, Ben, listen to me. I just . . . Talking to that journalist at the inquest, you really shouldn't have done that, OK? I appreciate all your help, all your compassion towards Max and me, but I'm asking you now, if you really want to do what's best for us, if you really want to do what Adam would have wanted, then you'll leave us alone. OK?'

'OK, Alice. I get it. I understand. Just . . . just be careful with the drink, OK?'

But she's already put the phone down and here I am, sat on the toilet at work, and it's all over. I head out of the cubicle, and George Taylor, the PE teacher, is standing at one of the urinals.

'You OK, bud? The missus causing you some grief?'

'Ha, you know what it's like. I'll pick up some flowers on the way home.'

I only manage to stay focused for the rest of the afternoon because it is pretty stressful. One of the girls in my class, Evie, has an 'accident', which in the context of a primary school only means one thing. The teaching assistant is off in the afternoon, so I have to deal with it myself.

I leave school at around 5 p.m. and the traffic is heavier than usual. I stop off at the corner shop and buy some ice cream and AA batteries and, while I'm there, I pick up three copies of the local newspaper, two for me and one for my parents. They don't get the *Watford Gazette* where they are and I think they'll be proud to see me in the paper again. While paying, I'm pretty sure the guy at the checkout is looking at me with some recognition and it occurs to me that life might be different for the next few weeks.

I didn't intend to speak to the journalist. He approached me. As I left the courtroom, I saw him crouched, doing up his shoelaces. A pen slipped out of his back pocket and I rushed forwards to get it for him.

'Excuse me, I think you dropped your pen.'

'Ah, thanks, buddy. Hey, really interested to hear more about what happened to you, if you're happy to talk to me? Can I buy you a coffee?'

I took a second to respond. My gut reaction was to decline, to walk away, not to give this journalist fodder to write something sensationalist about our personal tragedy. But then I also felt flattered, pleased that somebody was acknowledging my role in this, happy to have been offered a forum to tell my side of the story. This was my chance to show Alice, in black and white, just what this whole thing means to me.

I actually quite enjoyed our chat and, afterwards, a photographer who works with Ryan took a few shots of me standing outside the courthouse. Out of the corner of my eye, I saw a couple of old ladies stop and watch while my photo was being taken, but I didn't allow myself to be fazed.

When I get home from the shop, I sit on the sofa and eat the entire tub of ice cream. Not the most wholesome dinner, but tonight I've got more pressing things to do than cook. I put two of the newspapers in the drawer under my bed, take the third copy and tear out the article so I can pin it on the front of my fridge. Separately, I cut out the photo of myself and place it on the mantelpiece in my living room.

It's reassuring to see my picture there, next to photos of Maxy and Alice. It's not quite the same as us having a family photo together, but for the time being it will do. I've got a few photos up now: one of Maxy holding the papier mâché pterodactyl, one of Alice, which I took when we had that Italian dinner – our first proper date, the night that we slept together for the first time.

I'll leave the flat at about 9 p.m. and then I should be there by half past. I really want to get the presents to Maxy.

His birthday's almost over now and I don't want him to have to wait too much longer. He's probably wondering what's happened to them, and it's not fair that just because his mother and I are going through a rough patch, he should be deprived.

I sit on the floor of my bedroom and open any of the presents that state on the boxes that they require batteries. I remember, from my own childhood, that the most frustrating thing is to receive presents and then not be able to play with them immediately. So I insert all the batteries, make sure everything is working and then put all the toys back in their respective boxes.

I take all the bags down the stairs, load them into my car and then have a quick shower. I'm not expecting to be invited in – my plan is to leave the presents as a surprise for Maxy in the morning – but I'd rather not be caught off guard. I tend to sweat a lot during the day, particularly when I've been stressed, and while it is very unlikely, if one thing does lead to another I don't want to smell.

The roads are clear and there's a thrill as I watch the speedometer creep up, from 20, to 30, to 45 mph, and I feel in control, fully aware and ready to face any hazards in my way. I'm on an important mission to deliver some presents to a very deserving child.

I make a stop at an Esso petrol station just around the corner from Alice and Max's house to pick up a birthday card for him. Not the greatest selection. In the end, I go for a large one that is probably aimed at kids slightly younger than Max, but it comes with a large round 'Birthday Boy' badge and I know this is something he will like. Back in the car, I reach for a pen in the glove compartment and write a short message. Normally, I have to think really hard about what to write beyond 'Happy birthday', but in this case the words just flow.

By the time I reach their house, it's a bit later than planned. I park a good few doors down, outside number 77. I turn the ignition off, grab all the Hamleys bags and hesitate for a second before getting out of the car. Maybe I should just ring the doorbell and deliver the presents directly to Maxy. I have heard Alice loud and clear, but my focus now has to be on him. He was struggling, but with my influence has been thriving again. This separation will do him no good. I could just stride up there, with confidence, and ask Alice politely if I can see him for a few minutes and give him the presents he deserves. Even better, maybe Maxy will be the one to open the front door and I can deliver the presents without her getting in the way. But there's a good chance he's in bed now and I don't want Alice to refuse to take the bags, so I stick with my original plan.

I look in the rear-view mirror. There are no cars coming and I can't see anyone on the pavement either side, so I get out of my car, grab the bags and gently shut the car door. I lock it manually, putting the key in the door, because it beeps when it's locked automatically. I edge slowly towards the house and, from a distance, I can see that the hallway light is still on, but all the lights upstairs are off. Maxy must be asleep – it's long past his bedtime.

I bypass the driveway altogether and head straight to the side gate, because I know there's a motion-controlled light that comes on when you reach a certain point. I keep right to the side, in the shadow of a large hedge, push open the side gate and head towards the back garden. I've never seen this part of the garden before and, because there's a light on in the kitchen, I get a good look at it in all its wild, unmanaged glory. There are more dead roses. I remove the heads – that should give them another lease of life.

I can hear the TV blaring. It's selfish of Alice to have it on so loud when Max is trying to sleep. It's a school night and even if he's not being kept awake, I'm sure the quality of his sleep will be affected. Despite the noise of the TV, I'm conscious of being as quiet as possible, so I make a particular effort not to rustle the bags as I squeeze along the side passage. One of the bags is particularly heavy, so I'm holding it from the bottom to prevent it from splitting and the toys inside spilling out and breaking.

My plan is to leave all the presents on the patio, because there are French doors leading from the living room – where Maxy eats breakfast – to the garden, so when he wakes and runs down the stairs, they'll be the first things he'll see. It'll be like Christmas morning for him. He'll know exactly who the presents have come from, but they will have arrived under the cloak of night. I can't imagine Maxy ever believing in Santa Claus, or the tooth fairy, for that matter. He's too rational and sensible. More rooted in the real world than his mother.

If I stand on the far right-hand corner of the patio, I have a good vantage point. I can see most of the living room: the mango wood coffee table, which has two empty bottles of wine on it and a few unopened packets of salt and vinegar crisps. I can see the end of the leather sofa – the one I once lay on with Alice – and Alice's feet, hanging just over the edge. Her nails are painted a deep red, very tidy, and if you judged Alice just by her feet, you would assume she was perfect: dainty, feminine, discerning.

I gasp as she edges forwards and stands. Her eye make-up is smudged, her hair unkempt, thin and dirty, and she's stumbling around. This is not tipsy Alice but downright off-her-face, couldn't-possibly-string-a-sentence-together Alice. She pours another glass of wine, missing on the first attempt and spilling a fair bit, leaving a puddle of booze on the coffee table.

I feel a wave of rage. This woman, this drunkard, is the sole carer of Max. How irresponsible of her to drink so heavily, with her son upstairs sleeping innocently. And on his birthday, of all days!

She reaches for something under the coffee table and then walks out into the garden. I dart back, retreating into a bush behind me. I feel a prick on the back of my neck as I reverse into a cluster of thorns. She's so close that I can hear her breathing, so I'm all too conscious that if I don't control myself, she may hear mine. I think I can even smell the booze on her breath, that stale smell of ethanol.

I bundle all of the Hamleys bags behind me so that she doesn't see the white in the bushes. There's a rustle that I can't control, but she's so out of it that she doesn't flinch. She reaches into the pocket of her dressing gown and pulls out a long, thin cigarette.

Is this a new habit?

She takes a match out of a box and strikes it, lighting the cigarette and taking a long, deep drag, closing her eyes and pulling her head back in ecstasy. The fumes are potent and I watch as the smoke rises into the sky. If it were a bit warmer, if Maxy were to have his window open, these fumes would be wafting into his bedroom and into his lungs.

I watch Alice as she takes each puff of her cigarette. With each drag, I see the amber light at the butt rise and fall. I'm petrified that she'll see me, that the glow will shine on my face and she'll catch me, a pair of eyes peering out at her from among the shrubbery.

But the danger of being caught makes it exciting. Here I am, invading her private moment of transgression. I'm transfixed. And then all of a sudden I jump as she throws the cigarette in my direction. It lands about six inches from my feet, still burning, the smell now so strong that it makes me queasy. If she had aimed slightly to the right, turned her wrist just a few inches, the butt could have landed on my head, or in my eye, and I'm sure an involuntary scream would have blown my cover.

Alice turns on her heel, tightens her dressing grown and stumbles back into the house, closing the doors behind her. She looks out into the garden as she locks the door and for a moment I'm sure that our eyes meet, but she doesn't react. When she turns and makes her way back into the living room, I draw a long breath.

She pours herself yet another glass of wine, takes a big swig and then trips on the side of the table, lunging the wine glass towards the French windows. I watch as the glass smashes and scatters across the floor, but Alice seems unfazed. She turns round and heads out of the living room, leaving the shards of glass glistening, their edges like sharpened knives.

She must be going up to bed now, so it's probably safe for me to come out, but I wait a few minutes to be sure.

I see the light go on in the bathroom on the first floor – the bathroom that looks out onto the garden, the bathroom where I showered after the night we made love. Then it goes off and all is dark.

I wait for a few moments longer, to make sure that the coast is clear. I suddenly become aware of my own body and sense a huge patch of sweat at the top of my back. My head is banging and my ears are ringing – my whole body is rattling as if I've been shaken hard and I feel like I might faint. I take a few deep breaths, gather composure, and when I'm sure that Alice has definitely gone to bed and I won't be spotted, I emerge from my hideaway and place the Hamleys bags carefully, right in front of the patio doors.

I line them up neatly, each bag equidistant from the next, and I can feel myself grinning as I imagine Maxy's surprise when he sees them in the morning. I turn round and look towards the large shed at the end of the garden, its outline just visible in the evening's moonlight. Adam's studio. I've never been in, but I've often let myself imagine what it's like. How I long to see it from the inside.

The shed is at the far end of the garden and I make my way down, wading through long grass, careful not to crunch as I go. When I reach the outhouse, I place my hand on the handle of the door and feel the itch of cobwebs. My heart is beating fast and my hand is shaking as I press it down. And then . . . a light behind me.

I dart back into the shrubs and stride all the way down the garden and into the bushes, traipsing over flowers and feeling the prickle of nettles through my trousers, on my ankles. Alice must be coming back down for a glass of water and I don't want her to see the Hamleys bags now. In her state, she'll come out into the garden and smash everything to pieces. But it's not Alice who's made her way back downstairs. It's Maxy.

He's wearing his Spiderman pyjamas and he's clearly been asleep already, as I had thought, because he's rubbing his eyes and squinting as he adjusts to the light of the living room. He stands at the kitchen tap and pours himself a glass of water, which he downs in one gulp. Then I hear the TV switch back on and can see his legs dangle over the sofa. What a cheeky little monkey. Creeping downstairs after his mother has gone to bed to watch late-night TV.

I don't like the idea of him watching TV at this time and certainly not on his own. God knows what he could be watching. I don't think it's late enough for proper erotica: it's violence that I'm more worried about. He's at such an impressionable age, and exposure to guns and knives is not good for someone of his age.

Then Maxy stands and for a moment I think he's noticed the plastic bags on the patio. It would be ideal to be able to witness him discovering the presents – I had imagined that I'd be long gone by then. But he's not looking out. He's looking at the pieces of broken glass that are scattered by the window. He edges forwards, picks up one of the shards and lifts it towards the light, examining its contours and watching it glisten as he rotates it. This child is in danger.

I edge out of the bush – I need to go in there and put a stop to this. I need to catch his attention, shock him in some way. I gather a couple of pebbles from the patio and throw them at the window. I throw them gently, because I don't want to break anything, but I need him to hear. I need to scare him away.

It works. He reacts like a fox caught in headlights on a busy country road. He drops the glass and runs out of the living room, leaving the light on and storming up the stairs.

I'm fuming. I clamber out of the bushes, rustling plants as I go, striding down the side passageway and out of the garden gate. All previous precautions are now futile. I almost want to be caught now. I want Alice to find me. I want a confrontation, because if I don't step in then no one else will.

I march through the front garden, activating the lights on my way out, and I point my keys at my car over the road, opening the doors automatically and hearing the 'beep-beep' that earlier I had feared. I run across the street without looking and I hear the screech of brakes as I dart out in front of a blue Vauxhall Corsa.

The driver pulls down the window and shouts at me, but I'm so focused now, so single-minded, that the words pass right over me and he speeds off into the distance. I get into the car, start the ignition and drive. I'm going fast. Much faster than I should be. I'm so out of control on this journey home that I'm swerving from left to right, speeding, mishandling the clutch so that the gearbox groans like an old man's stomach.

When I reach my driveway, I misjudge the distance and hit the bumper on the front wall, jerking forwards and then back, hitting my head on the back of my seat. I pull the handbrake up without pressing the button and it makes a sharp croaking sound. I go to undo my seat belt, then realise that I never put it on. I climb out, slamming the door and locking it again. I put the key in the door to the building and as I do so, the door opens and one of my neighbours is just on her way out.

'Is everything OK? You seem . . .'

But I brush straight past her, shoving her slightly as I take two steps, four steps, six, up to my front door. I'm out of breath, heaving, wheezing. I can do without Alice; she can fend for herself. She can make all the mistakes she wants to make. But Max needs me. The time has come. Something needs to be done.

ALICE

Friday, 6 July

'Mummy, Mummy, wake up. Look what I've got!'

I open my eyes and Max is about three inches from my head, with a massive grin on his face. My head is spinning and my mouth feels so dry it's like I've eaten a whole packet of Rich Tea biscuits in a minute without a sip of water. My eyes are sore and heavy, and it's boiling hot. Under the covers, I can feel that I'm still wearing my dressing gown and there's a wet patch on the back of my nightie.

'Max, what time is it? Mummy's still sleeping. Can you get off the bed, please?'

'Mummy, you smell funny. I think you need to brush your teeth. Look at all these presents!'

I get out of bed and the floor is a bomb site. There's a mound of empty boxes and toys lying around. A remote-control car, a huge pirate ship made out of Lego and, in Max's hand, some kind of iPad or Kindle.

'Max, where did you get all of this stuff?'

'It's my birthday presents from Ben. He left them for me, outside.'

'What are you talking about, outside?'

'Outside on the patio. He left a pile of presents there and a card for me. You know, all the stuff that he bought for me at Hamleys.'

'What? What are you talking about? For God's sake, Max, go and get dressed immediately. It's eight forty-five, you're going to be late for school.'

What's he talking about? Has Ben had some presents delivered here? When did they arrive? My temples start to pulse with rage, but I feel so delicate that I can't think straight and have to hold onto the banister as I head down the stairs. Why am I feeling so rough? I have vague memories of getting through quite a lot of wine while watching *Love Island* on TV, but I don't remember going to bed. When I head into the living room, the patio doors are wide open and there are empty bags strewn on the lawn. Why is the patio door open? Then I see the broken wine glass by the doors, and I have flashbacks to last night, to going outside to smoke a fag. I must have left the door unlocked.

'Max, get down here. Now! It's nearly nine o'clock already, for fuck's sake!'

I take my dressing gown off and fling on the first coat that I find in the cupboard, grabbing my car keys from the kitchen counter. Max comes down the stairs, his shirt untucked and his hair a wild mess.

'Mummy, you said the F-word.'

'I'm sorry, darling. I shouldn't have done that. Have you had any breakfast?'

'I had two mini Mars bars. Sorry, Mummy.'

I usher Max through the front door and almost trip on the bottom step as we head towards the car. I turn on the ignition and I know that I'm not fit to drive, but we're already running late. The last thing I need now is a phone call from the school berating me about Max's absence.

There's traffic, which always happens when we leave a little later, and as we're waiting, I place my head on the steering wheel. I'm desperate to go back to bed. And then Max, who up until now has been silent, pipes up. I look in the rear-view mirror and see that he's trying to put some kind of badge on his jumper, holding a card in his other hand.

'Mummy, what is WhatsApp?'

'It's for people to send messages to their friends and family.'

'Can I do WhatsApp, Mummy? I've got someone I want to message.'

'Who do you want to message, Max? Maybe when you get home this afternoon, you can send a message from my phone, if you're a good boy.'

We pull up at the school gates and Max is still fiddling with the badge, on the verge of pricking his finger.

'Get out of the car, Max, come on. Leave that bloody badge, will you?! You're late. And if the teacher asks, tell them that there was a road accident that caused lots of traffic, OK?'

But Max is already out of the car and running up the path. He's left the car door open, so I get out to close it and when I do, I see a birthday card lying on the back seat. I pick it up and read the message:

Dear Maxy,

*Happy birthday! Sorry that you're getting these presents a bit
later than planned – but better late than never! I know you'll
be a good boy and open one present at a time. Next time I
come round I want to see the Lego ship complete!*

Love from Ben xx

*P.S. Here's my mobile number in case you ever need it:
07825 745412. Send me a message on WhatsApp!*

I tear the card into two, fling it onto the floor of the car, and
get back into the driver's seat. What, exactly, are his intentions? What kind of relationship does he hope to sustain
with my son? It's not right for a man of his age to be sharing
his mobile number with a child of eight. Where does he
hope this relationship will lead?

When I get back to the house, I head upstairs, ripping off
the coat and shedding it on the banister before entering my
bedroom and crashing on the bed. I take three paracetamol
from the drawer in my bedside table and swallow them without
water. I know that I should be clearing up all the debris from
last night before Max gets home, but I need to sleep.

I need to do something about Ben. This is not a situation
that I can carry on handling alone. Ben is everywhere, infil-
trating our lives, and I need to take action. I reach into my
bedside table and pull out a card that the detective inspector
gave me on the day of the accident, making a mental note
to call him later. Now, I need to sleep off this hangover
and get my head in the right place. I set the timer on my
phone for three hours and enter into a deep slumber.

When I wake, everything is a bit clearer. My head no longer feels like it's been invaded by an army of monkeys, hammering away at my brain, cell by cell, and I feel more rested. I get out of bed, change the sheets and head into the bathroom to run a bath. I empty three quarters of a bottle of bubble bath into the water, light a candle by the edge of the bath and spend a good hour in there, scrubbing off the grime, washing off the remnants of make-up from my face, feeling warmth inside my body.

I think of Adam and remember what it was like to be with him. He knew just how to touch me and when, gently at first and then with increased vigour, running his fingers over my neck, along my spine and down to the arch of my back. He'd kiss me gently on the forehead, once, twice, three times, and then go down on me. He'd use his whole mouth, holding me between his lips, never overdoing it but showing persistence, not pulling away too early or arching back in the middle of my orgasm. And today, remembering his touch and simulating it with my own, I come and I come again.

I get out and grab the towel that's on the rail. It's damp in the centre and crusty round the edges. As I wrap it round my dripping torso, the sour smell of mildew hits the back of my throat. I walk over to the bedroom, drop the towel and stare at my reflection in the full-length mirror.

I run my finger along the scar on my front, the mark that will always remind me of Max, then exhale deeply, my belly protruding and the button popping out, and sink to the floor. I sit there, staring, for five minutes, ten minutes or maybe even twenty. It's not until I hear the church bell strike three o'clock that I wake from my trance. I don't know where the day has gone and I'm running late, again. There is no homework club today and Mrs Turner is in Torquay with her bridge circle, so I need to go and pick up Max. I fling on the first clothes that I can find. No deodorant, no knickers even. Then I run down the stairs, grab my car keys and reverse out of the driveway.

I park at the school gate and make my way up the long, winding path that leads to the main building. The incline is steep, and after just a few strides I'm out of breath and I can feel the friction as one thigh strokes the other. I'm late, but not ridiculously so, because a couple of other women are running past me. Other mothers, and the occasional father, are crossing my path, heading in the opposite direction, kids five steps ahead, swinging their hands by their sides and throwing their heads back in laughter.

For a moment I feel a pang of jealousy, which takes me by surprise, and I even force out a smile as one woman scoops up her screaming toddler from the floor. Maybe I should make more of an effort with these people, join the PTA, start going for coffee with the parents of Max's school friends. What would we talk about, though? What would I have to bring to the party?

When I reach the top of the path, it feels like such an achievement that I stop for a moment on a bench at the edge of the playground. I reach into my handbag for my inhaler and take three big pumps. I find some lipstick in the left pocket of my dress – bright red – and slap it on in a pathetic attempt to brighten up what must otherwise be a pretty grim, grey appearance. I probably shouldn't

have left the house without my phone – not because I've
got anyone who I particularly want to ring or text, but
because without it I'm lacking my crutch. My phone is
so often a shield between the rest of the world and me, a
decoy. When I'm scrolling, I'm occupied, engaged, closed
for business with anyone else.

In front of me is a sea of boys and girls, pigtails and knee-
caps, a flurry of colour and a storm of yelps and screams. As
the minutes pass, the crowd dies down, so I pluck up the
energy to stand and head towards the main building.
The problem with school uniform is that everyone looks
the same. It would be useful, in a scenario like this, to have
a child with shocking ginger hair.

I walk the width of the playground, looking each child
up and down but doing my best to avoid direct eye contact.
Some of these kids are so scatty: shirts untucked, rips in
their shorts and scuffs on their shoes. I lock eyes with one
child who looks like he hasn't been properly fed in years,
scrawny and pale, and with a red crust on his top lip.

Max is obviously still inside. If he's anything like he is
at home, he'll be faffing around, taking ages to pack up
his stuff, daydreaming and chatting away, in his own little
world. I can see his teacher is outside, by the back door
of her classroom, nodding earnestly as a concerned mother
chews her ear off. Why on earth anyone would choose to
be a primary school teacher is beyond me. It's bad enough
to have to spend the best part of the day with a group of
children who aren't your own, fielding inane questions and
clearing up vomit. But then to have to deal with the parents,
the neurotic, overbearing parents with their insecurities,

having to distinguish between each child and give bespoke reports, individual analyses of each little darling, would surely be more than anyone could reasonably bear.

I decide to sit on the bench at the back of the playground. Max can take as long as he likes and then he can come and find me. I take a seat and close my eyes, feeling the gentle breeze on the back of my neck.

'Excuse me. Mrs Selby, isn't it?'

The sun is shining bright and I have to squint to see that it's the school secretary, Brenda.

'Hi. Sorry, I must have dropped off.'

Brenda looks me up and down, and I feel compelled to cross my legs and grab hold of my dress, scrunching it up and sitting up straight.

'Can I help you at all?' she asks.

'Well, I'm here to pick up Max. Is he still inside?'

'What? Max left about an hour ago. Your husband picked him up.'

'Is that some kind of sick joke? Max's dad is dead. You must know that.'

'Oh gosh, how terrible. Not Adam. The handsome chap who dropped off Max once before. You added him to the drop-off list. He said he was Max's stepdad?'

Stepdad? That word enters me like a bullet, as if Brenda has loaded it into a shotgun and fired it straight through me.

'Ben?'

'Yeah, that's it. Ben. Seems lovely. Mrs Selby, is everything OK?'

BEN

I knew that if we hit the M1 before rush hour, we should be able to avoid too much traffic. There was a bit of a hold-up as we joined the motorway and then, pretty quickly, Maxy declared that he needed the toilet, so we stopped at a service station. I didn't need to go, so while Maxy went, I bought a jumbo packet of wine gums and a Little Mix CD for the drive. I know Maxy is a fan because there's a poster of them on his bedroom wall. Jesy is his favourite.

It's a beautiful day for a long drive. The thermometer on the dashboard says 24 degrees, but it feels warmer. The sun is strong and a couple of times I've had to pull the sun visor down to avoid the glare. Isn't it funny how the weather, in all of its extremes, can put obstacles in the way of safe driving?

Quite early in our trip, we passed the exact spot where I hit Adam almost six months ago. Thankfully, there is no rain today and Max's stream of questions is keeping me occupied. Now, as I look out to the right, the sun is hovering and creating a deep yellow hue over the countryside.

'Ben, where are we going? Are we nearly there yet?'

Maxy is sitting in the back, behind the front passenger seat, so I can see him clearly in the rear-view mirror. He's still wearing his school uniform and there's a big blob of orange on the collar of his green polo shirt. It doesn't look like a fresh stain and I am ashamed at the thought that Alice lets him go to school in unwashed clothes. It's one thing for her to take no pride in her own appearance, but Max shouldn't suffer.

'I told you, Maxy, it's a surprise. It's going to be another couple of hours yet. Why don't we give your mum a call?'

This is an important part of the plan. This isn't some sort of kidnap. This is a temporary solution, an opportunity for Alice to realise that she's heading down a dangerous path. So I need to give her a ring. Let her know that her son is safe. Alice will thank me for this in the long run.

We probably should have made the phone call while we were at the service station. We could have done it from a café – found a quiet corner at the back, bought an ice cream and put her on loudspeaker. It's probably too far to the next nearest service station and we need to make the call sooner rather than later, so I indicate, pull up on the hard shoulder and stop. I put my hazard lights on, and the tick-tock, tick-tock sends a shiver of adrenaline right up my spine.

There's something about being stationary on the motorway that makes my ears prick up and suddenly I am hypersensitive. Cars are driving past us at top speed and each time another one crashes past, it sounds like I've plunged my head under a waterfall. A lorry honks three times as it passes and each is so deafening that I flinch, as if being hit over the head with a thick baton.

I take my phone out of my pocket and connect it to the car's Bluetooth. I want Maxy to be able to hear the conversation and I want Alice to hear Maxy, too. She needs to know that he is safe. My hands are shaking and I dial her number in full, even though I know I could just go into my most recently dialled to find her. It doesn't ring and I hear her voice right away.

'Hi, this is Alice's phone. Leave a message and I'll call you back.'

BEEP.

Fuck. I wasn't expecting voicemail. She must be on the phone to someone else. Who could she be calling? Lisa? Another man? My heart is pounding and there must be three seconds that go past, after the beep, before I start speaking.

'Hi, Alice, it's me. I . . . I don't know why your phone is switched off, or if you're on the phone to someone else, or . . . Anyway, I just want to confirm that I've picked Maxy up from school today and he's with me. Say hi to your Mum, Maxy!'

'Hi, Mummy! We're going on a trip. I've got wine gums.'

'Ha ha, don't worry; I'll make sure he has dinner, too. Anyway, yeah, so we're on the motorway, we'll be back in London on Monday. I thought you could do with some space to get your head in the right place. I'm worried about you, Alice. The drink and everything else. It's been such a hard year for you and I definitely don't blame you for needing a bit of a crutch, I completely understand. I just want to make sure we're all doing the best thing for Max, you know?

'I think you need to go and see someone. I dunno, maybe a GP, but I know it's the kind of thing that you have to come to on your own and so I thought that . . . Well, anyway, it's just a couple of days away and we'll be back on Monday. Go and treat yourself tomorrow – go to a spa or something. I'll transfer you the money for it. Get your head in order. And yeah, well, you know where we are if you need us. Call me anytime so we can talk all this through. Thinking of you.'

Done. I take my phone off Bluetooth and twist back to check on Max. I wonder what he makes of all of this. But he's silent, his little head resting against the window and his mouth wide open. He's content. All is fine. I take off the hazard lights, indicate and wait. I want to wait until there are no cars anywhere near. My right hand is shaking a little and I don't trust myself to judge the distance correctly if another car is approaching. When the coast is clear, I edge back onto the motorway and accelerate.

For the last half-hour of the journey, I think about Alice. I think about what I can do to help her get out of the mess she's found herself in, when we're all back together. I know that neither of us has been to the mindfulness centre in a while. Maybe it would do her some good to go back there. Maybe I'll go with her. I don't think I need it anymore, but I know that she needs my support.

By the time we pull up to the guest house, it's almost dark. Maxy has been asleep in the back seat for the last couple of hours. I hope this doesn't mean he's going to struggle to settle tonight. I park in the small car park by the entrance to the house, get out of the car and take the suitcase out of the boot. I've only taken my hand luggage bag because we don't need that much stuff. I popped to Primark this morning and bought Maxy a couple of T-shirts, a few underpants and socks and a pair of jeans. I think I judged the size right – he's grown so much, even in the short time I've known him, that it's hard to tell. I erred on the larger size because he can always grow into the new clothes.

I open the rear door of the car and nudge Maxy gently to wake him.

'Maxy, we're here. We're here. Come on, undo your seat belt.'

Max rubs his eyes and shuffles out of the car, still half asleep, before following me across the gravel path to the sign that says 'Entrance'. I grab his hand as we walk through the door and a barking Yorkshire terrier greets us. I wouldn't say I'm scared of dogs, but I'm not a great fan, either. Right behind the dog is a middle-aged woman wearing an apron. The owner, presumably, of both dog and house.

'OK, Maisie, calm down, calm down. Sorry about her, she gets quite overexcited when people walk in!'

Maxy is far less fazed than me and starts stroking Maisie with great vigour.

'You must be Ben and Max? How was your drive?'

'Lovely, thanks. Yeah, really nice. Beautiful evening.'

I follow her towards the reception desk, leaving Maxy playing with the dog by the fireplace in front of the sofas.

'So it's one room, two nights. Is that right?'

'Yes, please. Twin, ideally, if you've got one.'

'Sorry, I think we've only got doubles left. I can put up a camp bed for the little one?'

'No, it's OK. We can share.'

'Great. If I can just take a credit card now for any incidentals.'

I hand over my Mastercard and the dog runs off into the front garden. I don't want Maxy chasing after him; there might be other cars arriving.

'Maxy, come over here. Look, if you ask nicely, maybe this lady will let you have one of these sweets.'

'Please can I have a sweet?' asks Maxy on cue, and the lady smiles and nods.

Maxy takes a sweet, unwraps it and gives a big grin as he pops it in his mouth.

'Is your daddy taking you to Alton Towers then, young man?'

And before Maxy can correct her, I jump in.

'Well, there you go, ruining the surprise!'

The prospect of going to Alton Towers is, thankfully, exciting enough that Maxy is distracted, jumping up and down.

'Really? Is that true? When are we going?'

'Tomorrow, Max. First thing tomorrow. So we're getting an early night.'

And that look on his little face, the delight in his eyes, is worth every second of hurt and heartbreak that I've had to endure since this ordeal began. The chance to make this child so happy is worth everything. And I think of Adam. Of the role I played in his death. Of the duty that I am now fulfilling.

ALICE

Friday, 6 July

'If you can get your seat belt on, Mrs Selby. We can't leave until your seat belt is secured.'

I'm sitting right on the edge of my seat, in the back of a police car. I don't want to sit back. I don't want to be tied down. Somehow, sitting on the edge of the seat gives me more freedom, makes me more agile, ready to open the door and jump out as soon as I see him. If I sit back, with my belt on, I'm out of control. For the period of this journey, my son's fate is in the hands of someone else. If I sit back, I submit to the whim of fate.

'Please, Mrs Selby. The sooner you put the belt on, the sooner we can get going, the sooner we can get to your son. Unless you'd rather stay at the station?'

There's no way that's going to happen. I need to be there when they find him. I need to be the first to hold him, to take him into my arms and to promise him that he'll never, ever come into harm's way again. I'm the one who's put him in danger, by letting that creep infiltrate himself into our lives, so I need to be there to save him. Why didn't I call the police earlier? What was I waiting for? Why didn't I see how serious it was getting?

I sit back and feel the crunch as the metal of the seat belt enters the red slot. The stomach cramps were manageable while I was sitting forwards and now they're back, an aching feeling worse than the most excruciating period pain. It's as if Max's danger is hitting me in the very place where he first grew and I know that these pains will go away as soon as we're back together.

'That's great, thanks, Mrs Selby. Now, if you just try to sit back and relax, we'll be there in no time. And we've got our colleagues at Staffordshire Police already in the area where he last used his phone.'

'Sit back and relax? Sit back and relax! Is that some kind of joke? Don't you realise how dangerous this man is?'

I shouldn't have mentioned the voicemail to them after we swung past the house to pick up my phone. The second I did, they made me hand over my phone. I pleaded with them to let me call him back, to let me reason with him.

And now they're not going fast enough. My eyes are fixed on the speedometer as we hit the motorway: 20, 40, 50, 70 mph – come on, keep going. I'm staring, willing the little pin with the power of my own eyes to move further along the semicircle. I feel like reaching forwards and yanking the driver, shaking him into action. This is just another day at work for you, I feel like screaming. This is my life, my whole existence, my whole reason for getting out of bed in the morning.

And then we do go faster, and I feel a thrill as I see the speedometer go further and further. My stomach still stings, so I place my left hand on it and press it down. It feels tender and, as I push, a wave of nausea hits me and I gag. Nothing comes out. The police officer in the passenger seat, a stout older man with a cleft palate, looks back and hands me a sick bag, like those you get on a flight.

'If you're going to be sick, love, please try to do it in this bag rather than all over the seats.'

I catch him glancing over to his colleague and giving, I think, a shake of the head, and that's enough to set me off.

'Fuck you. Fuck you both. Sitting there in your shitty little uniforms, chatting away, laughing and joking. I'll get out of the car and drive up there myself, rescue Max and give that bastard what he deserves.'

The cleft-palated officer quickly loses his smirk, turns round in his seat and goes into stern mode. When most people get angry, their mouths move, but his lips stay put, so he overcompensates with his eyebrows. They seem to take on a life of their own and his reaction is cartoonish, exaggerated, theatrical.

'Listen, Mrs Selby. If you don't calm down, I'm in half a mind to turn round, drop you at the station and detain you for aggravating a police officer. Now, I think it's in everyone's best interests if you sit back, stay silent and let us get on with finding your son.'

I'm stunned by this outburst, but also finally delighted to see fire in his eyes. I adjust my seat belt, tightening it at the waist, giving the pain in my groin a sharp hit, which reverberates like a cymbal and then settles. I crack open the window and allow myself to get lost in the din of the motorway: that low, unrelenting whirr of engines, interrupted by the occasional bleat of a freight lorry as it chugs its way across the country, sluggish and reluctant, heavy and tired.

In the police station, I told them everything I knew about Ben and how this man came to be in our lives. Why did it have to be Ben who was driving that car, on that particular day? What are the chances that things would turn out as they have? If it had been any other car, on any other morning, how would these events have unfolded?

In a different version of this story, a little old lady called Mary hits Adam. Mary gets out of her car and is horrified to see Adam lying there, his white trousers stained with the deep red of blood. Mary gives a witness statement and is shaken, of course. She's horrified to hear that this man has been compelled to take his own life. She sheds a tear as she gets back into her car and, when she gets home, her husband, Lionel, makes her a cup of tea, and they sit together and watch a bit of telly. She tells her best friend, Marjorie, about it when she meets her the next day for a game of bridge. Everyone feels sad.

Months later, Mary dons her smartest Sunday dress – dark blue floral, matched with some cream kitten heels – and brings a hankie to the stand at the inquest as she gives a brief state-ment as to what she saw. Mary gives me a sympathetic smile on the way out of the inquest and I smile back. Mary never meets Max. Mary goes home. Mary gets on with her life.

A crackle and a hiss, then a slow, northern drawl comes through the police radio that is attached to the dashboard of the car.

'Hello, PC Lincoln here, are you receiving?'

PC Cleft Palate grabs the radio and responds.

'Receiving. What's the latest?'

'We've tracked them down to a little pub just outside Quixhill. Arrived at about 19:15. Owner remembers checking them in – a man who fits the suspect's description with a young lad of nine or ten.'

'He's eight. He's eight.'

The officer driving the car waves his hand behind him, shooing me away like an unwanted cat, and the conversation continues.

'Name of the pub, please?'

'The Boxhill Inn. Just off the B5030. My nan had her eightieth there, actually.'

'Sounds lovely. We should be there in thirty-five minutes. In the meantime, can you get some backup down there? Great job, officer.'

An acknowledgement, a crackle and the officer places the radio back on the dashboard.

'There you go, Mrs Selby. Nothing to worry about. We've located Max; he's safe.'

Nothing to worry about? My mind is going into overdrive. I look at the clock on the dashboard: 20:17. They've been in that hotel room for over an hour. What has happened? The world is spinning with a kaleidoscope of possibilities. As each scenario rushes into my mind, it becomes not a chance but a reality, a certainty, the most likely outcome. They've climbed out of the back window and gone even further, checking into this inn as a ruse, a decoy to take us off track. It was not Ben and Max at all who checked into this inn, but an innocent father and son, who are about to be caught up in a police raid, a farcical game of mistaken identity. And then, the most sinister possibility of all: an image of Ben and Max together in a double bed, sharing a duvet and . . .

Vomit. Not in the bag, or out of the window. All over my trousers, seeping between my legs onto the seat of the car. The officers are appalled, indignant, but I don't give a fuck because I feel an immediate sense of relief. A purge. A sudden resolve and clarity. Everything is coming to a head and, soon, Max and I will be ready for a clean break. A new beginning, far away from Ben, far away from that house that carries with it so much baggage.

As we come off the motorway, speeding around the country lanes, I feel a sense of exhilaration as we smash the speed limit. The sirens are on now – the heat is rising. We're getting closer and closer. I open the window as far as it will go and stick my head out, feeling the cool evening wind. And then we start to slow down and I see a couple of other police cars parked in a driveway. We pull up between the two cars and the crunch of the handbrake goes right through me. I swallow hard, wipe myself down, undo my seat belt and step out into the bracing countryside air.

BEN

Friday, 6 July

This is a strange little place. As we walk up the stairs towards our room, the mix of garish interiors, taxidermy, pots and pans and odds and sods that grace the walls transfixes both Max and me. It's like a theatre set, at once random but also thoroughly curated, and any other child of Max's age would, no doubt, be frightened by some of things we see. Most startling of all is the handmade doll sitting on the top of the banister, perfectly constructed but for her lack of eyes. A guard in miniature, perfectly positioned to watch over the guests, but stunted, disabled, haunting.

There are only three rooms and ours is located just to the right of the stairs. Maxy has got the key and he rushes excitedly to the door, turning it with care and then pushing the heavy door with all his might.

The interior of the room is less kooky. There is a bed in the centre – a small double – a tiny wardrobe on the far side by the window and a writing table at the foot of the bed. On top of the table is a TV that looks like it was purchased in the 1980s and a remote control by its side with a label that reads 'Do not remove batteries'. I put our bag down and look around, as if searching for hidden depths or a secret passageway. Maxy heads straight for the remote control and launches himself on the bed.

'Take your shoes off, Maxy! We both have to sleep on that bed and I don't want dirty footprints all over it.'

I'm surprised by my tone. I don't want to be one of those strict parents who shouts at every occasion and monitors every activity with huge scrutiny. Having said that, as delightful and polite as Max is, there are basic rules of etiquette that his parents seem to have let slip, so it falls to me to fill in the gaps.

Maxy kicks off his shoes and switches on the TV. It's such an old set that the picture is fuzzy and there's a low hiss, but this doesn't seem to perturb him and he flicks through the channels until he finds *The Simpsons*. I go about unpacking our little bag as he watches.

It's amazing when you leave London how different the air feels. All of a sudden, it is easier to breathe and there's a tangible silence. I sniff my underarms and it's not pleasant. It's been a long day and I could do with freshening up, so I take my washbag out of the holdall and head into the bathroom for a shower.

The door is stuck and when I finally eke it open, there is a stench of sulphur, coming from a cracked yellow-stained bath. I put my washbag down, switch on the water and take off my clothes. I go to lock the door, but decide to keep it open in case Maxy needs me. Climbing into the bath, I fling my head all the way back as the tepid water engulfs me. I pick up a half-chewed bar of soap that sits on a dish in the bath and lather my underarms, rubbing under my balls and feeling for any lumps or inconsistencies, and then I lean over for the small bottle of shampoo.

When I step out of the bath, I land on a great puddle of water because there's no curtain. I rub my hand on the mirror to clear the steam and reveal my reflection. I'm looking good, my hair's a decent length and my stubble is thickening. I reach up for the white towel on a rack above the bath, give my hair a quick rub and wrap the towel round my waist.

When I go back into the bedroom, the telly is still on and Max has put the volume up so that it's blaring. *The Simpsons* has finished and I recognise the distinct canned laughter of *Friends*. Maxy is no longer on the bed but instead is standing at the window and I go over to join him.

'What you looking at, buddy?'

'Look, the police are here. Those two cars over there. Is there a robber?'

'Don't worry, Maxy. They're probably just stopping for some dinner. Or maybe they're staying in one of the other rooms in this hotel.'

'I'd like to be a policeman one day. Or a teacher like you.'

That hits me in the chest and I have to stop myself from shouting out in glee. The fact that Maxy has even registered that I'm a teacher is joyful for me and then the idea that he idolises me, that he sees in me the man who he one day would like to become, is more than I can handle. I secure the towel round my waist and give him a big hug, holding him tight. He hugs me back, as if it's been months since he's been properly looked after. Don't worry, Maxy, I'm here.

And then we hear a siren. Max breaks away, turning back to the window and cracking it open, leaning his head out to investigate.

'Something's definitely happening, Ben. Look, there's another car coming down the lane. It's got flashing lights! Maybe there's been a murder or something. Like in Cluedo.'

I shut the window and push Max back. He falls onto the bed.

'Come on, Maxy, it's none of our business. I'm sure it's something pretty minor; there's nothing to worry about. Shall we call down to reception and see if they can bring us something to eat for dinner? What do you what? Fish fingers and chips?'

'I want Mummy.'

I wasn't expecting that. I can see he's welling up, but he needs to know the truth.

'Your mummy needs a bit of time off, Maxy. Since your dad died, it's been really hard for her, you see. And sometimes, don't you think maybe she has a bit too much wine? Does that sometimes make her a bit angry? Sometimes even mummies need some help, sweetheart. But don't worry; I'll always be here. And I'll never hurt you, or leave you, or forget you. Not like Mummy and Daddy.'

Now he's full-on crying. The tears are falling in huge streams and his nose is running. I've never seen Maxy cry and to see him this hurt, this vulnerable, breaks my heart. This is the last thing that I want.

'OK, Maxy. Why don't you go over to the window and see what's going on? Maybe you can help them to solve the crime.'

And, in a flash, Maxy is back up and pressing his face against the window again, his eyes gleaming with excitement. But I think I know why the police are here. There's something I've done that I didn't mention in my voicemail to Alice. There are steps that I've taken to protect Maxy that had to remain secret. A phone call to social services reporting Alice for putting an innocent child in danger. I hadn't expected everything to move so quickly, but I'm glad that it has. So what happens now? We sit and wait, I think. We sit and wait.

A hammering on the door: one, two, three. Maxy shoots me a glance and then darts across the room to open it.

'Get back, Maxy, wait! Wait!'

But he's opened the door and standing there are two officers in full uniform. One is much taller than the other and the shorter one has a cleft palate.

'You must be Max,' says the taller officer.

'Yes, yes. That's me.'

And then from behind the officers, a yelp and Alice bursts through, lifting Maxy into her arms and spinning him round. I can't believe my eyes. The whole point of this is to keep Max away from his mother, for his protection. What on earth is Alice doing here with them?

'And you are Ben Anderson, I assume. Get some clothes on, please, sir, you're coming with us.'

'What's going on? Sorry, give me a minute to get dressed – I've just got out of the bath.'

'OK, sir, just stay back from the young lad, please. PC Hardy, why don't you head back down to the car with Alice and Max? I've got it from here.'

I rush back into the bathroom and fling on the clothes that I'd shed before getting in the bath. I turn round and find that the tall officer has followed me and is standing less than a foot away. I brush past him to get my shoes from the bedroom and he follows me still, closer and closer, before I flip.

'Look – what is this? Can you give me some space?'

The officer reaches into his pocket and I see the flash of silver. He grabs my wrists that bit too hard and starts reciting his chant. The words wash over me and I feel detached, like Ben Anderson is someone else, like I'm watching this happen to someone else.

'Ben Anderson, I'm arresting you on suspicion of kidnapping. You do not have to say anything, but it may harm your defence if you do not mention when questioned something you later rely on in court . . .'

ALICE

Thursday, 9 August

'So what we need, Mrs Selby, is any information that might help us to understand how this all began. The first time you met Mr Anderson, how often you were in contact, when he first started showing signs of obsession. Anything you can think of that can help us to nail him. And we will nail him: don't worry.'

The word 'nail' makes me smirk, because they don't know the half of it and I'm never going to tell him that just a few months ago I was the one nailing Ben. I'm supposed to tell them everything, but that's something I'm going to leave out. No need to confuse things.

'Thanks, Inspector. Now, if you don't mind, I'd like to go up and read my son a bedtime story. That's the least I can do.'

Too much? I need to make it clear to these people I'm not a neglectful mother. I need to make them see that I love Max and would do anything for him. Because I can only imagine what Ben's defence is going to be. He's going to tell them I lost him in Hamleys. He's going to tell them how infrequently I used to pick Max up from school, how much I relied on Mrs Turner for childcare. But it's going to be his word against mine, isn't it? Who is going to believe the man arrested with a child in a guest house, ambushed with just a towel on?

That image makes my skin crawl. I've been reassured, time and again, that there was no evidence of any physical contact between Ben and Max, and Max has told me exactly what went on in that room. But that image of Ben in a crusty white towel, the threat that implies, is one that I don't think I'll ever shake off.

I've been doing my best to play the dutiful host all afternoon. A couple of police officers have been here for an hour, together with someone who is calling himself a family liaison officer but who, as far as I can tell, is just here to make the tea. I cleared up the living room before they arrived, flinging all the clothes that were strewn over the floor into the laundry basket and sweeping the crumbs leftover from yesterday's dinner under the sofa. I even went out to buy biscuits and ended up taking the most expensive ones – Viennese Melts. I bought three packets and, thankfully, only a couple of biscuits were eaten, so I can finish the rest once I've put Maxy to bed. I'm piling on the pounds at the moment, but I don't care.

I let the three of them out and stand on the doorstep, waving like a Stepford wife as the two police officers get into their car and the other guy into another. Once they've driven off, I turn back, close the front door and head upstairs to check on Max. It's late and his light is still on, but I'm delighted to see that he's reading.

'What you reading, sweetheart?'

'*The Witches*. Have you heard of it? Ben's read it. He's read everything. Some of his books are even more than 500 pages long.'

'Sweetheart, remember what we agreed about Ben? We don't talk about him anymore. And of course I've read *The Witches*. Are you sure it's not too scary for you, sweetheart?'

'No, I'm not scared. Not even of the Grand High Witch. She reminds me of Mrs Lacey.'

It's difficult to know how much of what's been going on with Ben Max really understands. The police did a great job of keeping him out of the way when Ben was actually arrested, and while there has been some coverage of the case in the press, I don't think Max has cottoned on. It's a tough balance to strike: I don't want to scare Max, but he needs to know that Ben is dangerous.

With Max tucked up in bed, I'm faced with a whole evening in my own company. I head downstairs to look for something to eat. I open the fridge and stand there staring at a bare selection. In the bottom drawer are a few shrivelled grapes that have turned a deep green. I finger them and shudder at the texture – like an old lady's bingo wings. There's an open packet of salami – I don't remember buying that and it's not something that Max would touch – and I hold it at arm's-length before throwing it in the kitchen dustbin.

I open one of the remaining packets of Viennese Melts. I want to focus on the warmth of the milk chocolate, the crunch of the shortbread, the sweetness. But as I swallow, my mind is elsewhere. I'm standing at the sink, transfixed on the garden.

I haven't been into Adam's study since that day in January last year. It's not that I've specifically avoided going in, but I just haven't felt the need. It was always Adam's space, a place of his own, and so there it has remained, untouched. I know there are some things in there that Adam would want me to hold on to – his manuscripts and that old porcelain lamp of his mother's. I remember seeing it smashed on the floor, but I could save it. Collect the pieces and find a shop to repair it.

I step outside. This garden has been wasted on us. Other families would live in this garden. They'd build swings for the children, put up goalposts and basketball nets. They'd plant apple trees, grow tomato plants and entertain their friends in the summer with lavish barbecues. I, on the other hand, have not stepped out here in weeks.

I am such a rare visitor to my own garden that as I edge further and further away from the light of the house, I'm more and more afraid. I wade through the grass, feeling the crunch and crack of snail shells. I hear a distant squealing – a fox, perhaps – and find myself scurrying quickly, not quite running, afraid that I'm going to get caught by an animal.

When I finally get to Adam's shed, I feel like I've come to the end of an army drill, an endurance exercise, and I have to stop to reach for my inhaler.

The door is stiff and when it finally opens, I burst forwards and almost trip on the step. It's dark and I can't even see my hand in front of me. There's a dreadful stench of mildew and the chill of somewhere abandoned, uninhabited. I feel for the light switch and I almost trip again on a large object, maybe a chair. My face hits a net of silk, like candyfloss on my lips, and when I finally find the switch and turn on the light, I see that the place is covered in cobwebs.

The chair by the desk, the ghastly green one that Adam treasured so much and never let Max sit on, has lost its colour and is submerged in a puddle of rainwater. I step over a pile of papers and the broken remains of Adam's mother's lamp and start riffling through the drawers. Pens. So many green pens. And stacks and stacks of paper. Scribblings that he's accumulated over the years.

And then I see it, out of the corner of my eye. The brown envelope. That envelope that I discovered on that fateful morning, with the words 'Tell Maxy I'm sorry' written so immaculately on the front. I tear it open and a bundle of papers fall out. Papers I've never seen before.

My hands are shaking, the tips of my fingers numb as I riffle through the pages. Everything is a blur, moving back and forth, and I can't focus on the words. And then I find the photos, attached in a bundle with a paper clip. I feel sick. I can't breathe. Each photo has a timestamp and I riffle through them, sweat pouring down my face.

06:15: A man getting into a red car.

06:35: That red car on the motorway.

07:08: A man getting out of that red car.

17:23: That man coming out of a school.

18:35: That man walking into his flat.

18:36: Close-up on a number plate.

18:37: Close-up on a pair of deep ocean-blue eyes.

18:38: A face. Younger, fresher, but unmistakably him. Ben.

ADAM

Tuesday, 2 January

The moment I first saw his face, I knew it could be him. There he was, in the *Watford Gazette*, crouching down, surrounded by a classroom of infants. A handsome lad. A symmetrical face, eyes equidistant from a perfectly straight nose, eyebrows groomed, eyelashes flared around two large almond-shaped blue eyes.

'Bricket Wood teacher is "best in the country".' The headline on page seven. It described how Ben Anderson had been given the Pearson Teaching Award, a national competition judged by head teachers and Ofsted inspectors invited to assess lessons by outstanding primary school teachers. Mr Anderson had been commended for his 'remarkable sensitivity and tireless dedication to the well-being of his class'. Dr John Patterson, Chief Executive of Pearson Education and the chair of the panel, said, 'We were all blown away by Mr Anderson's calm but authoritative teaching methods. It was very clear to see that all of his students – boys and girls alike – look up to him, admire him and see in themselves the adults they might become under his care.'

I opened the top drawer of my desk and got out the folder. I highlighted the words 'calm but authoritative', tore out the article and placed it inside. I'd gathered quite a lot of clippings and printouts by this stage, at least three potential candidates, but this one felt different. This time, I felt a rush of blood in my chest as I closed the drawer and I immediately opened it again, taking the clipping back out and looking straight into his eyes. This is a man I can trust. This is a man who is up to the job. This could be the man to take my place.

It's freezing in the car. The dashboard says minus one, but it feels colder than that. I keep the heating off, as I don't want the engine to make a noise. I can still feel my hands, but the tips of my fingers are numb. A fox could climb into the car and start gnawing on my pinkie, and I wouldn't flinch. I wish I could feel this numb inside, too.

The clock on the dashboard display blinks: 3 p.m. I hear the toll of the bells from the church at the end of the road. It can't be long now before the kids come running out. If he doesn't go to the homework club, Maxy finishes at 3.15 p.m. and so it can't be much later at this school. I've been here since 2 p.m., just in case, which explains in part why I'm so cold. But I don't want to miss him again.

When I came before the Christmas holidays, I looked and I looked but I didn't see him. I must have just missed him. I wasn't watching closely enough. I must have looked away for a minute, got distracted by something or someone, and missed my chance. This time, I'm going to see him. Today, I'm going to see him in the flesh for the first time.

The kids start swarming out at 3.14 p.m. There's obviously no uniform at this school, because it's a mad frenzy of colour: yellows and reds, greens and purples, and it's impossible to keep track of everyone. I consider getting out of the car, of going through the gates and standing among them all, to make sure that Ben doesn't slip away, but that's too much. Presumably, he has to wait for all the kids in his class to leave, anyway, before he can head off himself. No, I'll wait here. I might drive a bit closer to the gates once others start to leave, but I'm staying in the car.

It's 5.05 p.m. now and there's still no sign of him. I've watched just about everyone else come out of this building. A few young women, other teachers, I assume, zipping up their anoraks and running to their clapped-out cars. The last few children have left, glued to their iPhones, dragging their feet behind their besuited mothers or fathers, who have just about found the time to steal themselves away to pick up their children after homework club.

I've been biting my nails and I only realise this because I go too far with the nail on my right thumb. I've bitten it just that bit too low and I suck it to relieve the sting. I had been worried that I'd miss him if he didn't come out before it got dark but, luckily, the lighting is good throughout the playground.

Finally, at 5.12 p.m., the great door to the school opens and it's him: Ben Anderson. There's a white light just above the main entrance, so when he appears, he's in a spotlight and I can identify him. He's tall, which is something that I'd imagined but not been able to verify from the photos of him I've found online. He's clearly in good shape, not in a gym-bunny kind of way, but in an everyday, 'I go running at the weekend and play in an amateur five-a-side on a Wednesday evening' kind of way. He looks smart, in a tweed jacket that might be from Zara and blue chinos, and he's got a tartan scarf wrapped round his neck.

He strides across the playground and, as he passes my car, he looks in my direction and stops for a moment, but then keeps on going. He gets into a red car – a Volkswagen Passat – and I drive slightly closer so that my headlights glow on his number plate: Y488 VOH. I get out my phone and snap three times. I give him some time to drive out of the school and make his way down the small lane towards the main road. Then I start my engine and follow.

Ben Anderson is an incredibly slow driver. Who drives at 50 mph on the motorway? He sticks to the slow lane and I watch numerous cars overtake him. He's driving like a cautious old lady. What should be a journey of no more than ten or fifteen minutes takes over twenty, and when we finally come off the motorway, he gets even slower, taking each turn as if he's never driven in a town before.

I follow him all the way to a little cul-de-sac. It's a quiet road and I pull up a few doors down from where he's stopped, turning off the engine and headlights. I can still make out his silhouette as he gets out of his car and he looks back briefly in my direction before heading into his driveway.

I laugh about how slowly he drives, but, in truth, I like it. It's endearing. And it's reassuring to think I won't have to worry about him giving lifts to Maxy. I wait for a few minutes and then drive away.

Of all the men I've considered, Ben Anderson ticks the most boxes. For a while, I thought it was going to be Dr Schwartz, my psychologist. His wife passed away eighteen months ago – cervical cancer – leaving him with two young sons. For ages, I liked the idea of him being the one. I liked the idea of this widower falling in love with Alice, rescuing her, and these two broken families coming together. And I had no doubt at all that Dr Schwartz would be a good role model for Maxy. But then, in the end, I just couldn't see Alice going for it. He's older – late forties at least – and while he's not quite completely bald, his hair is thinning in most places, and I know how Alice feels about that.

And then there was Jason, the personal trainer at the gym. I bought Alice a few sessions for her birthday, in the hope that it might motivate her to kick-start a health routine, but she spent most of the time focusing on Jason's bum. She's not very good at subtlety and on more than one occasion I caught her pouting as Jason passed by. Then once, when I went to the gym on my own, I stood in the corner watching as he did his best to help an octogenarian onto the cross trainer. There was a gentleness about him, an understanding that struck me, and so I found out his full name from the reception desk and started doing a background check.

That was all fine, but I couldn't get over the niggle that he lacked the intellect, the academic grounding, that I wanted Maxy to aspire towards. And then also there were a few photos of him shirtless on Bondi Beach in Australia with another chap, so maybe he's gay, anyway.

So far, I haven't found anything to put me off Ben. First criterion: looks. He doesn't look dissimilar to me, I suppose, but everything is just that bit better. He's a couple of inches taller, his eyes a couple of shades bluer, and I have no doubt that Alice would find him attractive. Second criterion: relationship status. This is where Facebook is a blessing. He is single and interested in women. And then a character reference. What more could I ask for than that award? If a man is so impressive to a panel of school inspectors that he can be named primary school teacher of the year, he must have all the qualities to be a role model for my son. 'Calm but authoritative,' they said. Someone who can keep things in order, who can keep a cool head under pressure. And somebody for Maxy to look up to. To aspire to be.

He has 354 Facebook friends, which I think is quite a lot, and I spend half an hour scrolling through them to see if I can find anything that looks untoward in his friend-ship groups. Because it's not just about Ben. It's about the people he spends time with.

I spend a few minutes looking at an Amanda Anderson, who has a completely open profile. She looks like she's in her early sixties, a very smiley, happy-go-lucky kind of woman, because in every picture she is beaming: at a picnic with friends, on a motorbike with the Colosseum in the background, holding a baby who looks just delighted to be in her arms. And then I find a photo of Amanda and Ben, with the caption 'me and my handsome son', and I'm delighted at the prospect of Maxy finally having a grandma, a matriarch to cuddle him and guide him, to smother him and spoil him. If I choose Ben, I'm choosing a whole new world for Alice and Maxy.

When I get home from Ben's road, I walk towards the living room and stop at the door to listen. Is she watching TV? It's probably one of those documentaries about emergency vets or babies born too early – mindless shit, commissioned for people with nothing to do but indulge in other people's tragedies. She knows how I feel about this – she'll end up weeping into a tissue and making a fool of herself.

I open the door slightly, to get a better listen, and realise she's actually on the phone. Who is she talking to? I take a step forwards and my arm is shaking. I feel my pulse quicken, and notice my right arm has been clenching and unclenching. I'm edging closer and closer, and when she sees me, she drops the phone. 'It was just Lisa. We were talking about something to do with her work. It's nothing.'

I run out just before I lose control, up the stairs and into the bedroom. I punch the mattress and scream into the pillow. I can't control her. I know I'm going to hit her again. How long will it be this time before she pushes me too far?

If Alice and I are going to be apart, it will be on my terms. She's threatened to leave before, but I've always thought she wouldn't have the backbone to go through with it. When she was pregnant with Maxy, she packed a bag in the middle of the night and tried to creep out while I was asleep. I knew what was going on long before I opened my eyes. I could hear her thrashing around, opening drawers, zipping up the bag.

I waited. I wanted to see just how far she would go. When she left the room and headed down the stairs, I jumped out of bed and followed her. Then we tussled and she tripped and tumbled down the last few steps. She was crying hysterically, worried that she'd harmed the baby, and I was wailing, too. What had I done?

I drove her to the hospital and we had to drive round and round the block until we both stopped crying. We always keep some make-up in the glove compartment for times like this when we lose control, and so, by the time we walked into the hospital, everything was composed and calm. I sat with her, stroking her hand, while the doctor performed the ultrasound and confirmed that everything was as expected. Then we went home and made love, and we both apologised, so that was the end of that.

Then there was the time, two years ago, when she left me a note saying that she'd taken Maxy and gone to stay with Lisa for the weekend to 'clear her head'. She knew very well how I felt about Lisa, that manipulative, needy bitch who has always been so hostile towards me, so I drove round to her flat and rang the doorbell. When no one answered, I hammered on the door so hard that I nearly cracked a finger.

I stayed in the car, outside Lisa's flat, for an entire night, because I knew that at some point they'd have to come out. When Alice emerged at about 2pm the next day, I felt such a surge of anger that if she hadn't been with Maxy, I'd have run her over with the four wheels of my car. I controlled myself, composed myself, and followed her car all the way home.

That evening, Alice and I had a serious chat about commitment, about our promise to one another, about how close she'd come to pushing me to do something insane, and she vowed never to leave me again.

And for a few months now, things have been getting out of control again. We spent Christmas Day at each other's throats and I made her cancel plans for New Year's Eve because I couldn't trust her to behave. She's been taking liberties. Why is she so stupid to think that I haven't heard her, creeping downstairs in the middle of the night and going onto the computer? She hasn't even bothered to delete her search history, so I know that she's been on Facebook, looking through pictures of other men, imagining herself fucking them, being fucked by them, leaving me. It's as if she gets a thrill in me knowing that she doesn't love me anymore, that my needs and desires don't mean anything to her.

And, increasingly, I don't know where my anger's going to take me. If I don't take decisive action now, take things into my own hands, then I'm going to end up hurting her so much that she's never going to recover. When I was in the shower last night, I had images of myself going into the kitchen and grabbing the carving knife, that knife that she got me as a Christmas present the first year we were married. I saw myself really going for it, lunging at her with all my might, blood spurting from her insides and hitting me straight in the face. I heard Maxy, whimpering in the corner by the oven, screaming for me to stop. What would happen next? Would I turn the knife on myself, leaving Maxy alone in the world? Or would I have to take him with us?

It's time for me to make my exit, gracefully, before Alice does something that really makes me lose it. I know now, more than ever, that if I truly love them I need to leave them. The one thing that has kept me from killing myself is knowing that Alice is not capable of looking after herself, or Maxy. If I leave, she'll run straight into the arms of someone else and I can't trust her to find the right man.

If I have a dying wish, she will honour it. She owes me this at least. I can't leave without knowing I have done everything I can to make sure she and Maxy will survive. With the right person, they could thrive without me. So she needs to see my thought process. She needs to see the research, the documentation, and I need to guide her in the right direction. She needs to know that whoever runs me over has been selected, hand-picked. She needs to know there are specific, important, reasons. She needs to know that he has to hit me in order to force him, inescapably, into her life.

And then she needs to follow up on the lead. She needs to make an effort.

So I'll leave her a letter. Not a suicide note, but a letter of intention. And, with all the photos and press clippings, the proof that this man is good for her, maybe even a better version of me, without the violence, she will, I'm sure, give happiness a chance.

There's one final criterion that I need to check about Ben Anderson. A functional criterion, but one that is crucial to my plan. I need to ensure that he follows a daily pattern. I already know that he drives to and from work, but how can I pinpoint him to a specific time and place? I need to establish a predictability to his morning routine, which means I can get him at just the right moment. If my plan is to come off, I need to be scientific. So tomorrow morning

I'll go back to the cul-de-sac and confirm the timings. And if I need to go back the morning after, I will. And again. Until the pattern is set.

I put on an alarm for 5.15 a.m. Alice and I still share a bed, but we position ourselves at each extreme, as if we can't think of anything worse than accidentally brushing against each other in the middle of the night. Soon, she'll be able to go full-on starfish. She doesn't even stir when I climb out of bed, put on the same clothes as yesterday, then head downstairs and out of the house.

The cold hits me with a sting straight across the face and I can feel a dusting of snow underfoot. There's a whistling to the wind that goes to my very core, the only discernible sound on this dead, wintry morning. For a moment, this strikes me as the perfect setting for my denouement: a dignified, quiet hour to depart. But I must stick with my plan and lay the foundations for my replacement.

I turn the key in the lock of my car and the door is so stiff that I stumble backwards as it jars open. I turn on the engine and head over towards Ben's flat.

In just under forty minutes, I've arrived. At first, I park on the road, just a few inches from his front door. But it strikes me that this is not a good move – he will see the one car parked on this otherwise barren road and perhaps even remember me from the previous night.

After about five minutes parked there, I notice that there's a space in the driveway of the house opposite. Far more inconspicuous, I think, and so I move into the space. It's so early that even if the owners are in, I doubt they'll be awake to spot me. I take the risk. And I actually end up with a much better vantage point. I sit there, transfixed on the rear-view mirror, waiting for the door to open.

Sure enough, at six fifteen – earlier than I'd imagined – I see the door open and the porch light go on. I quickly make a note of the time on a piece of paper, snap another photo through the rear-view mirror, then watch him reverse out of his driveway and onto the road. I wait a few seconds before switching on my engine, reversing out of my spot and following him. He keeps to exactly the same route as the one that he had taken the morning before and, no doubt, the morning before that.

Even though it's so early in the morning, by the time we reach the motorway there are plenty of cars on the road, so his 50 mph is about the maximum anyone could reasonably manage in the slow lane. I wonder who all these other drivers are: where are they going? What are they doing up so early in the morning? Do they have families? What are their stories?

In a different version of events, the bald, tattooed man driving the white van that I pass on the inside lane could be responsible for ending my life. Or it could be the little old lady driving the green Ford Ka that everyone is overtaking. But no, it will be Ben Anderson. If there's one thing I'm still in control of, it's this. *I* will decide how this ends.

The time reads six thirty-two on my dashboard when I drive past the bridge that I have in mind. I'm sure it's a bridge that has seen its fair share of tragedy before. God knows, I won't be the first person to jump. I wonder, when this bridge was being constructed, whether the builders had any concept of what they were facilitating. Do you think that it occurred to them that there are forums online that keep track of such bridges, announcing their arrival, plotting their exact coordinates, giving advice on the best time to jump? A bridge has a primary function, of course, helping people to cross from one place to the next, but what of this secondary, sinister use?

I make a note of six thirty-two on my list of timings and as I do so, I almost swerve off the road onto the hard shoulder. I make an emergency stop, because impulse tells me to do that, and I'm reminded of the fight I've got on my hands, the fight against impulse that I'll have to win if I'm going to jump off that bridge.

I put my hazard lights on and stay on the hard shoulder, staring at the bridge. This isn't going to work, is it? For a start, I'm not the most agile person. In the heat of the moment, I could easily falter when standing on the ledge and end up falling too early, or too late. What if I misjudge it? This is a fast road: what if it takes me longer than expected to fall? What are the rules of physics here? Is there a time lapse between me jumping and me falling? After all this, after taking such care to select the right man, do I want to risk the laws of gravity letting me down?

I look ahead and see that there is an easy pathway from the field to the west of the road onto the slow lane. In everything I've witnessed so far of Ben and his driving technique, he *never* veers from the slow lane. So all I need to do is head through that field there and wait at the allocated time, then step out into the road. Much easier to time. Much more predictable. No room for error.

I get back on the road, then come off at the next exit and go into a scatty café called Joe's for a fry-up and coffee.

I've spent so many years watching my waistline, but now it doesn't matter.

I scoff down the fried eggs, bacon, hash browns, baked beans like it's the first meal I've had in years. I get back in my car and take a more scenic route, off the motorway, back to the house.

When I get back, I slip into bed with Alice and she's none the wiser, snoring now like an old drunkard. I close my eyes and feel content. Things are falling into place.

I repeat my mission, exactly the same, the following morning. Out of bed at 5.15 a.m., creeping downstairs, heading out into the bleak, wintry moonlight and over to Ben's little cul-de-sac. The same pattern emerges. Out he comes at six thirteen, just two minutes earlier than yesterday. He gets into the car, reverses out and takes the same route as always. The traffic is a bit lighter today, so we reach the bridge at six forty-one. Even though I'm not going to jump from the bridge now, it's a good marker – a landmark, so that I know exactly where I need to be on the side of the road and at what time.

All I need to do is stand there and wait for his car to appear. I'm going to have to be eagle-eyed: his car is not particularly unique and if he's driving too fast, I could miss it. When I was little, I used to play a game with my next-door neighbour, James. He was really into cars, much more than I was, and we would sit in his parents' house, looking out of his bedroom window, counting the number of luxury cars that we spotted. We'd have to shout when we saw a Jaguar, or a Porsche, or a Lamborghini, and the person who spotted the most would win. In some ways, what I have to do here is not dissimilar. Spot the red cars. Spot the Volkswagens. Spot Ben Anderson. Step out.

On this drive back home, I see everything afresh. I edge down the high street slowly, taking it all in. The old lady who runs the florist opening the shutters of her humble little shop and waving at the grocer next door. The school-children waiting, shivering, at the bus stop, rucksacks over their shoulders. The queue of commuters rushing towards the train station, clutching their coffees and croissants and walking with their heads down as if the stance could shield them from the bitter cold.

I drive onto our road and park the car in the driveway. I get out, stand back and look at our house. I'm happy to know that Alice and Maxy are being left somewhere they can be proud of, in a grand old place.

I walk inside, through the hallway, into the living room and straight out to the garden. Into my outhouse I go, straight to my desk. I connect my phone to my printer and watch the paper as it comes through the slot. Coloured photographs of Ben by the school. Ben outside his house. Ben on the motorway. I collate them and, with a paper clip, attach the cutting from the *Watford Gazette*. I place everything in a brown envelope before taking out my favourite green pen and writing on the front: 'Tell Maxy I'm sorry.' Then I start writing on a plain piece of paper, unruled. The last words I'll ever write:

Alice,

I love you. I have loved you since the first day, and more and more every day since. Without you, I am a half-formed man, a shaded version of myself. For me there is no Before

Alice and there shall be no After Alice. And I know you'll understand that I'm doing this for you – I'm ending my life for you, and for Maxy, to keep you safe, to keep you happy.

I'm making a huge sacrifice for you, Alice, so you need to do something for me. When you read this letter, you'll go to the police station. They'll tell you that there's been an accident. A collision. Ask about the man who ran me over. Ask for Ben. Because he's the one who will take you forwards. Chat to him. Get to know him. I've found him for you.

I don't want you ending up with someone unsuitable. I don't want you ending up with someone else like me, who can't control their own emotions. I've done my research. Take a look at these press cuttings. And I've left you some photos – your type, isn't he? Don't mess around. Ben's the one. Play your part, Alice. Do it for me.

I can't hurt you anymore, Alice. You'll find peace without me and finally have the life you deserve.

Adam
xxx

ALICE

I've thought about ringing a hundred times before. I've looked at the website so many times that I know the number off by heart.

But I've never had the guts. While Adam was alive, it felt like a betrayal. The second I said it aloud, the moment I said the words, it would be out in the open, real and acknowledged. And after all that Adam had done for me over the years: did he deserve such exposure?

And now, is it too late to be ringing Women's Aid for help? What am I actually asking of them? Adam's gone: I'm not in peril. And I've always been hesitant, cynical about asking for help from strangers. I can imagine what their first lines of interrogation are going to be. They're going to ask me to tell them about the first time that Adam hit me. They're going to ask me why it happened, what his triggers were and why I stayed with him for so long. But some of these questions are not easy to answer.

Of course, I remember the first time. It was a couple of

years before Max was born. We hadn't long been in the new house and had spent most of the day sorting through boxes, deciding which bed should go in which bedroom. We'd been bickering over boxes full of 'family heirlooms' that I was determined to send to the dump but that Adam wanted to keep for sentimental reasons.

He'd had a good few weeks, mood-wise, and we'd had a nice day: constructive, fruitful, and even if we'd been squabbling, it had been in good spirits. It was 8 p.m. and I'd wandered out into the garden with a glass of Merlot. It was just getting dark and I had my back to the house, delighted that we finally had bought a place with some outdoor space. And then I heard him shouting, and he was getting nearer and nearer.

'For fuck's sake, Alice! Why is Dave texting me that they're coming over on Saturday night? Why did you invite them over without asking me? You know I can't see people at the moment!'

I turned round and saw the rage on his face: his eyes wide and seemingly closer together, his cheeks scarlet and his forehead crumpled. For Adam, there was never a build-up of emotion. It was all or nothing – from calm to all-out rage in a matter of seconds. I stepped towards him.

'Sorry, I thought you wouldn't mind. You and Dave go way back and I thought you were in a good . . .'

He grabbed the wine glass from my hand and I can still hear the crunch as he smashed it in his palm. His hand was bleeding and I moved forwards to tend to it, but as I did, he flinched and hit me on my right eye. It was an unfortunate aim, because the hard corner from the cygnet ring on his pinkie caught it and that's why I got the cut.

Adam was clearly taken aback by his own action and regretted it immediately. He started stroking the back of my head, and I could feel the blood from his own wounded hand trickle down the back of my hair and onto my neck.

'Alice, Alice, what have I done?' He fell to his knees and sobbed, begging for forgiveness. 'Alice, I'm sorry. I don't know what came over me. I'm a terrible husband.'

I needed a moment on my own. I walked into the house and up to our bedroom. My face was sore, but the sting inside ran far deeper. I felt betrayed, like I had been tricked into loving this man who was only now showing his true self, like he was revealing a new side to himself when he knew that I was too invested to escape. But then Adam came up to join me, a bag of frozen peas in his hand, and he sat next to me on the bed, dabbing my eye and whispering words of apology.

'I'm so sorry, Alice. I just saw red and . . . I love you so much. You know I wouldn't hurt you.'

And I kissed him, feeling the ache as my face touched his.

'It was just a moment of madness, I know. We all lose our temper sometimes. I forgive you.'

I had to wear sunglasses for a week after that. Sometimes when I look in the mirror, really, really close, I can still see a tiny scar just above my right eyebrow. It reminds me of that first time. It reminds me of Adam.

I don't remember the second time, or the third, and it pains me to think that I became so quickly accustomed to Adam's temper that only a few instances stand out. The years after that are a blur, an ebb and flow of love and violence.

When I got pregnant with Max, I assumed everything would change. Adam was desperate to have a baby and wanted to start trying very early on, but I'd never wanted to be a mother. I'd never felt the impulse that so many other women harp on about and in some ways I felt like I wasn't cut out for the job. Because my own childhood wasn't exactly exemplary, I didn't feel like I had the tools or the precedent to raise a happy child. My parents died so young that I had no point of reference.

But I knew that as a father, Adam would come into his own. Adam needed someone to dote over, to mould. I thought that, with a child, Adam would have a focus, a *raison d'être*, and I saw it as my duty to make this happen for him.

And then, of course, when I did fall pregnant, I started to fulfil all the clichés. Against all the odds, I cried during our first scan. I would sit there for hours, rubbing my swelling tummy, waiting for Max to kick, to say hello, and Adam would sit beside me, massaging my ballooning ankles.

But pregnancy didn't stop Adam from getting angry. There was one particularly nasty incident, quite late on, when I thought we were going to lose the baby. When I think back to that night, it's just a series of flashes, an amalgam of snapshots that don't quite form a full image. It's as if my brain has vetoed that particular memory, considering it too extreme, too traumatic, to hold on to. I can remember the weightlessness of falling, and a sensation of warmth as piss trickled down my thighs and ankles. I can also remember the aftermath, the shouting, the vow that as much as Adam hit me, if he ever, *ever* laid a hand on our child, I'd kill him with my own bare fists.

When Max was born, the violence subsided for a time, but then there was a gradual crescendo as our son got older. Adam never did harm Max, though, and it was also important to both of us that he never witnessed the rows between us. I never wanted Max to see the wave of rage that suddenly swept over Adam's face when I did something wrong. If I ever had a bruise, or a cut, or a split lip, it was explained away, trivialised, brushed under the carpet. My son will not grow up to be like his father.

I imagine some women talk of extreme jealousy, of accusations of infidelity and lack of trust. But in our case it would be wrong to identify such simplistic cause and effect. Adam was a man who suffered from acute clinical depression and sometimes it would overwhelm him. Sometimes, when he was feeling particularly low, he'd lose it and take it out on the only person who was truly close to him.

Adam's violence was never malicious, premeditated or intended, but rather spontaneous and passionate, a symptom of his mental illness. And there would always be deep, deep regret. Over the years, the attacks may have changed – some were more serious than others – but the remorse was constant, the aftermath rehearsed and replayed. Adam would cry, wail, beg for forgiveness and plead for help.

When I think of Adam now, when I think of his moments of violence, I focus on what came afterwards. I picture him dabbing the frozen peas on my forehead that first time. How do I explain all this to somebody I've never met on a phone line? Because I've always refused to believe that my husband was a demon and I'm scared of being forced to admit that he was.

'You're through to the twenty-four-hour National Domestic Violence Helpline. If you're in immediate danger, please hang up and dial 999 for the police. All calls to the helpline are confidential but may be monitored for training purposes.'

My heart's pounding. What do I say first?

BEN

Tuesday, 28 August

As I walk along the high street, I can feel the sun beating down on the back of my neck. It feels tight, like the tip of a needle on my skin, scratching the surface but not quite piercing. I'm wearing a shirt, trousers and blazer, because I think it's good to be smart when checking in at the police station. The blazer also hides the patches of sweat that invariably form at my armpits, getting wider and wider as I approach, my pulse quickening and my throat closing.

It's been a baking-hot summer so far and I've really appreciated being back living with my parents because they have the most amazing garden. I sometimes sit for whole afternoons, watching as robins come and pick at the feed. I cherish these moments, because I know full well that in a matter of weeks, I could be behind bars.

Mum has been up in her room mostly since I first came back to them and she's been crying so much that Dad says it's best for everyone if she just rests in bed. This has meant that it's been Dad and me pottering around on our own and, actually, it's been rather nice. Mum bought Dad a Paul Hollywood book for his birthday last month, so on Sunday we made a chicken and mushroom pie. We've been watching lots of TV as well, because what else is there to do in the evening? Dad and I have different tastes when it comes to idle entertainment, so it's been a case of allowing for both of our preferences.

I've not wanted to be left alone, so much so that I've even sat through a couple of football games. Dad is a proper football fanatic and he's only just about come to accept that this is not a passion I share. He used to drag me to watch live games when I was younger and I'd spend the whole time looking up at the clock, calculating what percentage of the game had elapsed and how long we still had ahead of us. I can't stand the sounds. That horrible din of the crowds is so relentless, so feral, and it gives me a headache. Still, I've decided that, on balance, I'd prefer to sit with my dad to watch a game or two on the television than sit by myself and think about what's happened and what's going to happen next.

On the day of my arrest, I was given the opportunity to make a phone call, so I called Dad. It's the default solution in a moment of crisis and, scrolling through the recently called numbers on my phone, I realised just how long it had been since we'd last spoken. I'd been so caught up in this new world, the world of Alice and Max, that I had neglected the things that had previously been my anchors.

My parents, who would always wait for me to call them rather than vice versa, for fear of catching me at a bad time, suddenly felt a bit distant, like old university friends.

People who had done enough to secure an indelible spot in my sphere of acquaintance but who had fallen down the priority list. And I can't remember the last time I went for a drink with my uni mates.

Before Alice and Max, we'd go out on a Saturday night, to a bar or a comedy night in Covent Garden, even occasionally to a club, and I'd spend the whole of Sunday recovering. As time went on, the group of friends dwindled as we paired off, and I wonder if I got back in touch with them whether or not there would be anyone left. It is, I suppose, irrelevant right now. I'm likely to be otherwise engaged for a year, or even more – and then, when I'm released, who will want to go out with me?

Dad sent his lawyer to the police station and his advice was to say nothing. It felt clichéd to say 'no comment' when questioned, but I felt so numb from the whole ordeal that it was as if I were living someone else's life, like I was watching a true crime documentary on Netflix. As I sat there being questioned, I could see the footage, a bit grainy, the camera not quite at the right angle. I imagined the clock in the top right-hand corner and the booming tone of the voiceover: 'Anderson was slumped in a chair, looking dazed, refusing to cooperate with the investigators.' I was playing a role that had been forced upon me.

When they charged me, it made sense, so I didn't resist. I didn't cry, or scream, or try to deny anything. I just remained silent, unmoved and unmoving. Dad and I drove back together to their house. No conversation, no explanation, no apologies or indignations. Just going through the motions.

But now, with the trial approaching, I'm on my way to the police station to set the record straight. I'm going against all the legal advice I've been given, but I know that I need to confess. I need to make this as straightforward as possible, both for Alice and for Max. If I plead not guilty at trial – which, according to the script, is the next logical step – it's just the beginning of yet another ordeal for this poor family. Alice will have to appear as a witness. She'll have to relive everything from the very beginning. And every effort I have made to make life bearable for her, every endeavour to make it all better, to fill the void left by Adam, will be undone.

If there's a trial, there'll be press. Journalists, maybe even TV crews, will be waiting at the entrance to the courthouse, ready to pounce, spreading our story further in time and place, imprinting it into the history books, immortalising it on the Internet. I owe it to both Alice and Max to make this go away as quickly and as quietly as possible. And, God knows, I deserve any sentence that I face.

There will be something cathartic about pleading guilty, as if by pleading guilty to the kidnap I'm also pleading guilty to the original act on the motorway. Because I'm the only one who hasn't had to sacrifice anything in this whole thing. I haven't lost a husband, or a father, or a lifetime of security. So now's the time for me to pay for what I've done.

As I walk across the high street towards the bus stop, it's all go. An old lady pushing a shopping trolley into the super-market, walking with such temerity in the wintry conditions that it's unclear whether she's actually moving forwards or backwards. A man in a pinstriped suit with gelled-back hair, striding down the high street with great intention, clutching a bunch of keys and letting himself into a small car. A mother ushering two small children across the road in a hurry to get to school. The little boy can't be much younger than Max, but he's screaming and shouting like a toddler. Behind the mother and children is a woman in one of those electric wheelchairs. I give her a big smile and she gives one back. I like that she's noticed me, because this morning I feel invisible, like the world is moving around me, dodging me, avoiding eye contact and hoping I'll go away.

It's about a twenty-minute bus ride to the police station and when I step off, I trip, falling down the step, grazing my face and arm on the pavement. A few passers-by stop to help me up and I bat them away, because I'm fine, I'm fine. I think I must have twisted an ankle, because as I walk towards the police station I'm limping – and then I see some drops of blood drip onto the pavement in front of me. I reach for a tissue in my pocket and wipe the blood off my nose.

The automatic doors open and I stumble towards the reception desk. The friendly Scottish lady is on duty and she gives me a sympathetic smile as I lunge forwards, putting my fist onto her desk.

'I'm here to report in for my bail, but I'd like to speak to my assigned officer, please. It's Ben. Benjamin Anderson. I've got something I'd like to say.'

And you'd think that if someone came in with such purpose, he'd be seen right away. But there's no urgency here. I feel exhilarated, like this whole ordeal is reaching a climax, but the staff at the police station don't seem bothered.

I help myself to a cup of water and catch a glimpse of myself in the glass door leading out to the street. I look a right state, like some kind of drunk who's been brought into the police station at the end of a heavy night. And when they call my name, I don't immediately respond, because I don't recognise myself. I don't answer to my own name.

'Mr Anderson. Ben. Please, come with us.'

It's the same officer who questioned me last month and he looks angry. Maybe he's in the middle of something else, something more crucial, and I've caused him an inconvenience by asking for his time.

I follow him into an interview room, take a seat and draw a deep breath.

'Sorry to disturb you, officer.'

'Oh, here he is, the luckiest man in England right now.'

'What do you mean?'

'Have you not been informed? Mrs Selby is refusing to give evidence against you.'

'She's what? Alice?'

'Yeah. And without evidence from her, the Crown Prosecution Service are refusing to go after you.'

'Really? I mean . . .'

'You're free to go. But you listen to me: if you touch her, or go anywhere near her, or that son of hers, I'll have you. I'll get you locked up for years, you fucking pervert. Do you understand me? Just leave them alone.'

He gets up, shaking his head, and slams the door behind me. And I'm sat here, alone in a police room, paralysed, with my mouth wide open. Why has Alice changed her mind? Why is he calling me a pervert? Where do I go from here?

I stay there, my head in my hands, for another five minutes. Then I swallow a whole mouthful of saliva that has gathered in my mouth. I stand and leave the room. I go into the toilet by the exit and sit down for a while, but nothing comes out. I pull up my trousers, flush the toilet, wash my hands and head back out into the corridor. And then I leave the police station, for the last time, and make my way back home.

ALICE

Wednesday, 7 November

'Look at Syrup, Mummy! Look how fast he's running!'

It would have been hard to imagine, this time last year, that there would be a golden hamster in a pink plastic ball, rolling down the stairs of our house.

'You should race him down the stairs, darling. See who's faster.'

'Syrup is definitely faster, Mummy! He's like a hamster version of Mo Farah!'

I can't say that having a rodent as a pet would have been top of my wish list, but just seeing the joy that this glorified rat gives Max, the smile that it puts on his face to have a companion, is worth the bother of a few droppings here and there.

'Don't forget that we need to clean out his cage before the removal people get here, darling. We can do it together.'

The removal vans are arriving at 10 a.m. tomorrow and the house is still a tip. Organisation has never been my strong suit, but, to be fair, packing up this house single-handedly would be a mean feat for even the most accomplished and officious project manager. I've had to clear out rooms that I'd never been in before. Rooms filled with shit that Adam's mum collected before she died. Grotesque antique cabinets, piles of Adam's grandmother's evening gowns and other family heirlooms that I'm just going to send to the dump.

It's been almost three months since I went back into that outhouse and read the suicide note that I'd been avoiding. I knew that to open it, to read it, would make me confront the role that I played in Adam's downfall. As long as that envelope remained in the shed, sealed, nothing was set in stone. I could guess why Adam had jumped in front of a car, but I couldn't say so with any certainty.

After reading his letter, I can better understand his death and process it. In many ways, I was relieved: overwhelmed by his admission of guilt, surprised for the first time to see the abuse acknowledged. The real shock, though, came when I saw those photos of Ben. How manipulated he has been in all of this. It makes me feel angry to think that Adam, as disgruntled as he was with his own existence, should drag an unassuming stranger into our lives in this way.

That's why I decided not to give evidence against Ben. Not because I believe he was innocent of the charges that were ultimately levelled against him. But because Ben was also a victim in all this – another casualty of Adam's abuse. All things considered, I decided to give Ben a get-out-of-jail-free card as an apology on behalf of my manipulative ex-husband.

That's not to say I don't still feel afraid of Ben, and I'd be lying if I said that our big move is not, in part, an escape from him. I find myself looking out of the window from time to time, checking up and down the street for his little red car. Sometimes, when I'm sitting in the living room and it's dark outside, I peer into the garden and search for his silhouette, convinced that he's watching us from the bushes. But he's never there. We haven't seen him, or any trace of him, since that evening at the guest house.

After I dropped the charges against Ben, I promised Max that we'd draw a line under everything that had happened. That we'd no longer have to speak to journalists, that he'd be spending far less time being looked after by other people like Mrs Turner, and that he and I would be able to start a new life, far away, just the two of us. And so off we go to the countryside.

I've found a gorgeous little cottage in a village on the edge of the Cotswolds. It's small, just three bedrooms, but it's more than we need. It's only a rental, which gives us time to see how we find it up there. I like the idea of being in a small village, of getting to know other families in the area. I like the thought of being able to pop into the village pub, have a lime and soda and bump into familiar faces. I want Max to make friends and I want to be friends with their parents. And yes, just a lime and soda. I'm going alcohol-free for a while.

I've even applied for a job at a local accountancy firm. Because now there's no one there to stop me. No one to get paranoid if I arrive home from work a little later than planned. No one to shout at me if I pick up the phone and talk to my one friend. No one to keep tabs on me during my every waking hour, or to worry that I might meet someone new at work who I prefer. And who knows? Maybe I'll meet someone else, in time, but for now I'm happy that's it just Max and me, forging a new future together.

On the night of the discovery in the shed, I made a bonfire. This is not an area of expertise for me. I was a Girl Guide for a while, but to say that I was unengaged would be the understatement of the century. I found a video on YouTube entitled 'How 2 Build the Perfect Bonfire in Less than 1 Minute' and was subjected to five minutes and fifty-nine seconds of Jessica walking me through, step by step, the process of how to use household items to build a bonfire. I wondered what Jessica needed to destroy so urgently. Jessica had laid the make-up on thick and was sporting a white blouse that was definitely too small for her, her tennis-ball boobs protruding. I wondered whether Jessica appreciated the irony of asking me to watch her waffle on for six whole minutes in order to communicate a task that was only supposed to take one minute.

I headed back outside into the garden, grasping two plastic bags' worth of material to get the fire going: scrunched-up newspaper, chewing gum wrappers, kitchen roll, a packet of cotton buds, half a packet of long matches, some birthday candles that I found at the back of the cupboard, left over from the time we threw a party for Max's fifth birthday. I even threw a packet of unopened tampons into the mix. I went right to the end of the garden – as far away from the house as possible, to avoid any fumes wafting into the house and upstairs while Max slept – dumped everything into a pile and set it on fire, retreating to a safe distance.

The flame started small, an orange triangle, and I watched as it grew, engulfing the kitchen paper, sizzling as it lit the candles, popping and flashing as it ignited the matches. I then darted back towards it, as there was a sudden surge. I could feel the heat of the flame, a roasting sensation on my arms, and a trickle of sweat dripping all the way from my forehead down to my chin.

My face was illuminated, and as I started throwing the pages of Adam's letter into the flame, one by one, I felt exhilarated. I threw each photograph in, then watched as the edges curled and the photos shrank. This was a thing of beauty: performance art, curated by me. A moment of reckoning, of creation and destruction, which would mark the end of one thing and the start of something new.

After a few minutes, I could see that the fire was dwindling, so I turned round and headed back towards the house. I went upstairs, stepping over boxes and crates, into my en suite. As I approached the mirror, I could see that my face was black, ashen, and the deep pink of my dressing gown was now a muted salmon colour. I took my clothes off and stood in the shower, like a killer washing blood off their skin.

I stepped out, covered myself in a towel and went into Max's room. His bed was empty and, for a split second, I felt that sharp pang of panic.

I quickly found him standing at his window, looking in amazement at the bonfire that I'd created.

'Mum, have you seen the fire at the end of the garden? Do we need to call the fire brigade?'

'No, darling, don't worry. You only need to call the fire brigade if a fire is started accidentally or it gets out of control. I just wanted to get rid of a few things tonight, that's all.'

'Why didn't you just throw them in the dustbin, then?'

'Well, darling, when things are really special, really precious, then sometimes it's a good idea to make sure that they are destroyed completely.'

'Why would you destroy something special?'

I went over to him, kissed his head and drew his curtains.

'You'd better go to bed, Max. It's late.'

And he left it at that. Maybe one day, when he's older, I'll remind him of that time at the window and I'll tell him everything.

'Mummy, I just want to take a selfie in front of the removal van!'

Selfies are Max's new thing. I gave him my old iPhone when I upgraded a couple of months ago and now he's a real budding photographer. I know he's a bit young to have a phone, but given everything that's happened recently, it felt like the right thing to do. I've put some parental settings on, so he can't browse the Internet, and all he's interested in is taking photos and playing Monsters Unleashed, anyway.

Max and I watch the last removal van head off into the distance – it takes four whole loads to gather everything, in the end – and then we stand there, beside a suitcase each, waiting for the taxi to pick us up and take us to the train station. It's cold, but the sun is out and it's shining on the white facade of the house. I'm glad that our last image of this house, the enduring snapshot, will be a bright one. And I've got a surprise for him.

'Here, Max, take this.'

I hand Max a shopping bag containing a large red box. I've always been too lazy for wrapping paper and it never seems to have bothered him.

'For me? But it's not even my birthday or Christmas! What is it, Mummy?'

'Just open it, sweetheart!'

I smile as he tips the bag upside down in excitement and the box falls to the floor. He opens it and lifts out a little yellow hard hat, with his name written on the front in big black letters. He screws up his face.

'What is it, Mummy? A hat?'

'It's called a hard hat, Max. For builders. It's for you, look.'

I take the hat and place it on his head. It's a little small for him and I have to squash it down slightly, which makes Max giggle.

'But what's it *for*, Mummy?'

'When we get to the new house, darling, we're going to finally build you a tree house. And not a small, child's tree house like the one you started with Daddy all that time ago. A proper, grown-up tree house for you to spend time with all the friends from your new school. It's a big project, though, are you to up to the challenge?'

Max's mouth falls to the ground, he lets out a little yelp of joy and then he launches himself straight into my arms.

'Of course, Mummy! Have you *seen* how good I am at Lego?'

BEN

Friday, 14 December

'This is the final call for all passengers travelling on BA285. Will passengers please proceed to gate B46, where boarding is almost complete.'

Shit. Where's all the time gone? I arrived at the airport three hours and fifteen minutes before departure, what am I still doing sitting here eating? It's been such a long time since I've been abroad, let alone on a long-haul flight. And it's the first time I've ever booked a single flight without the return leg. By the time I arrived and queued up for check-in, bought everything I needed at the chemist and got through security, I was flustered and thought I deserved a proper sit-down meal. Then I took ages deciding what to order because I was hungry, but, equally, I didn't want to eat too much, because I knew there would be at least one, if not two meals on the plane. And I didn't want to eat anything with too much fibre, because the last thing I wanted was to have a stomach ache. And then when I did order – fish and

308

chips – it took at least twenty minutes to arrive, which is not acceptable in an airport restaurant.

I look at my watch and see that I now only have twenty-five minutes until the scheduled take-off, and the sign for B gates says ten to fifteen minutes' walk, so I'd better get a move on. I put my rucksack on my back and run as fast as I can through the terminal.

When I reach the gate, I'm relieved to see that there's a queue of at least thirty people in front of me, so I'm clearly not going to miss the flight. I join the back of the line and reach into my pocket for my passport and boarding pass. The top right-hand corner of my passport has creased over and the perforated section on my boarding pass has torn slightly. I see a member of BA staff, helping to manage the queue, and check that this isn't going to be an issue.

'I'm sorry, mate, I must have torn the boarding pass in my pocket. That's not going to be an issue, is it?'

And the guy takes a look at the boarding pass, without even taking it out of my hand, and says, 'Not to worry, sir. I think we'll still let you on.'

There's a condescending tone to his voice and I realise that I'm probably a bit more jumpy than most travellers. As I put my passport and boarding pass back in my pocket to keep them safe, I see the BA man give a little smirk to the passenger in front of me and I feel put out.

It was Mum who first suggested that I go and stay with my cousin, Andrea, in Australia. She and I were good buddies when we were kids. Her mum and my mum are sisters, and although we've always lived on opposite sides of the world, every time Andrea came over with her parents, they'd stay at our house and we'd get on well. As kids, we were both really in to music and we'd spend hours sitting on my bedroom floor listening to Destiny's Child, TLC and other stalwarts of the nineties R & B scene.

We only went over to visit them as a family the once. I was fourteen, and I was envious of their proximity to the beach and their happy-go-lucky outlook. I went to a party on a Saturday night with Andrea and some of her school friends and, for the first time in my life, I was the centre of attention. There were beautiful girls, the kind of girls who wouldn't even look at me back home, firing questions at me.

'Have you met the Queen?'

'Have you seen snow?'

Andrea and I have remained in touch. She ended up going into teaching as well, although university teaching in her case. She lectures on English literature at the University of Brisbane. She got married four years ago to a lovely guy called Steven and they have gorgeous twins who, judging by photos, look just like Andrea.

So I sent Andrea an email, saying that I fancied a new start and asking if she knew of any teaching opportunities in Brisbane. I had tried to get primary teaching jobs in and around London after I was let go from my old job and, although I was never given the feedback explicitly, I'm getting the impression that no school here would hire me now. Even though I was never convicted, there's obviously a black mark next to my name, on some register, somewhere.

I had talked to Andrea previously about how many colleges there are in Australia teaching English as a foreign language and I thought I might as well give that a go. Businessmen coming in from Tokyo; keen grown-up students doing their best to perfect their business English. Surely my black mark would not travel with me all the way to Brisbane, out of the primary sector and into the mature-student market.

In my email to Andrea, I kept the details of the reasons for my proposed move as scant as possible. I'd spent weeks coming to terms with the events of the past year. I know that I wasn't to blame for Adam's death but that my subsequent behaviour, my obsession with Alice and Max, was unhealthy, unhelpful and, ultimately, could have led to a criminal conviction, were it not for Alice's compassion.

I never definitively found out why Alice refused to give evidence, but I can only assume that she came to see that my heart was always in the right place, that all I wanted to do was help them. But still, there was no excuse for breaking into their garden. No defence for picking up a child from school who wasn't mine and checking him into a hotel. With the benefit of hindsight, I know that I overstepped the mark.

And I don't feel sad about it anymore, either. I accept the way things have turned out. I don't believe in God, or anything particularly supernatural. But life is what it is, I am what I am, and as I wait here, in a queue to board a plane towards my next adventure, I'm pretty happy.

The queue moves slowly, and although they don't announce that there's a delay, there obviously is one because by the time I actually step onto the plane, it's ten minutes later than the departure time. It's going to be a long journey, twenty-two hours and forty-five minutes in total, including a stopover in Singapore, so I've got a whole bag full of books, crossword

puzzles and Sudoku collections to keep me occupied. I'll probably watch a film or two as well – although I always find it
hard to concentrate on anything too serious or involved. I've
opted for an aisle seat, partly to give myself as much legroom
as possible but also because I don't know how nervous I'm
going to be when we take off and, if I am, it's only going
to be worse if I'm by the window.

I'm surprised when the air stewardess starts the safety
instruction routine, because the plane only looks to be about
70 per cent full – surely there must be more passengers still
to arrive? There's a real mixture of people on this flight. In
front of me, to the right, is a man in a suit, no tie. He's
tapping away furiously on his laptop, hitting the keys way
too hard. I try to get a quick look through the gap in the
seat at what he's working on – I'm always curious – but it's
just an Excel spreadsheet with a sea of numbers. Three rows
ahead are a couple of very excitable teenagers. I'm not sure
exactly how old they are, but judging by their conversation
and general attire, I think there's a good chance they're just
about to embark on a gap year. There's a woman in the
window seat of the row across with long dreadlocks and
seven piercings in the ear that faces me.

The air stewardess has just put down the life jacket and
is pointing out all the nearest exits, when a woman bursts
through the door and runs down the aisle. Strictly speaking,
they shouldn't have started the safety demonstration before
everyone had boarded and it makes me nervous that this
crew don't know what they are doing. The late passenger
is followed by a small child, a little girl who can't be older
than five or six, who is dragging a Peppa Pig wheelie bag

behind her. She's a pretty little thing, full of life, chirping away and smiling at old ladies as she saunters down the aisle. The mother has an Australian accent and as she stops right by me, I feel a sharp pang of excitement.

'This is us! Sorry to disturb you – we're these two.'

She points to the two seats next to me and I jump up to let them through. The girl takes the middle seat, next to me, and I give her a smile.

'What's your name, young lady?'

She goes scarlet, sticks her thumb in her mouth and buries her face in her mother's dress. The mum smiles at me.

'Why have you gone shy all of a sudden? This is Victoria.'

'Hello, Victoria, it's nice to meet you. Does anyone ever call you Vicki? I'm Benjamin, but most people call me Ben.'

Vicki removes her thumb, looks at her mum and nods.

'My best friend calls me Vicki.'

'Well, Vicki it is, then.'

Vicki's mum squeezes back past me with her hand luggage, and then struggles as she tries to fit their bag in the overhead compartment. I do the valiant thing.

'Here, let me help.'

I take the bag from her – it is quite heavy – and notice the tag. I make a mental note of the address:

Carol Whittaker
8/142 Upper Rome Street,
Brisbane

I wonder how close they are to where I'll be staying. I don't think Brisbane's a massive place.

I sit back down next to Vicki and she takes a packet of wine gums out of the seat pocket.

'Victoria, darling. I told you, they need to last you all the way to Brisbane.'

Carol has a strawberry blonde bob and a distinctive face: chiselled cheekbones and a strong, square jaw, which softens when she smiles. I glance down instinctively at her left hand. No ring.

'I'm Carol, by the way.'

'Nice to meet you, Carol. Long flight ahead of us, eh?'

'Oh yes! Vicki, why don't you offer Ben a wine gum?'

'Wine gums are Maxy's favourite. He's a bit older than you, I think.'

Carol smiles, her eyes widening to invite me in.

'Oh, you have a son? How old is he?'

Do I correct her?

'That reminds me, actually – I promised to take a selfie on the plane before take-off.'

I reach into my pocket for my phone, switch on the camera, smile and click.

'His mum gave him her old phone after we split up. He's on a special plan for kids – you know, family filters and all that.'

Carol raises her eyebrows and lowers her voice, turning away from her daughter.

'Oh, it'll be years before I let Vicki have a phone. You hear such horror stories, don't you?'

I check the photo and send it to Maxy. He'll in bed by now, I should think, but he'll reply in the morning.

Acknowledgements

Before anyone else, I would like to thank *you* for reading *The Wreckage*, and for getting as far as the acknowledgements. There are lots of books to read; thanks for spending time with mine. I'd love to hear from you and find out what you think of Ben and Alice. Feel free to drop me an email at hello@robinmorganbentley.com, or you can find me on Twitter, Facebook or Instagram.

I've been lucky enough to work with many talented people in the process of bringing *The Wreckage* to life, and I will start with my peerless agent Madeleine Milburn. I'll never forget the email I got from Maddy after she read the first draft of my manuscript: her passion, determination and drive have been a huge inspiration to me and I thank her for all the doors she's opened. It's also been great getting to know Giles and the other members of her equally brilliant team – I can't wait to spend more time together in the future.

And then a HUGE thanks to Phoebe Morgan for signing me, and for her editorial guidance: her enthusiasm and vision for *The Wreckage* bowled me over from our very first meeting. Thanks to Anna Valentine and Katie Brown also for being such champions and being so lovely about this little book that I wrote on Sunday mornings and weekday evenings in the tiny study at the back of my flat. I feel very lucky to have found a home at Trapeze and Orion, and can't wait for all the adventures to come.

In my day job at Audible, I've worked with some of the most inspiring, exciting authors out there, many of whom have been a big inspiration to me in one way or another. Listening to their books, and chatting to them about their own writing careers, has given me the impetus and drive to pick up the pen myself, and I'm grateful to all of them. I'd like to give particular thanks to Fiona Barton, whose warmth and encouragement in the very first stages of my writing really spurred me on to persevere.

I'm not the kind of person that is able to keep things to themselves, and so many people read early drafts of *The Wreckage* and gave me feedback along the way. I'd like to thank everyone who loved it, but also everyone that gave me brutal feedback – this has helped me make it better! So, thanks to Sam, Alex, Philly, Adam, Harriet, Henna, Nicola, Sophie, Aaron, Michelle, Deborah, Tanya, Eli, Linda, Johnny, Hadassah, Max, Imogen, Holly, Jez and my in-laws Simon and Esther for all their thoughts. And thanks to Matt Lucas, John Marrs and Matt Nixson for reading early versions and giving their much-valued stamps of approval.

Thanks to Melanie Brown and Louise Gannon, and Teresa Parker from Women's Aid, who let me ask them difficult questions while researching some of the more sensitive areas of *The Wreckage*. Thanks to Adam Jacobs for his guidance on the legal/court bits, and to Rachel, James, Charlie and Jack for the inspiration for Maxy!

To my amazing Mum and Dad: I didn't have the easiest start to life – I have cerebral palsy, and was very ill as a baby. It was their stoic determination to crash through obstacles that I have to thank for everything. Mum, I know you usually don't read thrillers, but I think you'll like this one!

One of the reasons I wrote this book was that I was keen to read a thriller with anxious men at the centre. With so many books out there where the protagonist is troubled and female, as a man who has been living with anxiety and depression for over twenty years, I wanted to redress a balance and write a story about men in turmoil. I hope that men and women reading this know that it's OK to be anxious, and it's OK for things to take you off-kilter. For me, talking about my anxiety is an important part of managing it, and I think one of the reasons that Ben spirals out of control in *The Wreckage* is that he doesn't share what's on his mind with people that might be able to help. There are lots of great resources out there – I think the mental-health charity Mind is a great place to start.

And finally, thanks Pauly. My first reader, my sounding board, inspiration, (harshest) critic, my husband and my best friend. I couldn't even have started this book without you, and I dedicate every word to you. I love you.

Credits

Trapeze would like to thank everyone at Orion who worked on the publication of *The Wreckage* in the UK.

Editorial
Phoebe Morgan
Katie Brown
Ru Merritt
Sarah Fortune
Charlie Panayiotou
Jane Hughes
Alice Davis

Copy-editor
Claire Dean

Proofreader
Jade Craddock

Audio
Paul Stark
Amber Bates

Contracts
Anne Goddard
Paul Bulos
Jake Alderson

Design
Debbie Holmes
Lucie Stericker
Joanna Ridley
Nick May
Clare Sivell
Helen Ewing
Jan Bielecki
Henry Steadman

Finance
Jennifer Muchan
Jasdip Nandra

Afeera Ahmed
Rabale Mustafa
Elizabeth Beaumont
Sue Baker
Tom Costello

Marketing
Tom Noble
Lucy Cameron

Production
Claire Keep
Fiona McIntosh

Publicity
Alex Layt
Maura Wilding

Sales
Jen Wilson
Laura Fletcher
Esther Waters

Rachael Hum
Ellie Kyrke-Smith
Ben Goddard
Georgina Cutler
Barbara Ronan
Andrew Hally
Dominic Smith
Maggy Park
Linda McGregor

Rights
Susan Howe
Richard King
Krystyna Kujawinska
Jessica Purdue
Louise Henderson

Operations
Jo Jacobs
Sharon Willis
Lucy Brem
Lisa Pryde

Reading Group Questions

What were your impressions of Ben and Alice in their first chapters? How did these impressions change over the course of the novel? Did your sympathies shift?

Could you understand Ben's response immediately after the crash? Or is Alice's attitude that life is too short to dwell on other people's tragedies more understandable?

How did Alice come across as a wife and mother? How do you feel she copes following the crash? Were there any of her behaviours/actions that you found questionable?

How did you feel about Alice and Ben's relationship?

Was it easy to understand the connection they forged or did it feel unsettling?

Max's head teacher, Mrs Lacey believes a male role model would be beneficial for Max, which angers Alice. Whose opinion do you agree with?

Did you have any suspicions about Adam and Alice's relationship? Were you surprised by what was revealed? Did it change your attitudes towards Alice?

What feelings did you have towards Adam? Did you sympathise because of his mental health condition, or did some of his actions make him a villain?

What did you think of Alice's decision not to provide evidence against Ben?

Alice gives eight-year-old Max a mobile phone – how do you feel about young children having mobiles?

Should there be an age limit?

How did you feel about the ending of the novel? Would you trust Ben with your own children?

The title of the novel is The Wreckage. What types of wreckage occur in the novel?